THE CLOCK IS TICKING!

A devoted nursemaid braves mythical Japanese spirits to save a little girl's life, only to bring down the wrath of a demon on the child's father.

Two daredevil American adventurers encounter a Chinese demon who styles himself as the Lord of Death, and they must race against time to stop his murderous plan to eliminate London's top industrialists.

A set-maker's apprentice delves the depths beneath Paris's famed Opera House and unwittingly discovers an opera equestrienne's secret lover, a man all believe to be only a legend.

An Academy romance turns deadly when two young cadets encounter clockwork horrors in Edinburgh's underground city.

A lady archaeologist turned adventurer finds herself saddled with an unlikely partner and must use all her cunning and guile to save both Britain and herself.

Make a wish. Count to three. Is the Polychrome Wishing Jar everything it's supposed to be?

Twenty-four stories. Twenty-four hours of steampunk action and gripping adventure steeped in myth, legend, and lore. Race the clock with our stalwart heroes and heroines.

FIND OUT WHAT HAPPENS TWELVE HOURS LATER!

TWELVE HOURS LATER

24 Tales of Myth and Mystery

Edited by
BJ Sikes
Dover Whitecliff
AJ Sikes
&
Sharon E. Cathcart

Thinking Ink Press
Campbell, California

Published by Thinking Ink Press

P.O. Box 1411, Campbell, California, 95009

First printing, 2017

Ebook edition ISBN 978-1-942480-17-4

Print edition ISBN 978-1-942480-18-1

Printed in the United States of America.

This anthology was inspired by the 2015 Clockwork
Alchemy theme Myths, Legends, & Lore.
The editors would like to thank the staff and owners of
Linde Lane Tea Room in Dixon, California,
without whose wonderful atmosphere and tea service
this project would not have been conceived.
We dedicate the work to librarians and literacy trainers
everywhere.

THE STORY BEGINS

THE STORY BEGINS

In the Midnight Hour

By Lillian Csernica

12:00 AM, Kyoto

Olivia Danforth hurried down the Sannen-zaka toward Kiyomizu Temple. She had no interest in the shops offering sandals, dolls, fans, and knickknacks. The tea houses called to her with their warmth and light. Her kid gloves, two extra petticoats beneath her taffeta walking skirt, and her heavy cloak kept out the chill of the autumn night. A hot cup of tea would be such a comfort. All around her the russet maple leaves shivered and whispered in the wind.

Back at Dr. Harrington's residence, little Madelaine lay dying. Dr. Harrington's brave words could not conceal the shadows under his eyes and the wasting thinness that had gripped him these past weeks. Nothing in Western medicine could combat the illness that had seized Madelaine just days after Dr. Harrington and his household arrived in Kyoto.

Beneath all the layers of propriety and respectability, Olivia was terrified. Only the worst kind of desperation could have driven her to seriously consider what she was about to do.

Olivia's grandmother had told Olivia tales of people who went to the crossroads at midnight to offer their souls to the Devil in exchange for whatever it was that drove them to make such a hellish bargain. It had to be at the crossroads, the traditional burial place of hanged criminals, suicides, and others guilty of the most terrible crimes. Olivia loved Madelaine with all her heart as the daughter she could never have. If it meant giving up her own life, her own soul to save the child, then Olivia saw it as the one act of maternal devotion that would do Madelaine real and lasting good.

The maid Akiko and the cook had taken to Madelaine as if she were their very own. Every folk remedy known for miles around was brought forth and offered to "Harrington-*sensei*." Olivia had caught Akiko giving poor little Madelaine a drink of supposedly magical water. Olivia chased the maid out, berating her in terms that surely translated regardless of Olivia's very limited Japanese and Akiko's total lack of English. Dr. Harrington tried to soothe Olivia's outrage by explaining the "Pure Water Temple" was named for the Otowa Falls. The Japanese people believed that to drink from one of the three streams of water falling down the cliffs would bring prosperity, success in scholarship, or good fortune in love. Olivia tsked. Such superstition. As if some unseen spirit living in the water could really grant such wishes. Prosperity, scholarship, and love all came from hard work, devout living, and strength of character.

Now Olivia chided herself. She had no business mocking the superstitions of the Japanese people, not when she herself had come to a strange part of Kyoto unescorted in the middle of the night on an errand that would consign her soul to the farthest depths of Hell. Fortunately the Sannen-zaka was busy even at this hour with pilgrims who'd come to visit Kiyomizu Temple. That meant the shops were still open, their lanterns casting a reassuring light.

Olivia hurried on until she left the cheerful noise of the Sannen-zaka. The temple loomed ahead, high and imposing on the mountainside, the moon rising behind its curious pointed rooftops. She paused in the darkness, listening for anything that might be lurking nearby. Foxes and deer lived in the woods around the temple grounds. Fireflies flickered here and there under the maple trees. The Japanese love of nature and gardens had done much to thaw Olivia's cold disapproval. When she'd first learned Dr. Harrington had been posted to Japan, by Queen Victoria herself, and intended to move his household to the East for the entire four years, she considered giving her notice. Dr. Harrington's medical expertise in the area of geriatrics would expand greatly in this land where living to an advanced age was to be expected, even among the lower classes. Yes, becoming an advisor to the Emperor was a most admirable post, but what did it matter if the family lost their beloved daughter to some foreign disease?

Olivia reached the crossroads where the Sannen-zaka met the Kiyomizu-zaka. Were the old legends true? If you called the Devil to the crossroads at midnight, could you strike a bargain with him? For Madelaine's sake, Olivia took herself firmly in hand. A deep breath, a squaring of her shoulders, and she spoke.

"My name is Olivia Danforth. I have come to speak to the spirits who reside here at the crossroads. I wish to ask for your help in a most urgent matter." Olivia steadied herself. "I am willing to pay whatever price you ask."

The fireflies continued their flashing dance. The wind rattled the branches of the tree closest to her, sending bright red maple leaves spiraling downward. Olivia waited, her heart pounding.

"Please!" she cried. "I'm sorry I can't speak to you in the language of your country. I am desperate. A child lies dying." Olivia's voice broke. "Please, I beg you. Nothing we've done for her has made any difference. Please, please don't let my little girl die."

Tears ran down Olivia's cheeks. She was mortified, but this was no time to cling to pride.

"Konbanwa, gaijin."

A deep voice behind Olivia startled a cry out of her. She spun around. No one stood behind her, yet she knew something was there watching her. The darkness gathered into the shape of a man wrapped in shadows. Where his eyes should have been gleamed flashes of starlight.

"Who—what are you?" Olivia asked.

"I am Amatsu Mikaboshi, the August Star of Heaven."

Olivia gasped. The Morning Star? Could this be Lucifer himself? She knew he was speaking Japanese, yet she could understand him.

"What offering do you bring me, *gaijin*, that I should grant your wish?"

An offering? That sounded like the incense or oranges or the other items piled up by the shrines Olivia had seen.

"Don't listen to him, English lady." In the exact center of the crossroads stood a young man dressed in the kimono and long divided skirts of a samurai. His thick black hair was bound up in a topknot. He wore the traditional swords tucked through his belt. "Your priests have told you your Western Devil can be found anywhere in this world, *ne*? I tell you this is not that person. This is a creature older than any of the stories in your holy book."

Olivia studied him. "Are—are you human or spirit?"

The young man bowed. "I am Chimata-no-Kami. My brothers and I are what you would call the gods of the crossroads."

"Silence, puppy!" snapped the voice from the darkness. "I could smash your statues and leave you groaning in the rubble!"

The young samurai appeared right beside Olivia. "You can do nothing, Mikaboshi, not without a human to torment and corrupt."

"Stop this!" Olivia's fright gave way to outrage. "Is there no place on this earth where men can keep from strutting about and declaring themselves mightiest of all?"

Mikaboshi barked out a mocking laugh. "This from you, woman? Your queen rules countries she will never live to see. All over the world, her soldiers enslave the people of those countries and pillage their wealth. The English are the most elegant of thieves."

"Mind your tongue, demon!" Olivia snapped. "You will not speak that way about our beloved Queen Victoria!"

"Dee-mon." Chimata-no-Kami pronounced the word slowly. "*Hai.* This is what you seek, English lady? A demon? Believe me when I tell you Mikaboshi is not this Devil you seek."

"My precious little girl is dying!" Olivia cried. "Is there no one, no spirit, no human, no angel, no demon, no one in this entire wretched world who will give me the help I need?"

"Christians," Mikaboshi sneered. "The Tokugawa were right to kill as many of you as they could find. In your temples you light candles, you burn incense, but you come here in the dark without so much as a rice ball to lay before me."

"I have brought you something far more precious than a ball of rice wrapped in seaweed."

"Tell me, *gaijin.* What is this treasure you bring?"

"My life. More than that, my immortal soul."

"*Nani?*" Mikaboshi turned to Chimata-no-Kami. "You seem to understand this *gaijin*, boy. What is she saying?"

"When Christians die, part of them stands before their god awaiting judgment. If that part is found to be pure and righteous, it is allowed to join others of its kind in paradise."

"Do these Christians honor their dead with prayers and incense?"

"Not as we do. Their ancestors do not become *kami.*"

"Then what happens to them? What is this 'immortal soul' worth to me that I should take it as payment for healing the child?"

"Some of us are so diligent in our obedience to our Lord that we become filled with His grace," Olivia said. "Such people become saints. They perform miracles, healing the sick, answering prayers, bringing comfort and salvation to those suffering the torments of the Devil."

Mikaboshi looked at Chimata-no-Kami. "Bodhisattvas?"

"*Hai.* I have heard these 'saints' perform miracles while they live, and after they die and go to this paradise, still they can work their wonders."

Mikaboshi grunted. "These 'saints' must be feeble indeed, if this *gaijin* has come to me."

"Don't you think I've tried? Don't you think I've burned dozens of candles?" Rage and grief tore at Olivia's heart. "Would I offer my very soul to the Devil himself if I had not already hammered at the very gates of Heaven until my hands bled?"

"*Yokatta!*" Mikaboshi laughed. "This, this is what I value! Keep your soul, *gaijin*. Give me this pain that tears apart all the careful rules that govern your life!"

Chimata-no-Kami stepped between Olivia and the laughing darkness. "Begone, Amatsu Mikaboshi! This is my place! I am god of the crossroads, god of this crossroads that leads to Kiyomizudera itself!"

"Stupid boy," Mikaboshi snapped. "Roads lead two ways. You think it leads toward the temple? I say it leads away from it!"

Chimata-no-Kami seized Olivia's hand and pulled her toward the temple. "Jizo-*sama*! Jizo-*sama*! Hear the plea of one who loves a child more than life itself!"

Olivia ran with him. "Who is this Jizo-*sama*?"

"The protector of children. If any of the greater gods will answer you, it will be Jizo."

Mikaboshi appeared before them, barring their path. "She called me, boy! The chaos inside her belongs to me!"

Olivia dropped her cloak, wrenched open the high collar of her blouse, pulled out the delicate gold cross that had belonged to her mother and thrust it at the evil-eyed shadow.

"In the Name of Our Lord and Savior Jesus Christ, you will not stand between me and any hope of saving Madelaine!"

Moonlight struck the cross, flashing golden light across the darkness where Mikaboshi stood.

"Your Christian god doesn't frighten me. I will see to it you die before the little girl does!"

Out of nowhere a huge sword appeared in his hands, shaped like cold silver lightning.

"Amatsu Mikaboshi." A new voice rolled out across the night like the tolling of a great bell. "Amatsu Mikaboshi, you will not mock the light that burns inside this woman's heart."

Chimata-no-Kami fell to his knees and bowed down until his forehead touched the grass. Olivia clasped her cross between her folded hands and bent her head.

"Olivia Danforth." The great voice spoke. "You have come here at what you think of as the darkest hour of the night. You have come to call the Christian Devil, willing to offer up what is most precious to you if it will save the life of the child you love."

"Yes," Olivia whispered, more tears running down her cheeks.

"Is it not said in your holy book, 'Greater love hath no man than this that he lay down his life for his friends'?"

Olivia nodded. "The Gospel of John, Chapter Fifteen, Verse Thirteen."

"Go home, Olivia Danforth. Heaven sees your courage, your devotion, your willingness to sacrifice all to save this child."

"Then—will Madelaine be all right?"

"The fever has broken. Both mother and child need your care."

"Thank you! Thank you so much!"

Olivia snatched up her cloak and flung it around her shoulders. Chimata-no-Kami remained in full prostration before that great voice.

"Thank you, Chimata-no-Kami. If not for your help, I might have made a serious mistake." Olivia felt at a loss. Something more was needed. "May I—may I bring you some rice balls? Is there something you would prefer?"

"You are most kind, Danforth-*san*." Chimata-no-Kami stood up, then bowed to Olivia. "When the little girl is well, bring her to the temple. Jizo-*sama* is not the only *kami* who loves children."

Olivia smiled. "I'll do that."

LORD OF DEATH, PART I

By Steve DeWinter

1:00 AM, London

When the massive bell of Big Ben chimed only once in the still of the night, Nicholas "Nick" Steele was still wide awake in the upper floor of his rented flat. Illuminated by a single oil lamp, he tugged on the hoses that ran from the faceplate to the oxygen tanks on the back of the breathing apparatus. The tanks themselves were welded to a brass vest that looked like the breastplate from a suit of armor. He poured water over the various connections of the hoses and listened intently for the bubbling sound that indicated a leak. When nothing happened, he smiled in satisfaction.

The door opened and he looked up to see the stern face of the creator of this particular contraption, Jonathan "Jack" Flint, looking at him with a mixture of confusion and irritation.

"What are you doing up at this hour, Nick?" Jack whispered to keep the meddlesome landlady in the room below them from waking up. They had instigated her wrath on more than one occasion, and she had assured them that one more occurrence would result in them being put out on the street with nothing more than the clothes on their backs.

Nick placed a finger over his lips, reminding Jonathan to stay quiet as he responded. "I'm going to find that guy and bring him to justice."

Jack's mouth gaped. "No you're not."

Nick stood up. "We've got him this time, Jack. I feel it."

Jack was shaking his head. "You almost died last time, Nick. I can't let you. While we're not blood relations, you're more than a brother to me. I couldn't live with myself if something happened to you."

Nick grabbed Jack by the shoulders and grinned. "That's why you fixed the breather. I won't be affected by the white powder this time. Look, no leaks."

Jack shook his head even more forcefully. "We should just let the police handle this."

"The police are blind to what's really going on. They only see this as a string of suicides. They won't even try to listen to reason. We have to do this ourselves."

"I don't think the police are going to appreciate your vigilante actions. We're not out in the wild American frontier anymore, Nick. We are in the heart of greatest civilized empire in the world."

"Don't you see? If we catch this guy, then we can write our own ticket. Maybe even become consulting detectives to Scotland Yard."

Jack let out an exasperated breath. "We didn't come back to London to make the same mistakes all over again, Nick. We didn't start out trying to become outlaw rangers in America, and we certainly aren't going to try to become Sherlock Holmes and Doctor Watson here."

"And why not?"

"Well, for one, we're still wanted dead or alive in three Union states. Dead or alive, Nick. And two, there's no such thing as a consulting detective for Scotland Yard. That was made up for the books. Nobody really does that."

"That's only because nobody else can do what we can do."

"And what can we do, Nick? What?"

Nick smiled bigger. "We can show the world what we are made of. I'll get this guy and, at the very minimum, the streets of London will be safer for it. Even better, we can start getting paid for doing what we love. You can have seed money for your inventions …"

Jack cut him off, finishing his sentence. "And you get to run around playing the hero again."

Nick's smile threatened to split his face in half. "Now you're getting it. You'll see. I'll find this guy, bring him to the police, and everything will be okay. No, everything will be better than okay. Tonight marks a change in our fortunes, Jack. Are you with me?"

A tiny smile played along the corners of Jack's lips. "I think I'm close to formulating an antidote for the powder that makes people kill themselves."

Nick patted Jack's shoulders, fine black soot lifting from the woven fabric of his nightgown as he did. "Atta boy. Now, help me get this on."

Jack held the backpack while Nick put on his overcoat before slipping into the metal vest. Jack moved around to the front and made some final adjustments to the faceplate which, this time, completely covered Nick's face. Now that Nick was wearing the breather, the illuminated eyes and the thin hoses reaching back to the oxygen tanks on his back made him look like more like an automaton and less like a man.

He took a step back and admired Nick in the suit. "Maybe the sight of you alone will be enough to scare that villain straight," Jack said.

Nick turned and looked at himself in the mirror. "I sure hope so," he said, his voice muffled by the airtight faceplate. "Pray that he falls to the ground in terror and I won't have to chase after him. This thing feels much heavier than the last one."

Jack pulled on the straps and tightened the contraption around Nick's torso. "It is. I reinforced the tanks. Don't want them to explode if you get shot at."

Nick's head snapped toward him, but Jack couldn't see how big Nick's eyes were behind the metallic mask. "Shoot at me?" his anxiously muffled voice echoed a little too loudly in the room.

"Shh," Jack reminded him before continuing. "There's no reason to think he will do anything different from his current modus operandi. Just be careful, that's all."

"Aren't I always careful?" came the muffled response.

"Said the man with a hundred pounds of pressurized oxygen strapped to his back."

೫ಿಲ್ಲ

Nick stepped out into the chill of the night. At this hour, everyone decent had long since drifted off to sleep. Not to say Jack and Nick weren't decent fellows, but they were on a mission. A mission to rid London's foggy streets of the creature the newspapers had, tongue-clearly-in-cheek, dubbed the Lord of Death based on eyewitness accounts that reported seeing a ghost prowling the streets at night and surrounded his victims in a white vapor cloud.

Still reeling from the backlash of the unsolved murders in Whitechapel, the police denied the newspapers' allegations that they were unable to protect the city from yet another mass murder, and instead blamed the growing unemployment rates from the modernization of manufacturing as explanation for the increase in suicides throughout the greater London area in past months. Nick and Jack had discovered that most of those who had killed themselves were not unemployed line workers, but high level managers in various industries throughout the city. Something else was going on, and it had nothing to do with the despair of being replaced by machines in the workplace.

The Chinese immigrants in Limehouse, a district in East London, were calling him by another name: Mrtyu-mara. A Buddhist demon that is said to possess humans so that they suddenly want to commit suicide. While trying to disprove the working theory that it was a supernatural being, Nick had come across someone dressed in a Chinese opera mask who had engulfed him in a cloud of white powder. Planning for this, Nick was wearing a filtering mask over his mouth and nose, but the powder still got into his eyes. Within minutes, the feeling of hopelessness so overwhelmed him, it took all of Jack's coercive powers to talk him down off the roof of their rented flat. If he had ingested a full dose directly into his lungs, he was certain he would have jumped.

Once the drug had worn off, and Jack had run some tests on the powder residue still on Nick's clothes, they knew they were dealing with an ordinary man and not a ghost. Someone was using a new drug to drive people mad enough to kill themselves.

Nick passed a house with several bowls of food set out on the front steps. This was the seventh month of the Chinese calendar: the Ghost Month, according to ancient traditions held by the sailors stranded in London by the Blue Funnel Line, which offered no free return passage home to the East. It was the one month of the year that spirits supposedly walked freely on the earth. To honor their deceased, the Chinese celebrated the Hungry Ghost Festival by leaving out plates and bowls of food for the ghosts to eat so that perhaps they might leave the living alone.

Nick was a scientist and did not believe in ghosts or spirits, evil or otherwise. Despite the frightened and superstitious views held by an entire section of the city, he knew that the truth was far more terrifying. Someone was systematically killing influential people in the city, and the police were not willing to see it, encumbered by their own superstitions of the modern detective. All they saw was a clear-cut case of suicide with no need for a murder suspect.

If it was a suspect that they wanted, he would hand him to them, wrapped up neatly in a bow. Armed with his new full-face breather, Nick was ready to find this mythical Lord of Death and unmask him for the very real human villain he was.

☙❧

The light enhancing optics of the faceplate made seeing in the dark easier. Unfortunately, the field of view was greatly diminished and Nick found himself swiveling back and forth at the waist just to see the world around him. And with the increased weight of his back-mounted oxygen tanks, he was starting to feel his sides stitching up in cramps from the unanticipated exertion.

After the daily newspaper mentioned that this was the fifteenth night of the month, and that all the other suicides had taken place on the fifteenth of the month, the streets were deserted. Everyone had barricaded themselves in their homes to protect themselves from the most evil of spirits. It didn't matter that some of the higher profile victims had been at home. People always felt safer in their own houses than on the gritty streets of London at night.

After nearly half an hour of walking through one deserted street after another without encountering a single soul, Nick was beginning to wonder if the Lord of Death was going to be selecting a victim tonight. At first, the empty streets seemed like a good idea. It would just be Nick and the ghost, going mano a mano once he found him. But after spending the last half hour all by himself, it seemed that he was the only one in the world not safely nestled in bed.

Maybe Jack was right.

Maybe he should have stayed home tonight.

A flash of light at the end of yet another empty street caught Nick's eye. He focused on the corner and the lenses on his faceplate whirred quietly as they rotated and zoomed in on the corner that held his attention, letting him get visually closer without physically moving forward. He had to hand it to Jack; there was no invention too gratuitous for that guy. He let the lenses zoom in and refocus on the corner.

Another flash of light glinted in the darkened corner. Only this time, he recognized it as the flash of steel from a long bladed weapon. His optics struggled to see into the shadows, pulling every ounce of light from the widely spaced street lamps.

Suddenly, a figure stepped into view on the corner. No wonder he had such a hard time seeing who it was in the deep shadows. The man was entirely cloaked in a tight-fitting black suit that left only a sliver of skin exposed around the eyes. Gripped in the man's hands was a long sword that glinted when it caught the gaslight and reflected it back in its mirror finish.

Nick had never seen a sword like that. It looked more like a three-foot-long dagger than a sword. Just as quickly as he had appeared, the man faded back into the shadows. Nick was about to move when he saw what the black-clad man had been watching.

Coming around the far corner was someone dressed in a long black cloak, and wearing the same Chinese opera mask that was burned into Nick's memory from his previous encounter. Nick watched as the cloaked figure glided forward, moving so smoothly that he doubted if the man's feet even touched the ground. In fact, as his optics zoomed in, he noted that the man's feet were indeed several inches above the ground. The cloaked man wasn't walking on the ground. He was floating above it as he moved down the street toward Nick's position.

Maybe he was dealing with a ghost after all.

The ghost stopped at the door of a house and looked up at the open window on the second floor. He raised his arms and floated up until he was level with the window. The ghost then glided forward and hovered just outside the open window.

The flash of steel drew Nick's attention back to the ground. The black-clad man was moving silently down the edge of the street and stopped under the floating ghost. As Nick looked back and forth between these two strange figures, his optics zoomed out to let him see both at the same time. The ghost suddenly looked down at the sword-wielding man.

A cloud of white dust fell from the ghost and landed on the black-clad man's head, exploding into a larger cloud that surrounded the swordsman. He dropped his sword on the cobblestone street with a loud clatter and started weeping openly as he ran down the street.

The Lord of Death had claimed another victim.

The ghost returned his attention to the open window, landed softly on the edge of the windowsill, and climbed inside. Nick took off in a dead run, skidding on the white powder that dusted the street all around the front of the house. He looked up. There was no way he was going in the same way. He charged the front door, kicking out as he did.

The door shattered inward and Nick strained with the weight of his armored tanks as he vaulted up the stairs, taking two steps at a time. He kicked open the bedroom door and interrupted the ghost who had already awoken the man in bed. They both looked in Nick's direction in surprise as he charged forward to foolishly tackle the ghost before he could unleash his powder on the hapless victim.

Nick slammed into the ghost and heard him grunt as he knocked the wind out of him. Nick kept driving forward, using the momentum he had already built, and they both went out the window. He clung to the long cloak as the ghost roared in anger, sounding more human than mystical being.

They tumbled out the window, but instead of falling to the ground, they swung across the street in a low arc and slammed into the side of the house across the street. Nick maintained his grip as darkness fell over him, his vision blocked by the white powder that covered the optics on his faceplate. They swung back out to the street again, but no longer had enough momentum to reach the building they had fallen out of. Slowly, they swung back and forth like a pendulum in the middle of the street.

Nick reached up blindly and his hand found the edge of the opera mask. His fingernails scraped against flesh as he pulled the mask off. A ripping sound accompanied his stomach flipping as he felt himself fall. His legs hit the ground first and splayed out in opposite directions on the slick cobblestone right before the back of his head smacked against the uneven stones, knocking most of the powder loose.

As he lay on the pavement, he looked up and thought he saw the shadow of something large in the sky above the ghost as it rose out of sight into the night. Before he lost consciousness, his last thought was to ask Jack to completely surround his head with the protective mask for the next time.

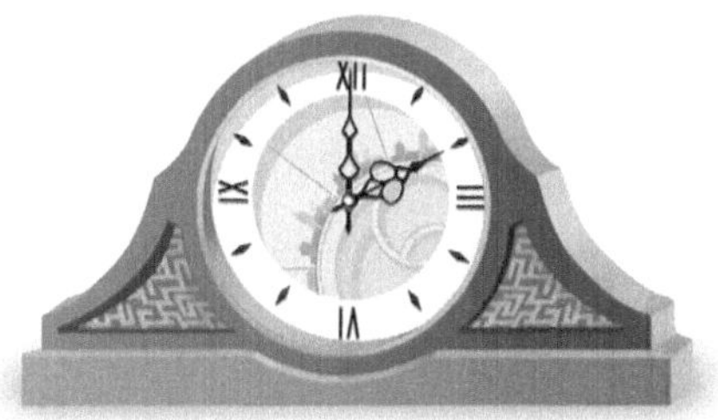

Nous Sommes Deux Heurs

By Sharon E. Cathcart

2:00 AM, Paris

Lucien Dubois was always glad when the ormolu clock set in the fireplace at his end of the Opera Garnier's Grand Foyer rang the two o'clock hour. It meant that the patrons and their parties were long gone and that he could remove his wig and livery. His work was far from over, though. There was the floor to sweep and the ashes to be cleared away so that a fresh fire could be laid before the next performance.

Lucien enjoyed serving in the Grand Foyer; it gave him a chance to hear the well-to-do folk talk about the sets he had helped build. Servants were treated as though they were invisible, but no one knew his name anyway.

At twenty years of age, Lucien was also one of the senior apprentices in the set shop; he was a gifted woodworker already, specializing in the miniatures used to create a set. He sometimes joked that it was in his blood; Dubois literally translated to "of the forest."

Usually, Lucien finished his duties in the Grand Foyer and then went back to the dormitories where he lived with his fellow apprentices. Tonight, he had other plans.

Lucien had heard rumors of an actual house in one of the lower cellars of the opera house. Tonight, after all of the chandeliers were dark and the fireplaces empty, he planned to find out the truth of the matter.

"If it is true," he thought, "I will use the house-within-a-house design in a set model someday. If it is not true, at least I will know for certain."

Sunday was Lucien's one day off for the week. No one cared how late he slept, or where he went. Sometimes, he would go to mass with his family; they all favored the priest at Saint Sulpice. Sometimes, he read a book. Sometimes he walked around the beautiful city that he called home. In these ways, he was like most of the other apprentices.

What set him apart from his fellows, more than anything else, was his nearly insatiable curiosity.

Off came the white gloves; it was time for the dirty work. The metal ash bucket felt heavier than usual, simply because Lucien was in a hurry to be done with his sweeping and cleaning. The refuse was hauled out to the heap, where the ash would be wetted down to make lye for soap and the trash carried away by the rag and junk man.

Lucien was proud of his work, even in the steward's serving role. He was able to give money to his family, and the hard work made his body strong. The women of the costume shop had remarked on his handsome face and dark curls and deep blue eyes more than once and always loudly enough for him to hear. He was tall and well-built.

Despite the attentions of the seamstresses, Lucien kept largely to himself. He preferred the opera's library, with its collection of set models right alongside the books, to carousing with his fellow apprentices. Lucien had dreams of becoming known for his designs, and thus spent what little spare time he had in study.

Lucien was one of the few apprentices who did not spend his money in the cribs of Place Pigalle. Not that he was priggish; he knew his funds were needed at home and could not see the point of wasting money on whores and absinthe.

That was not to say that he had no dreams of romance. Lucien had fancied himself in love a few times. There had been the chorine who enjoyed his company until she found a wealthy "sponsor" amongst the opera's male patrons. And there had been a scullery maid who eventually went back to her home in the country, saying the city was "too fast" for her.

And how his fellow apprentices teased him over his fondness for the dark-haired equestrienne who rode the big black mare! He loved watching her practice; the horse seemed to float across the ground with no visible command from the woman on her back.

Lucien knew her name: Claire Delacroix. It had appeared in many a program at the opera house. He also knew that, for a long time, she had been very sad. Lately, there was more light in her eyes and in her step. She did not seem the sort to take a sponsor, so Lucien decided that she must be in love.

She had been in the Grand Foyer that evening, dressed in a blue ball gown trimmed with fine black lace, enjoying a drink during the entr'acte. Sapphires sparkled at her ears and in her hair; a heavy collar of the blue stones wrapped around her throat and cascaded toward her bosom.

"You look beautiful this evening, Mademoiselle," Lucien said as he took her empty champagne glass.

"Thank you, Monsieur …"

"Dubois. Lucien Dubois." He bowed over her hand, wishing that he were wearing anything but the absurd, old-fashioned livery and wig.

"Monsieur Dubois," she smiled and nodded, then left the Grand Foyer. He wished that he knew where she was sitting, imagining himself inviting her for something to eat after the performance.

But that was pure fantasy; he had to put her from his mind. Besides, up close he could tell that she was at least ten years older than him. He had nothing to offer her.

Maybe she had a sponsor after all; how else would she have such jewels? Working in the set shop meant he could tell paste when he saw it, and those were no fakes borrowed from the costumers. These jewels were costly gifts from a patron.

"She is not for you, Lucien," he thought as he returned to his dormitory to change clothes. Tonight's plans called for simple brogans, cord trousers, and a rough shirt. He donned his laborer's attire, collected a lantern, and went to the library to look at Charles Garnier's plans for the building.

The drawings showed him all of the connections he needed to make in order to plumb the lowest depths of the building: the fifth cellar. The only part of the building he'd never explored.

Down stairwells and hallways he went, his lantern lighting the way in the darkness. The quiet was disconcerting; the usual bustle of the busy opera house was absent in the wee hours.

After what seemed an eternity, Lucien reached his destination, only to find a lake. Engineers had never successfully drained the fifth cellar, despite their efforts. Lucien shone his light on the water and watched a sleek shape glide past. Dear God, a sturgeon, of all things! There had to be a stream coming in from the Seine somewhere.

He lifted the lantern and peered into the distance. He saw lights across the way; surely that was more than mere reflection!

There was only one way to find out. He took off his shoes and stockings; they remained behind with the lantern as he entered the cold water.

Lucien was a strong swimmer, but the lights ahead were further away than he'd thought. A quick look back toward his lantern showed he was about halfway; turning back would take just as long as moving forward.

The water was much colder than he had anticipated, and every now and again a fish—the same sturgeon, perhaps—bumped into him.

He kept swimming.

℘つℭℛ

A bell chimed in the distance; the signal had not rung its alert in a long time. Erik LeMaître kissed Claire one more time—would he ever feel sated where her lips were concerned?—and got out of bed.

"What is it?" Claire murmured as she sat up, pulling the coverlet over herself. She wore nothing but the sapphire necklace.

"There's something outside, and I don't think it's that sturgeon," her lover replied as he drew on his trousers and slipped a mask over his face.

Claire reached for Erik's discarded shirt and pulled it over her head. She got out of bed and followed him out of his underground home and into the cavernous cellar.

"God in heaven!" she exclaimed as Erik turned an unconscious body over on the walkway. "It's Lucien Dubois, the steward from the Grand Foyer!"

"Yes, and also one of the set shop apprentices." Erik peered into the distance, seeing a speck of light. "The idiot swam here! I'll take the gondola to bring back his lantern before a rat upsets it and burns the whole place to the ground." His tone was one of disgust.

Claire, in the meanwhile, was examining Lucien as though he were one of her horses.

"He's chilled to the bone," she said. "Look at his skin; it's almost blue."

Erik rolled his eyes and picked up the unconscious youth as easily as though he were an infant.

"You start the caldarium, my love," he said. "I'll bring the lost sheep so that you can warm him."

Erik pretended more impatience with Claire's compassion than he felt, and both of them knew it. Claire smiled and ran ahead to the deep stone basin to open the tap.

Erik deposited the shivering, unconscious youth on the top step of the caldarium.

"You'll have to get him out of these foul clothes," he said. "I'll be back soon to help you with him."

"Lucien, you foolish boy," Claire murmured. "What on earth were you thinking?"

Practicality was the order of the day; she used a pair of shears to cut the shirt and trousers at the seams as the hot water filled the tub around her. Erik's linen shirt clung to her uncorseted curves.

Claire was quick and efficient in her work; before long, Lucien wore nothing but his pants and was coming to as the hot water rose around him, his eyes rolling a bit.

"Slip down one more step, Lucien. No, no. Don't stand. Just slip down. There you are."

Claire sat on the step Lucien had just vacated, her arm around the boy's shoulders. She spoke to him in the same tones she used with an injured or frightened animal.

"What … where?" Lucien's eyelids fluttered again.

"Just stay where you are; you're chilled to the bone."

"Mademoiselle Delacroix?" His quiet question showed his confusion. "How?"

"Never you mind what, where, or how, Lucien Dubois."

"My clothes!" His awareness was returning.

"Never mind those as well," Claire replied. "They were ruined by your swim."

Lucien pushed his sopping dark hair away from his face.

"They would be, I suppose." He groaned. "I don't suppose I could have some soap?" He was suddenly conscious of how he might smell.

"Of course."

Claire got out of the tub and retrieved a cake of Erik's sandalwood soap. Lucien gaped as he realized how little she wore.

"I'm sorry," she said as she handed him the soap. "I was more worried about warming you than about dressing myself. And I'm not leaving you alone."

"There is no need, my love." Erik had returned, holding an extinguished lantern and Lucien's heavy shoes. "Please, go change into something dry. I will watch our intruder."

Lucien had never seen anything like Erik LeMaître's face. When he took off the mask, the skin under it was discolored … a reddish-purple birthmark stained thin skin, one eyelid was nearly gone, and the nare on that side of his nose completely so. Scars that could only have come from a stinging lash covered his back. He stepped out of his trousers and into the tub.

"Go ahead and wash up, boy," he said. "And stop gawping like a fish. If you slip under the water and drown, Claire will never forgive me."

When Claire returned, clad in riding breeches, boots, and a shirt, Lucien's teeth were no longer chattering. Color had returned to his face and lips, and he was responding in a rather lively fashion to Erik's pointed questions about his early morning swim.

"What you have here is amazing," he was saying. "I must incorporate it into a set design."

"Lucien," Claire said quietly, "That is exactly what you must not do. Neither Erik nor I would be safe."

The youth started to protest, but fell silent. He gave Claire a beseeching look and spoke at last.

"He's your patron, isn't he?" Lucien's tone was glum.

"No, he isn't. He's my lover, certainly, but I am not ..."

"She's a lady," Erik interrupted, his voice like ice, as Claire walked away. "Her circumstances are reduced. That is all."

He got out of the tub and reached for a nearby towel.

"Dry off and follow me." His tone brooked no resistance, and Lucien obeyed.

In the main part of Erik's home, Claire waited with hot tea and cold beef sandwiches. When the two men reappeared, Lucien was wearing one of Erik's nightshirts. He fell on the repast gratefully.

"Might I have another cup of tea?" he asked.

"Of course," Erik replied, taking the youth's cup and saucer. With his back to Lucien, he tipped a small vial of powder into the hot tea. Claire saw what Erik had done and nodded her acknowledgment.

They didn't have to wait long for the drug to take effect. Once Lucien was sound asleep, Erik slung the youth over his shoulder like a sack of potatoes. With Claire carrying the lantern, they made their way back to the opera house dormitories by way of the Communard road.

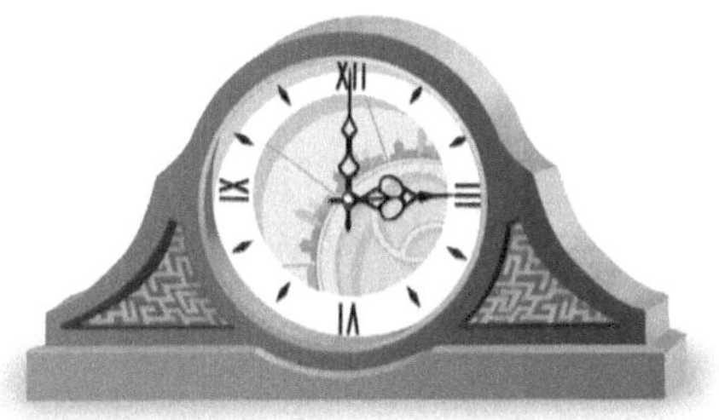

THE HOUR OF THE WOLF

By Anthony Francis

3:00 AM, Edinburgh

Jeremiah Willstone ran full tilt down the alley, the clockwork wolf nipping at her heels.

Her weekend had started pleasantly enough: an evening's liberty from the cloisters of Liberation Academy, a rattling ride into the city on a battered old mechanical caterpillar, and eluding the proctors for a walking tour of Edinburgh with a dish of an underclassman.

Late that night—or more properly early Halloween morning—the couple had thrown themselves down on the lawn of the park, and his sweet-talk had promised far more than this ersatz picnic of woven candies and braided sweets; but before they'd found a better use for their Victoria blanket, Jeremiah's eyes got them in trouble.

"Whatever is that?" she asked, sighting a glint running along the edge of the park.

"Just a rat," Erskine said, proffering her another twisted cinnamon scone.

"Of brass?" Jeremiah asked, sitting up. "With glowing eyes, I note—"

"Perhaps you imagined it, Jeremiah," Erskine said, but his eyes were following the glint, too, now; he was already slipping the scone back inside its woven bag. "Or perhaps this is a clever ploy to lure me into a dark alley for some mischief."

Jeremiah popped to her feet. "I'll take that," she said, crooking her finger.

"That worked?" Erskine asked, surprise spreading over his face; funny that, Jeremiah'd had the same thought. Without waiting, she strode into the underbrush, finding, just out of view, a cool, dark path, a tree to lean against, and when she turned about, him. He said, "Well met, Cadet."

"Well met, indeed," she replied, eyes flashing, drawing him to her.

Cadet's blues, assembled mix-and-match from parts designed to mock the functions of a full Expeditionary's tailored kit, peeled off easily: blue grieves and bracers easily unbuckled, ruffled white shirts that bloomed when freed, and durable black pants that rarely wrinkled.

Even on the coolness of a dark path, while young skin met the rough bark of a tree.

Even after that delight, discretion demanded a quick return to uniform, particularly donning their blue cadet's vestcoats— heavy Faraday mesh, expensive, mass produced, one-size-fits- most, adjusted with buckles. Cadets could trade vestcoats, despite their locator brooches, a dalliance scowled at by the red-coated student proctors, but when Jeremiah saw Erskine putting on her coat and adjusting it to size, she understood why young lovers risked it.

"Well met, indeed, Cadet," Jeremiah said, pulling on *his* coat. "I—oh, bugger me."

"Again?" Erskine asked, then whirled, drawing his thermionic blaster as he followed her gaze. A thousand beady eyes glowed in the dark, shining numerous and brightly enough to glint off each other's brass gears—and white teeth. "Bugger me twice!"

"Later," Jeremiah cried, drawing her blaster even as the clockwork rats reared. "Run!"

Jeremiah and Erskine bolted down the path, trying to regain the park, but were corralled into the underbrush by the squealing horde. Forced down a streambed into the warren of drainage canals undergirding Edinburgh's financial acropolis, the cadets cried for help, but found none in the shuttered windows of the tottering skyscrapers above. As the lanes grew narrower and the swarm grew closer, they whirled, took aim, and unloosed green electrodynamic fire.

Thermionics rarely killed, so the Academy taught its cadets to be liberal with the trigger, and they mowed down the first wave of half-machine rats with gusto. But soon Jeremiah found her blaster's gas canister running thin while the horde got thicker, herding them into the corner of two crumbling warehouses.

"Cast off!" Jeremiah cried, kicking one of the rats away.

"I second the sentiment," Erskine said, popping a discharged canister and pulling out another—his last, from the look on his face. He opened the breech of his blaster, worrying at a spring. "If I pop the limiter and discharge the canister all at once—"

"Oh, bloody hell," Jeremiah said, shrinking back. "What the hell is that?"

A spiky brass *thing* the shape of a wolf but the size of a bear padded toward them down the narrow alleyway, its metal claws scraping against the cobblestones. The outline of its body was almost lost in the mess of gears and spines, but its glowing eyes pinned them.

"—I'll wager the blast will … set them back," Erskine said, voice trailing to a quaver.

"Failing a successful defense," Jeremiah said, "we need to sound the alarm."

"Agreed," Erskine said, as the thing clanked forward. "I'll fight them off, you run!"

And before Jeremiah could say "hang that," Erskine ran forward, discharging the blaster at full, spraying the clockwork rats with thermionic fire. They twitched and fell, and he advanced on the clockwork wolf even as his blaster sputtered out—and fallen rats started to rise.

"Go!" Erskine said, as the things swarmed him. "Hang sentiment—get help! Go!"

Cursing her cowardice, Jeremiah turned and ran, dodging through narrow, twisted alleys. The horde of clockwork vermin followed, but their rattles and squeals were drowned out by the swift, heavy, springy footfalls of the metal wolf rapidly gaining on her.

Jeremiah dodged through lanes barely wide enough to pass her—then her ankle turned. She tumbled and slid down a steep, narrow ramp that was little more than a waste sluice—then impacted in a pool of brown, muddy muck, which splashed out, then closed back over her.

Briefly stunned, Jeremiah struggled to surface—until a metal paw fell on her chest.

Only the pressure of the clockwork wolf's paw prevented her from screaming: it had caught her on the exhale, leaving her no air to scream with. A few bubbles popped the surface, but were lost in the muddy squelch as the mechanical monster set another paw upon her.

Horrified, arms pinned beneath its paws, only her eyes visible above the muck, Jeremiah stared up at the underside of the monster's throat as it scanned the alley. What was it looking for? Friends? Foes? Then she realized, from this angle … she couldn't see its eyes.

It was looking for *her.*

Lungs burning, Jeremiah remained absolutely still as the hybrid monster, half brass, half flesh, scanned, sniffed, snarled—then planted one paw further forward, cutting her temple, but continuing its advance. It had lost sight of her when she'd slid down the sluice into the muck.

She resolved to never complain about Edinburgh's sanitation again.

The monster took another step. Now the thing's chest was above her and, inside its brass armor, she spied a wonder: within its metal ribcage, she could see an emaciated, hairless, *human* chest—and, where a heart should have been, a spinning, glowing thermionic engine.

Oh, God. The rats appeared to be rats inside their spiky, gear-encrusted exoskeletons, but this wasn't a wolf in clockwork clothing. There was a *person* in there: this strange construct was a human being encased—enmeshed—in the electromechanical semblance of a wolf.

She started to scream, but the thing planted its hind foot on her chest, and then moved on. The water closed over her face again, and she spluttered as it splashed over her; then she lay perfectly still in the muck as a thousand clockwork rats swarmed over her—carrying something heavy.

What seemed like an eternity passed as Jeremiah lay there, submerged beneath muck filled with godknowswhat, hearing her heart pounding in her waterlogged ears, feeling her lungs burn with growing fire. Were they gone? Dared she move? Was that another approaching tread?

A strong hand seized her and Jeremiah struggled, spluttered, and sat up.

"Are you all right, Cadet?" asked a streetsweep. "A bit late for a swim …"

Jeremiah flopped and lunged, flipping over, looking after the direction that the monster had likely gone. No monster, no horde, and no Erskine, but she saw muddy tracks paralleling a heavy serrated tread … a trail which quickly petered out on the cobblestones.

"No," Jeremiah said, kicking herself up out of the mud, seizing the street sweep's hand and levering herself upright, watching—as Erskine had predicted—faint thermionic blasts in the distance, as raucous cadets started Halloween celebrations a bit early. "Not right at all."

Fearing arrest as a rowdy drunk cadet, Jeremiah ran back to Academy grounds. Full tilt was no longer in Jeremiah's arsenal, but she kept thinking of Erskine and made good time to the Electromechanical Relay building, where she could raise the alarm—or triangulate her brooch.

Bugger! Two red-coated proctors stood guard at the door. Even more likely to think a muddied, bloodied cadet talking monsters to be a drunken cadet talking nonsense. Still, she'd have to give it a go, and limped up to the stair beneath the flickering gas light.

"Hold up, Cadet, computers and support staff only," said the taller redcoat.

"I've been attacked," Jeremiah gasped. "We have a cadet down—"

"Drunk and disorderly will land you in the can, Cadet," said the shorter proctor.

"Not drunk," Jeremiah wheezed. "He's got my locator brooch. A computer can—"

"And blues-swapping will get you disciplined," the shorter proctor said, standing straight. The red vestcoat, identical to hers but for color, made the effort look ridiculous. "Look at you, blathering on to upperclassmen. Attention, Cadet! What's the proper form of address?"

Jeremiah despaired, and then resolved on a desperate chance. She snapped to attention.

"Sir, sorry, sir," she barked, and decked the shorter proctor, who fell unconscious against the tin side of the building with a rattling thump. Jeremiah whirled on the taller redcoat, who put his guard up and leapt back out of range. She cried: "Sir, stand aside, sir …"

"Good God, you've struck a proctor!" said the taller proctor, who was thin as a stick, but had half a head on her and a fighting form that wasn't bad. Taking him out would be quite the trick, but then he said: "You're serious! We have a cadet down?"

"Sir, yes, sir," Jeremiah said. "Sir, please, there's no time, sir, he held them off …"

Did her lip tremble? Jeremiah stiffened, but the proctor just opened the door.

"Drop the 'Sir, yes, sir,' bit, Cadet, we've work to do," he said, leading her down a narrow corridor. Glass-windowed doors granted peeks at vacuum tubes taller than she was. "And forget about Chadwick, he's a prick. I'm Proctor Evelyn Davidson. What's your name, Cadet?"

"Jeremiah Willstone, sir."

"Well, Jeremiah," Evelyn said, stopping before a heavy, insulated door, at which he tapped a combination before opening the latch and throwing it asunder. "Even if you recall your own locator code, it may take some work to convince the computer to cough it up."

"I think we're in luck," Jeremiah said. "This computer owes me a favor."

At the center of racks of electromechanical equipment three stories high, sitting on an elaborate throne and wearing an even more elaborate buckskin and crinoline dress—but with dozens of cables climbing out of her hair—sat the Lady Georgiana

Westenhoq, Jeremiah's Academy roommate, and the computer who drew night watch for Halloween weekend.

"Mya? Why are you here?" Georgiana asked, turning her head with the grace trained into Mahican aristocrats and required of computers; embedded in her dark, stacked curls were dozens of vacuum tubes plugged into her brain. "Proctor—Vellon, isn't? Have you a good reason …"

"It's Jer-eh-MI-yah," Jeremiah muttered.

"And it's Evelyn, Lady Westenhoq," said the proctor. "We have an emergency."

"My—ahem—lover was just taken by a horde of clockwork rats," Jeremiah said.

"Good God," the proctor said. "And we're given to think he has her locator brooch on."

Georgiana stared at them for a moment, her dark eyes enigmatic in her exotic ruddy skin.

"Well," she said, her throne rotating without any visible command. "Let's find him then."

"His—my locator brooch number is two one, oh nine …" Jeremiah recited, as Georgiana projected Edinburgh's narrow streets upon the wide, crackling dial of a spectroscope screen. Soon the computer had located the brooch's trail, and found its end. "*Destroyed?* Oh no …"

"No, deactivated," Georgiana corrected, highlighting the surge at the end of the signal. She expanded the map view and projected the trail forward. "Smart. They didn't want us finding their lair. They're not likely to have killed him. Not after all that effort to get him—"

"What?" Jeremiah said. "Those clockwork rats know of our locator brooches?"

"That trail projects out over a quarter of the city," said Evelyn. "Into the slums …"

"An ample supply of rats," Jeremiah said, thinking. "Focus on the end of the trail!"

Georgiana obliged, and Jeremiah stepped close to the spectroscope, peering at the truncated silver trail with her name on it, following its likely course out into the glowing green lines of the map, and finding streets which, to her, were all too familiar.

"How far back does my trail go?" Jeremiah asked. "Say, a week?"

"I can show you the whole month," Georgiana said—then gasped as the backwards-growing end of the line crossed in front of its truncated termination, then again, then again, stopping repeatedly at a point not three blocks from the end of the trail. "Jeremiah?"

"The Mechanical Assembly Workshop," Jeremiah said, pointing at the large, isolated building where her trail crossed over itself. "An older Academy building, infested with rats, filled with enough cylinder-directed arms to wind gears through the lot of them—"

"And the location of your assistantship, I see," Georgiana said, calling up the details of her portal crossings. "Fortunately I doubt anyone will be there at oh-three-thirty—oh, bugger, there's at least one locator beacon in the building, a faculty member—"

"The professor I assist, Feldkirch, keeps an office there," Jeremiah said. Her eyes bugged as she realized that assembly arms that could operate on rats could operate on people, too. "God, there was a person in that clockwork wolf. Erskine or the professor could be—"

"—could be in immediate danger," Chadwick finished, holding his jaw. Jeremiah whirled; she wondered how long he'd been listening, and how slack she'd gotten for letting him sneak up. "I overheard clockwork rats, and wolf. Bring me up to speed, Cadet."

Jeremiah explained the swarms of rats, the clockwork werewolf, and the person she'd seen inside it. When she described how Erskine was taken, she liked to think she kept the quaver out of her voice as she thought of what might be happening to him.

"Sirs and my lady," she finished, "the cadet recommends we strike while the iron is hot!"

"Sound the alarm," Evelyn commanded, galvanized. "And fetch the autocart!"

"With dispatch," Chadwick said, whirling and running out. "And arm yourselves!"

"I need to reload," Jeremiah said, checking her blaster. "I'm just about drained—"

"Fetch spare canisters, Chad," Evelyn called after Chadwick, who called back an affirmative. Evelyn turned back and his face paled as Georgiana rose. "Ah, my Lady Westenhoq, if you handle the alarm, we'll handle—"

"Fear not, I'm an excellent shot," Georgiana said, stepping down from her throne, cables unsnapping from her head and spine with sharp whipcracks. "And if you've a computer who's also a member of the Peerage with you, the Academy will send reinforcements."

"Capital strategy, but we need to go," Jeremiah said, helping Evelyn close the buckles on an aerograph pack as Georgiana strolled to the spectroscope's dial and punched keys. "You should have done that when plugged in. We need to go, quickly. I mean, quick, now!"

Georgiana pulled a red handle, the lights themselves turned a flickering red, and the powerful, mournful howl of the air raid siren rose over the campus—but, of course, theirs was the closest building. Georgiana turned, raising a deranger, checking its charge. "Ready."

Outside, Chadwick roared up in one of the bumpy old Ellis autocarts all miscreant cadets knew well from the inevitable proctor's roundups. But tonight, two cadets and two proctors tore off together toward the farthest part of the city—and the Mechanical Assembly Workshop.

"Shouldn't we wait for reinforcements?" Chadwick asked, even as he sped through the streets so quickly that he'd knocked off both of the mirrors and part of one fender. "Or drum up silver bullets for that clockwork werewolf—"

"We need speed, not silver," Jeremiah said. "Erskine and Feldkirch are in mortal danger from these monsters, but we don't need to defeat them all by ourselves—we've already called for reinforcements, so we only need delay whatever malfeasance is afoot—"

"Not stop it," Georgiana said. "You're using us as cannon fodder—"

"Hush, now, you're using yourself as bait," Jeremiah replied, as the autocart slid to a stop before the looming façade of the Mechanical Assembly Workshop. Half the windows were broken out, and glowing red eyes peered at them. "No need for stealth, then. In we go!"

They poured out of the autocart, the two proctors tackling the door with their shoulders while Jeremiah helped Georgiana down. Adding two more shoulders knocked the doors asunder and, inside, Jeremiah zapped a half-dozen clockwork rats before darting up the stair.

But halfway up, blasting away at an increasing swarm of reinforcement rats, her eye was caught by the stair's ornate balustrade—supported by long, narrow, wooden spindles, with a lower bulge that would do as an ersatz handle—but with the top end tapered to a point.

She kicked out one of the spindles and hefted it like a wooden stake.

"This might do the trick," Jeremiah muttered.

"What's the spindle for?" Georgiana cried, blasting away.

"Following a hunch; that wolf thing had a thermionic heart," Jeremiah said, zapping one off the rail as she crested the stairs, but what she saw through the narrow window of the catwalk door was not encouraging, and she crouched down. "Everyone, hang back a bit."

"What's wrong?" Evelyn asked, tapping out a call for reinforcements on his aerograph.

Jeremiah peered through a crack in the door. "My lady, sirs: we've a bit of mixed luck," she said, glancing at her compatriots and slipping the spindle into her belt while she reloaded. "Our foe has poor strategy: a strong core with a weak perimeter. That let us in—"

"But we're in for a fight," Chadwick said, raising his blaster.

"We are indeed." Jeremiah said. "On three, my lady and sirs; one, two—"

Her own words were lost as their four combined thermionic blasts blew open the door to the Mechanical Assembly Workshop Floor, a cavernous warehouse filled with hulking machine-building machines—all covered with endless gear-infested furry bodies with glowing eyes.

"It wasn't like this last week," Jeremiah said.

They ran out onto the catwalk as swarms of clockwork rats began looming up in masses, building gear-and-fur pyramids to reach them. Jeremiah blasted away, a little more cautiously now, trying to husband her shots, and then, rounding the corner, she sighted Erskine.

He lay arms out atop an assembly line, moving closer and closer to the cylinder-directed arms that built Mechanical Sciences' largest constructs. Those assembly arms were covered with new, strange circuits, loaded with glass jars of blood, and tipped with surgical blades, cutting her cadet's blues away from his chest. At the end of the assembly line, the clockwork wolf looked up and snarled, but the eyes behind the lenses were weary and bloodshot.

"Spent, and need a new host?" she said, clenching her teeth. "Not today, sir!"

"What the hell?" Evelyn cried, even as he fired. "Is that your clockwork werewolf?"

"It is indeed," Jeremiah said, running down the catwalk, rage granting her full tilt once again. The clockwork wolf stomped toward her, sometimes on two legs, sometimes on four. She cried: "Everyone, lay suppressing fire, guard yourselves—and touch nothing metal!"

The wolf leapt up at her as she leapt down on it, ramming the pointed spindle into its chest. They tumbled and rolled, but she kicked herself away, taking the spindle without a second thought, running forward as her compatriots blasted away the rats nipping at her heels.

The blades lowered toward Erskine's heart, and Jeremiah rammed the spindle into the core of the machine, shattering its thermionic engine. The spray of green thermodynamic fire knocked her off her feet and knocked the spindle from her hands.

But it had a greater effect on the mechanical arms, which jerked and twitched, their strange circuitry sparking, spewing out new waves of energy that spread out further, frying the clockwork rats, which squealed and died as their crackling green energy killed their kin.

The concentric ring of sparking death spread out over her, rattling every muscle with pins and needles, but Jeremiah paid no mind; she staggered to her feet and, with a shove of her shoulder, forced the blades of the cylinder-driven arms away from Erskine's bare chest.

He was out, bruised, almost still—but breathing, and she patted his chest.

"Well," she said. "Glad to see this again, still whole."

There was a groan behind her, and she turned to see the clockwork wolf trying to rise to its feet. The huge thing's framework of gears and wires made it much bigger than a man—but she could still see the shape of the man inside it, emaciated, half eaten by the machine.

And the machine was recovering: rebuilding itself, tearing into the flesh that supported it, a great paw with a skeletal hand inside it reaching aside to pick up a dead rat, which it threw into its maw, disassembled into parts, and began reincorporating, even as she watched.

"No, sir," Jeremiah said, pulling the stake out of the machine. "We have no do-overs at the Academy."

Jeremiah ran at the monster as her compatriots rained electrodynamic blasts down on it, but the thing just shrugged them off, grabbing more rats, gaining more strength, struggling to rise—even as Jeremiah rammed the wooden stake into its thermionic heart.

Green fire tore at her, and Jeremiah found herself frozen there, even as the thing slumped forward, its great metal maw inches from her face. The glow behind the lenses died, but behind the glass, she again saw those bloodshot eyes—eyes she'd glimpsed before.

"Professor Feldkirch," Jeremiah cried in horror. "What ... what happened to you?"

"A story for another time, Cadet," Feldkirch wheezed from within. "Thank you."

Then the eyes glazed over, and the man within the machine sagged as it, too, died.

"This is *quite* Foreign," Georgiana said, inspecting the strange, jury-rigged network of wires and gears spider webbed over the ruined assembly machine. Abruptly she pulled a scorched punch card out of a reader. "Jeremiah—these punches look like your locator code."

Jeremiah snatched it up. "Bugger me, this is my attendance card. You don't think it was targeting *me*, do you? The rats, homing in on my brooch, but taking him after I fell in the muck because it was a warm body with my signal?" At Georgiana's worried look, Jeremiah swallowed, but then Erskine groaned, and she went to his side.

"Capital," Chadwick said, as voices cried from outside. "Reinforcements."

"In the nick of time," Evelyn said. "Did we just kill a clockwork werewolf?"

"I think so," Georgiana said, extracting from the nest of gears a strange circuit: glittering, filigreed, and foreign to anything built on Earth. She passed it to Jeremiah, who quietly pocketed it for further action as Georgiana said to the proctors: "Without even a single silver bullet …"

"Bugger silver," Jeremiah said, relieved to find Erskine had a steady pulse. "Paid you no attention in Philip's mythology class? Rat familiars, a collector of blood—and I killed it with a wooden stake! Wolf form or no, it was never a werewolf. It was a vampire."

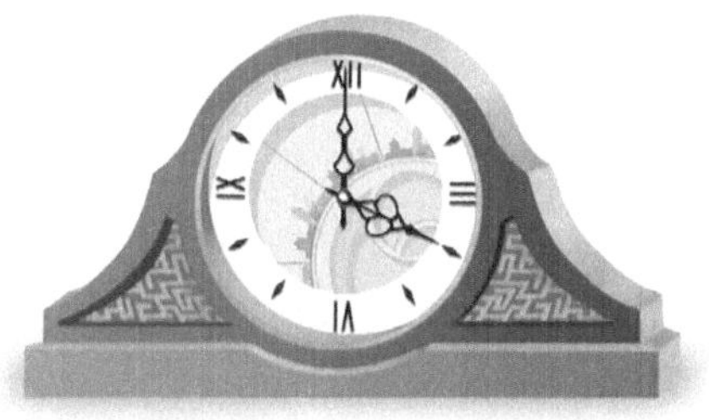

THE DUELING FIELD

A Miranda Gray Mystery

By T.E. MacArthur

4:00 AM, Bath

Damn it all, I was promised support—protection. Where is that so-called colonel?

Crouching low under the holly tree, she pushed her back against the twisted trunk and prayed that the branches, which fell from the top like an umbrella, would hide her sufficiently. *Just wait.* A good plan: she was nearly out of breath having run uphill to the Dueling Field, below the Royal Crescent. Hills—always hills in Bath. Where was her protector; *where is he?*

There was something wrong in Bath, and it wasn't only the dreadful weather. *Wait. No mistakes. This has to go right.* Of course, as things went with Miranda Gray, "right" might be impossible.

The old spa town was not prone to the screams and howls that marked London's bleak atmosphere; it was quiet. Even for a sultry night, with all the students in residence and the pubs over-flowing with human folly, it was quiet. Well, at least she would hear her prey approach, wouldn't she?

Where is the Colonel?

Minutes, only minutes at best. She must be calm. It would be essential. There was a fight coming.

Bloody nasty humidity. Bath was not known for being tropical, but Miranda sat watching the fog roll in sheets above a distant gaslamp and found that every dank breath reminded her of those days she had spent in Ceylon. Reflexively, she ran her fingertips down the grip of a pistol strapped under her arm. Strange. Eeven in this heat, it remained cold to the touch.

Something moved. Leaves? Gravel? What was it?

Her hearing expanded protectively. Her eyes saw something move in the distance. Flickering gaslight from the path above the field, failing moonlight frequently hidden by the fog, and shallow winds guaranteed that she would misinterpret what was out there if observed by sight alone. She listened, as they say, as if her life depended on it. And it did.

Is it the Colonel? Has he finally shown up?

Or was it the other man—her prey? No. No one was there. It was probably only a rabbit or a branch or something: common sounds in a wooded area. Maddeningly, it was definitely not the man she'd been promised would provide her with protection. Were she not a lady, she would have cursed in mariner fashion and spit. Stupid, unreliable, self-aggrandizing men. Liars. *Well, enough of that,* she thought, forcing her body to relax and her heartbeat to slow, as she'd been taught. She could, and thoroughly expected to, do this alone.

Miranda shifted her position so that the borrowed Italian boots wouldn't cut off the circulation to her feet. The blue-striped trousers had bunched slightly at the knee. *Lord Almighty, it is hot. And sticky. And grotesque.* What had Jane Austen said of the occasional, bizarre weather of Bath? It left one in a constant state of inelegance. *Ha! Madam, if only you knew.* A bead of sweat ran out from under the short-cropped wig, down her collar, and under her shirt and waistcoat. Her face was doing far more than "glowing" as a lady's might, and the wetness was causing the actor's paste holding her fake sideburns onto her skin to dissolve. Her disguise was under assault. But then, so was she. So was Britain if she failed.

Patience? Yes. She would wait in her safe warren until her prey caught up. It had been quite a task getting his attention and drawing him from the relative security of Garrick's Head Pub. He would follow her, once he mistook her for his contact. But he wouldn't follow too closely. That would be imprudent. He might be too experienced for that. She estimated he would take a good ten minutes to follow her up toward the Royal Crescent and the secluded grove called the Dueling Fields. *I wonder how many men died here—and for some ridiculous reason.* Five minutes at most remained.

A rather unladylike business, but then she hadn't exactly volunteered. She had, what was it they called them, "skills of particular nature in a peculiar combination," even for a woman? Most unladylike. Of eight persons in the old library two nights ago, six were men used to the free exercise of power over the multitudes. The two remaining were simply dismissed as part of the "multitudes": one woman, with particular skills, and a colonel—a dishonorable one, to be sure. If he showed up now, she would be genuinely surprised.

The Colonel, now forced into her association, had been disheveled, dirty, and bloodied. He had the look of a man who'd been spared the noose in exchange for services, but not before someone had made certain he paid some minimum for his crimes with a beating. The Colonel had been no more pleased to meet her than she had been to meet him, though likely for less cultured reasons. He had piercing eyes, eagle-like, and a lean, narrow body. His hair, had it been clean, might have been a rich brown. His hands were not worn by trade or labor, thus he was either a fallen gentleman or knew how to live as one. Just because they called him "Colonel" didn't mean he was one or qualified to be any sort of officer.

She reached up and wiped the back of her neck, flicking away the perspiration.

The Colonel was more likely a man of some limited means drawn into the lure of easy money in crime, caught, and forced to deal with the Ministry for his life. Hardly qualifications for the job. They had been foolish allowing him the freedom to choose his own methods to protect her. It was far more probable that he had boarded a train south to Dover and was already on the steamer, half way across the Channel, laughing as he went.

Movement. Footsteps on the fallen leaves. Miranda suddenly heard the sound of every beat of her heart, loud ringing, and every drop of moisture that fell from leaf to leaf.

"All right, Mister, come out." Her prey had arrived. "I isn't stupid. I know yer here. If you got the directions, then I got the map. Come on, mate, we can work it out." A knife was slowly removed from its sheath, a distinct sound regardless of the patience with which it was drawn. The blade caught dull glints from the gas lamp. Her prey was a professional thief, possibly a murderer. "There'll be plenty for the both of us. All we got to do is find it. We don' need to share no more beyond you and me."

Her prey moved very carefully, but his direction said he didn't know where she was. His voice displayed a slight shake; he was nervous or excited. Probably both. At the Garrick's Head, she'd sized him up to being less than six feet tall, under-nourished, and overly prone to drinking. Typical. How he had become embroiled in the business of national security and clues set in complex hieroglyphic codes was quite the question. He moved very deliberately, as a man would when sober. She'd hoped he'd been drinking; it would have given her some advantage, but that was not to be. No matter. She'd planned for his sobriety too.

"Treasure for us both. We'll be kings," he said with false sweetness.

Treasure? The Ministry had sent her to track down gold and goods? Ridiculous. They wouldn't send her for anything less than the needs of the nation. "Shut up and get over here before someone sees you." She needed more information.

The prey seemed startled. He probably hadn't expected cooperation.

"And put that thing away. Unless you can read Egyptian and do math," she said, keeping her voice low and lightly accented in the manner of West county speech.

"Where are ya?"

Miranda pressed her hands down on the false side-burns, adjusted the male-styled wig, and hoped that the heavy eye-brows would stay put over her own. From her coat pocket she removed a box of matches. Her hiding place glowed from the match but dully. She needed to keep her disguise from being brightly illuminated.

He walked over quickly, knife still in hand, and looked under the holly tree. He did not enter and appeared as concerned about the tree as he was of the disguised Miranda.

"What's the matter?" she asked in a whisper, keeping her gender hidden as much as she could.

"Don' ya know what this is?"

"It's a tree."

"No, mate. This is that tree what grew in the blood of the dead. I 'eard the stories. Toff like you should know. Duels 'ere and plenty of dead—I ain't for staying in this haunted place."

Miranda tried not to roll her eyes. "You want treasure, don't you?"

The prey shook his head, then nodded, but backed away all the same.

Fine. The close quarters might have kept any wild slashing movements or powerful knife thrusts limited, but she could deal with him in the open. She was armed, among other things.

He was genuinely afraid of the tree. He kept backing up until he had distanced himself enough to get back to business. As she stood there, looking annoyed, and holding the last of her lit match, he put away his knife. As slowly as he had approached the glade, but with none of the original bravado, he removed from his ill-fitting coat a large folded piece of paper, and laid it out on the ground.

She lit another match, revealing that the paper was a rubbing. It looked just like a rubbing from a tomb or sarcophagus, only the marks were too crisp and clean. Whatever he had copied was new, not ancient. It was made to look like it came from a statue in the British Museum. The unfolded paper was particularly large. At the top stretched a female form, with her legs providing the right side frame of the picture and her arms the left side. Beneath her were stars in irregular patterns. That is odd, she thought. The Egyptians loved symmetry, and random star patterns would have been considered disordered and ugly. And another thing she found odd: the starry sky took up more than three quarters of the illustration. The obscene deity of the Earth, with his "interest" in the sky goddess jutting straight up toward the female, only accounted for a tiny portion. No, she couldn't blush or shy away as a lady would from such a pornographic image; that would destroy her masculine disguise.

Her eyes must not have moved from the dramatic phallus for a second or two because her prey found her stare rather funny. "Damn Fuzzy-Wuzzies like to draw 'em big?" He laughed. Miranda just made a foolish-looking grin then went back to frowning.

"There." She pointed to a set of cartouches in the lower left-hand corner. They were completely new hieroglyphs; quite different from the ones she'd been originally shown. The whole coded business had been quite clever about giving only so many clues at a time.

"'Ow's a bloke like you know all this stuff?"

"I know people." She kept a new match aloft and maneuvered the rubbing with her left hand. It was difficult with gloves, but she didn't dare remove them and reveal the soft, dainty hands beneath.

"So, 'ow's this go now?"

"The man what made these codes is smart. See, the figures in the circle here and here," she pointed back and forth, "they're supposed to be names. They aren't. They're not 'picto-somethings' that mean exactly what they look like. See? Hashes and dots. I was told these aren't real Egyptian scribbles." Lord, how the accent and poor wording were hard to use for concepts she'd studied all her life. She hated not being able to fully explain how Egyptian written language had developed from the Old Kingdom to the Greek period.

"That's what my boss thinks. 'E got wind of this from someone what isn't here no more. So, I got hired to do what I do."

"Right. You got into the house that had the stone, copied it here, and now we got ourselves a full picture. The new parts aren't pictos, they're numbers. But you have to put them through some formulas to get the real numbers. That's the genius of this thing."

The prey looked up, concerned. "An' you got the real numbers right?"

"I will."

"No. You got 'em right now."

"You gotta give me a chance to …"

The knife was back out. "You're stallin'!" He began to look around frantically. Apparently, Miranda had overestimated his cool composure and intelligence. She had not properly estimated his paranoia or his sense of survival.

"This is the first I've seen of this, mate." Her reply had been too quick, but he was still looking for companions that sadly had never arrived to support her. She had to calm him down. "Look. I'm not playing games. You got a reputation and I won't risk my life by trying to fool you." With complete confidence in the truth of what she was saying, she added, "I came here alone. Nobody's hiding in the bushes. I'm playing you straight."

Apparently that didn't help. "I don't trust no one. Everyone wants the treasure. You best not kill me—I know something about those stars you don't. You and your gang ain't the only ones to figure stuff out. We're smarter than you."

Unlikely.

Without hesitation, her prey lashed out with his knife. Miranda stumbled back, snuffing out the match. The grove went nearly black. The gas lamp was insufficient for a fight but it was all she had.

She drew her pistol. "Calm down, will you!" She could still try to get more information out of him.

"Ain't nobody gettin' this treasure but me!"

"I'm not trying to steal it from you. Fair shares, right?"

He waited, clearly confused that he hadn't been shot yet. "You can't kill me."

"I don't wanna. Now shut up before someone hears us."

He moved suddenly, and in the poor light slashed the top of her hand, accidentally rather than purposely. She dropped the pistol. *Stupid*, she called herself, backing up and clutching her stinging hand. He'd cut her substantially.

She could see him swiping the blade back and forth, trying to adjust his eyes in the inconsistent light. She dropped her shoulders and allowed her coat to fall down her arms. Grasping the coat in one hand, she whipped it around that arm, creating a thick armor of wool, and turned her body so that her covered arm was closest to him. Planting her feet, she shifted into a flexible position with the only light behind her, now shining directly into his face, what little there was of it. She was wholly in shadow.

Before he could try to relocate to his advantage, she began the methodical movement of hands, up and down, catching attention while she assessed her next move. It was a style of defense from the Indies, which she had not even come close to mastering. Still, it was useful. Her prey was unable to discern what was happening with so much constant, distracting movement.

"You shouldn't want to be killin' me."

"Not my way, mate." Her prey moved to get around her, but she kept him facing the light. "You got information. So do I. We've gotta work together or neither one of us will get the treasure."

"You don' know what I know." He leapt forward, and Miranda allowed him to fly past on his own momentum and to land awkwardly on the ground. He began to stand up from where he'd fallen. Miranda stepped in sideways and slammed her foot into the side of his knee. He stumbled back howling, but still clutching the knife.

Once more, he lurched awkwardly at her. The blade sliced into her coat and she twisted it hard, enough to flip the knife out of his hand.

He came straight at her and locked his hands around her throat. She shoved one arm between his but couldn't free the coat from her other arm. He kept squeezing as they fell. Her ears rang; she couldn't breathe. She thrust her free hand up, slamming his nose. He reacted by grabbing at her head.

The wig came off.

He seized her again by her real hair and pulled her toward a pale spot of gas light between the bushes. Without the male styled wig, she suddenly looked very much like a woman disguised as a man, even in the poor light.

He leaned back, trying to figure out what happened. His hands reached out to grasp her throat again. "Who the hell are you? Who sent ..."

The report sounded just as his body jerked to the side and he fell into the grass.

Miranda rolled away from the body and crawled back to her feet. Something wet had sprayed across her face.

She reached for another match, but moonlight finally found a gap in the fog and lit the grove in a pale glow. *Oh, he's dead alright.* What had entered as a small hole near his left temple had exited as an enormous cavern on the right side of his face. Frankly, she was glad she didn't have better light to examine it.

She'd seen dead bodies before, but it always shocked her if the bodies were not ancient ones. After a moment of trying not to become sick when she realized the wetness on her face was his blood, she looked at her dead prey with every bit of logic she could summon. That was one large caliber round that hit him. But from where?

On the high building in the distance, she could see a tiny glow—a cigarette being lit? No one went to their roof to smoke. Was he pointing his rifle at her now, or was it her imagination? Would he kill her too? No. It would be wasteful at best to kill her now. She waited to see what he would do.

Well, at least you finally showed up for work, didn't you, Colonel?

GODS

By Vicki Rorke

5:00 AM, Crete

80—1876 AD—cs

Shay thrashed side to side, kicking the soft woolen blankets into a pile at the foot of her bed. The dream persisted. Her subconscious, full of anxiety over what her minds' eye was seeing, tried to comprehend, but couldn't. "No," she mumbled aloud. But her mind was telling her to continue. "I must not fear. I must allow the dream to continue." Shay rolled herself toward the bulkhead of the ship. Her hand reached out to the wall as if to steady herself. She drifted back further into the dream state. She could feel the cold of the morning air around her, hear the far-off thunder, and feel the soft breeze wafting through her hair. "Dream. You must allow yourself to dream …"

80—1562 BC—cs

The ground shook beneath her feet, a low, steady trembling from deep in the earth. Rumbling sounds reverberated off the brightly painted stones above her head. She felt the vibrations in her chest. It wasn't like the mild, rolling earthquakes that were so common on her island home. The warm Mediterranean air grew thick and muggy. It was getting hard to breathe. She looked toward the east and saw black, angry clouds forming at an unnatural pace, obscuring the barely risen sun and moving swiftly toward the city high on Kephala Hill. She crouched down even further in her hiding place. A storm was brewing, larger than any she could remember. Was HE upset at them? This year's harvest was bountiful, the sacred rites performed, and the festivals joyous. Now this, the most sacred of all, was about to take place. Why would HE be angry?

A chill ran down her spine, causing her body to shake involuntarily. Fear began to creep up from the farthest reaches of her mind. She swallowed hard and fought off her imagined horrors. After all, this had been a part of her culture, her people's traditions, for centuries. You have nothing to fear, Ari, she told herself. That's why she was here. It was just plain silly that children should be banned from the annual festival and sacred rite. By no means was she going to wait another six years to attend. Why shouldn't she be allowed to watch? She was a citizen. It was her right! Indignation made her brave.

Ari took a deep breath, let it out slowly, and stood up. The oversized storage vessel, painted brightly with red fish and blue dolphins, was the farthest one of four sculptures that stood on one side of the entrance to the Great Court. It had a narrow neck but its wide bulbous body had hidden her well. Now standing, Ari was several inches taller than the vessel. Even in this low light, she couldn't stand there long without being seen. Her only hope to go unnoticed was to find a large group of festival-goers and attach herself. She was tall for her age, and, draped in her mother's fancy silk and gold garments, jewelry dangling from her neck and wrists, hair piled high and entwined with flowers, and with a touch of face paint, she knew she could blend in.

There! Ari spotted a group amongst the crowds walking the well-worn path into the Great Court that would be perfect.

Talking and laughing, they seemed unaware of their surroundings. She walked quickly toward them, the bouquet of flowers she carried held high and close to her body, hoping to hide her face and not-yet-developed chest. She fell in line closely behind the group, and nodded to a couple as they passed by. So far, so good, she thought. But all good plans tend to go awry and so did hers.

Ari wasn't accustomed to her full-length garments and her sandals caught the hem of her dress. She stumbled. Before she could fully comprehend her soon-to-be position of lying face down on the smooth paving stones, humiliated, caught in her deception, a strong hand gripped her upper arm and kept her upright. Ari tried to lower her voice as best she could to sound older and softly muttered her thanks. She kept walking. The hand that had saved her retained its grip as its owner leaned over, bringing his head close to hers. The voice was edged with irritation … and familiarity.

"Ari, what in Hades do you think you're doing? Your father will tan your hide if he finds out you're here." His grip on her upper arm was beginning to hurt. She wanted to yank her arm from his grasp, but was afraid someone would see and inquire about the situation.

"You're hurting me," she growled.

Ari knew it was nothing compared to the wrath of her father if he discovered she was here. As the Minister of Trade, he was used to being obeyed, and he expected his daughter to act as a high-born, well-brought-up young lady should. Sneaking out at dawn to attend the Festival tou Taurou against his express orders would not be tolerated. Ari hoped her parents would be sitting with the other Ministers and their wives, high in the palace viewing room overlooking the Great Court, and wouldn't be able to see her face amongst the crowd below them.

"I said, let me go, Timais." Ari shook off his grip, surreptitiously glancing around, wondering if their harsh yet hushed tones were attracting attention. "I have every right to attend the festival, and no one is going to stop me!"

"Oh? One word from me and you'll be dragged out of here in chains, young lady," Timais threatened, an edge to his voice that Ari had not heard before. Timais was the elder brother of her best friend, Clio, and she always looked up to him as if he were her own sibling. He was on the shorter side for a young man, but was athletic and strong, with a handsome, kind face. Ari enjoyed listening to his tales of competitions in which he participated in faraway lands and the different peoples he encountered. Timais had always listened to her when she needed advice, and never treated her like "just a friend of my little sister." No, he treated her with respect and true friendship. She did not like pulling him into her deception, but she wouldn't back down either.

"Please, Timais, just go on and enjoy the festival. Don't worry about me," Ari pleaded, hopeful that Timais would leave her be— and keep her identity secret. Voices, followed by girlish giggles, broke the tension. Ari looked in the direction of the voices. Two young girls were waving enthusiastically at her friend, smiles wide, displaying the overly large bouquet of flowers they held.

"Timais! Timais! Come sit with us!" Bedecked in their finest gowns of silk, in colors chosen with great care to emphasize their sun-tanned skin, and with matching ribbons woven into their long, dark braids, the young ladies were planning on more than just attending the festival. No opportunity to showcase their beauty for potential suitors would go untaken. At 16, they were ripe for marriage, and what better place to make their societal debut than the biggest festival of the year. Timais smiled and waved back, then turned to Ari. His smile was gone.

"I'm warning you, Ariadne. This is no place for you! Pray the Gods don't strike you down for your impertinence." He turned and stalked off, heading toward the young ladies waiting for him. Ari watched as Timais joined his friends. They were soon enveloped by the crowd, lost to her sight. The ground shook again, though not nearly as harshly as the first time.

Ari let out a deep breath, not realizing she had been holding it. She squared her shoulders, head held high, stood as tall as she could manage, and walked through the twin pillars into the Great Court. It was already filled with people, talking excitedly, stopping to purchase fresh flowers to shower upon the performers in appreciation or buying fresh fruits and drinks from the vendors to sustain them throughout the day. Ari's stomach growled at the aroma of spices and fresh cooked meat. She chastised herself for not thinking to pack some food or bring any money. Oh well, she thought. Her people were generous, and she was certain someone would be happy to share. She looked about, decided where she would sit, and confidently strode toward the far end nearest the stage.

The Great Court was rectangular in shape with stone block terraces for seating on each of the long sides. Large pillows, crafted by the palace's best weavers, lay across the stone for festival goers to sit upon. One short end of the court was the entrance Ari had just walked through. The opposite short end was where the stage had been constructed. On non-festival days, the area was open to a pathway which came to a fork a few hundred meters down the hill. The right fork was the well-traveled path that meandered down Kephala Hill to the lower settlements and the seaport at Candia. The left fork, however, was seldom used; weeds had grown up through the cracks in the gray, uneven, weathered stones. This path led to the forbidden area; the place only the high priests were allowed to even come near, much less enter. The place where the legends had begun centuries ago; of fear, myth, and mystery. The Labyrinth.

Ari walked, head slightly bowed, hoping not to be scrutinized too closely, toward the far end of the court, and climbed the stairs leading to the fourth tier. She sat down next to an elderly woman and her husband. She noted they had a covered basket at their feet: food, Ari hoped. "Enough to share, with any luck," she muttered under her breath. She nodded to them politely while she fumbled with the flowers she held, not only to use as a shield from curious eyes but because she was getting nervous. The darkening skies and occasional rumbling of the earth beneath her were adding to her anxiousness. When will the festival begin? she thought to herself. Let's get on with it! Her patience, and her nerves, were wearing thin.

The crowd noise suddenly died down and Ari's attention was drawn to the entrance of the festival grounds opposite where she now sat. Dozens of young women were stepping precisely into the center of the court. Attired in the finest of linens, sandals made of leather and painted gold, matching sashes across their chests and golden hair hanging in ringlets, each dancer carried poles with streamers floating gaily behind them, blowing in the breeze that had come up in the last few minutes. They made intricate patterns in their dancing around the court, and crisp, synchronized pole movements with fluttering streamers made it all the more entertaining. The crowd was enthusiastic and cheered them at every up, down, left, or right swish of the pole.

The tension in Ari's shoulders began to melt away as she realized all eyes were focused on the dancers and no one was paying any attention to her. She sighed in relief and allowed herself to actually enjoy the performances. The next group of dancers performed their set using large rings, about two to three feet across, twirling them on their arms, legs, and even around their necks. They finished in a standing five-circle formation, their rings held high above their heads. The crowd erupted in cheers and applause. Flowers rained down onto the court amongst the dancers. Ari stood, cheering, pulled a flower from her bouquet and threw it as far as she could onto the court. Three more groups of dancers performed, each as dazzling in their costuming and movements as the one previous. Ari was thoroughly enjoying herself, wondering what was so terrible about this festival to make it prohibited for children to attend. She mentally shrugged off the question and instead vowed to enjoy every moment of the day.

Music was next on the agenda, with every act showcasing a specific instrument, culminating in a combined orchestral performance. Ari tapped her foot in time with the beat and heartily joined in when the music leader asked the audience to sing along with the music. Ari watched as the musicians gathered their instruments and filed out through the pillars at the far end of the court. A voice broke through her concentration.

"I'm sorry. What were you saying?" Ari inquired of her neighbor. An older woman, about fifty, with ringlets of graying hair peeking out under her headscarf, wrinkles around her eyes, and a soft mouth framed by naturally cherry-red lips, smiled warmly at Ari.

"Are you enjoying yourself, my dear?"

"Oh, yes, ma'am, very much! I had no idea how wonderful this would be!" Ari replied, her exuberance obvious to the woman who sat beside her.

"This must be your first time at the Festival tou Taurou. I couldn't help notice that you didn't bring a basket."

Ari cast her eyes downward, embarrassed to not only be green, but to be so obviously green. "Yes, ma'am, it's my first Festival, and I was so excited I completely forgot to pack any food or bring money for the vendors." Ari hoped her lie sounded believable.

"Not to worry, my dear, we have plenty to share and will be very happy to. In fact, my husband teases me every time that I bring enough food to feed the entire Cretan navy!" Her laugh was inviting, and Ari couldn't help but giggle at the woman's joke on herself.

"Thank you so much. You're very kind." Ari watched as the woman opened her basket and pulled out a bowl with several kinds of fruit cut into bite sized pieces, perfect for snacking. Ari gratefully selected a piece of each fruit and a cloth napkin to hold them while she ate. "Do you know what comes next?" Ari inquired of her neighbor.

"After this break, the vocal groups will perform, then the acrobats. Another short meal break in between and then the big finale, the bull jumping. Lastly, the priests will perform the Sacred Rite. On your way out, the various guilds will be demonstrating their arts at tables along the pathway outside the entrance to the Great Court. Maybe you saw them setting up when you came in this morning?"

"No, I didn't. I'm afraid I was too engrossed talking with my friend, Timais. But I should very much like to see them this afternoon when I leave. I've always been interested in spinning and weaving. My teacher, Lamia, has been wonderful, even tutoring me after hours on embroidery styles. I wish I were as talented as she is." Ari always loved to talk about her needlework.

"For many years I did fine needlework for the palace, before my hands became too stiff and my eyesight began to fade. It forced me to give up my position earlier this year. I embroidered many different things, the fine linens for Palace dinners, dresses for the queen. Many of the costumes you've seen today have been embellished by my hand. But time takes its toll on the body, and we must all accept change within our lives." The woman seemed a little saddened by her situation, but, at least to Ari, she seemed to have adjusted well enough. They continued the conversation on needlework, fibers, where around the seas the best cloth was to be found, what lands to get the best dyes from. The woman had several of the merchant ship captains willing to bring her whatever she desired—at a price of course.

The afternoon seemed to fly by, with choral concerts, followed by acrobats running, jumping, flipping, and twisting their way down the length of the Great Court, all to the pleasure of the crowd. Another meal break followed. The vendors had been grilling and smoking their meats all day, sending delicious aromas into the air. Ari, famished, was glad to partake of the cheese, flat bread, and strips of meat she was offered. The day had been quite enjoyable, even the weather. Though the skies remained dark and brooding, the rain had held off.

"Why are you here alone, my dear? Don't you have a young man yet? You're certainly pretty enough to have a bevy of young men vying for your hand." Ari wasn't sure how to respond, what lie to tell. Was he a sailor and rarely home? Was he studying in Athens? She was about to respond when the crowd once again erupted in a cacophony of cheering, shouting, stomping feet, saving her from deceit yet again. May the Gods forgive me my lies this day, she thought.

Looking down the court, Ari saw a young man and woman entering. Behind them, another young man was leading a bull into the court. Black as midnight with massive, wide horns, and weighing more than eight grown men combined, the bull was obviously not happy to be here. Ari watched the bull swinging his head from side to side, and decided the tips of the bull's horns looked rather deadly. She correctly surmised that this was to be the finale, the bull jumping event. Several times she had heard Timais describe the techniques on how to successfully throw yourself over the back of an angry bull. Once he even scared her with stories of failed attempts. Ari shook off the visual image of failure and refocused on the scene before her.

The young maiden, tall and muscular, dressed in a tight fitting, makeshift loin cloth that covered the upper part of her body as well as the lower, gracefully walked to the end of the far court. The second young man led the bull to center court, prodding it by taking a large tree limb with fan-like leaves, and hitting the bull's flesh just above the shoulder. It snorted in annoyance and danced sideways, then moved forward, flinging his head, and deadly horns, upward. The second young man was now standing a few feet behind the bull.

The crowd grew silent, collectively holding their breath. The young woman began to run, heading full speed toward the agitated bull. She gathered all her speed and strength, and jumped as high and as angled forward as she could. At the apex of her jump, she folded her body, soaring over the head and horns of the black beast below her. She stretched out her arms, bringing her legs straight up, and landed on the bull's back. Pushing off with her hands, arching her back and bringing her legs backwards in one smooth motion, the woman completed her somersault over the animal.

As she landed in a crouch with both feet underneath her, the crowd erupted like a volcano, spewing cheers, shouts, and applause. She stood erect, hands held high in triumph. Flowers rained down like a waterfall, covering the floor of the court. Several young girls, barely old enough to attend the festival, scurried around the court, gathering the flowers and clearing the floor, ready for next bull jumper.

The two young men were next to try their skill, hoping to win favors and please the Gods. The King was generous to those athletes who performed well in competitions, and the festival bull jumping was considered the epitome of athletic performance. The first young man landed on the bull's back with his torso slightly twisted but managed to land on his feet and beyond the reach of the bull's hind legs. One would not wish to survive the thrashing horns only to be kicked in the back.

To say the bull was now enraged was an underestimation of the bull's demeanor. A second and third handler were now needed to keep the bull from charging. Ropes lassoed each horn to help them steady his head, while the original wrangler leaned backward, bracing himself, holding the rope around the bull's neck with all his strength. All eyes turned to the far end of the court and rested on the fellow taking on the beast.

The young man, tan and muscular, with long limbs and a handsome face, shook his arms trying to release the tension and anxiety out of his body. He took several deep breaths and began to run down the court, the bull thrashing and bucking just a few feet in front of him. He leapt just as the bull yanked a rope loose from the handler and twisted his head. The left horn swung upward and connected with the jumpers' bare flesh, ripping open a gash along his side. The crowd inhaled, a collective gasp of surprise and horror at seeing blood fly from the young man. He managed to continue over the back of the bull and landed in a controlled heap on the stone floor of the Great Court. The wranglers quickly regained control of their charge and pulled it off the court, heading toward the fields where the livestock were grazing.

As the crowd waited silently, the young woman rushed to attend her fellow athlete. He raised himself, supported on the arm of the female bull jumper and came to a standing position. With blood streaming down his side, he raised his arms triumphantly. The crowd went wild, screaming his name, flowers raining down seemingly out of the sky.

Ari jumped up and down, thanking the Gods for his safe leap in her loudest voice. She turned to her seat mate, threw caution to the wind, and tightly hugged her new friend. "I didn't think he'd make it!" Ari screamed over the crowd noise.

"Nor did I!" Ari's friend screamed back at her. "I'm so thankful that young man wasn't seriously hurt." They both turned to watch the bull jumper walk off the court under his own power, holding a rapidly turning red piece of cloth to his side.

Ari sat down, relieved, yet exhilarated by the performances she had just witnessed. She couldn't imagine how the Sacred Rites could top that, but paying tribute to the Gods, even in their small-scale home rituals, were very fulfilling to her inner spirit. She was anticipating great things ahead of her.

Thunder clapped overhead and rain began to fall ever so lightly as the priests entered the far end of the court. The festival goers, who just moments before were boisterous and cheerful, grew silent. The priests pulled down the giant fabric curtains that covered the stage at the far end of the court, revealing an oblong table-like stone structure in the center, an altar off to the right holding bowls full of something, and several other objects that Ari could not see from her vantage point. Lastly, several bull statues stood on the left, the largest almost life size and apparently made of gold.

The priests made themselves busy, hoisting bowls toward the heavens and gesturing wildly. Ari was far enough away that she couldn't quite hear their chants but assumed it was something special for the Sacred Rites, maybe even in her peoples' ancient language. One of the three priests left the stage while the other two unfolded a silken red cloth onto the oblong table. The other priests returned with a young lady that made Ari sit up and take notice. She recognized her. Lamia! But she hadn't told Ari anything about her participation. What's going to happen? She wondered aloud.

"Hush, dear. But be prepared." The old woman grabbed Ari's hand. Foreboding was barging into her mind, and she grew increasingly agitated. The dark sky had opened up and the thunder was more menacing than before. The rain drops grew bigger and Ari was acutely aware of the rain rolling down her face, dripping onto her mother's gown. Lamia lay down on the oblong table, face looking up toward the sky, the thunder, and the rain. She reached her arms upward, as if trying to touch the Gods being honored. The three priests stood beside her, chanting louder than before. The crowd remained hushed, not a breath was exhaled.

Before Ari knew what was happening, the priest, in the finest red silk robe to be seen, pulled from behind him a large knife with an ivory handle and plunged it into the young maiden's chest, below her outstretched arms. Blood flew out of her body and covered the priest who had wielded the knife. The crowd exhaled in relief that the sacrifice was over, and the Gods would favor them another year.

Ari barely heard herself screaming before collapsing unconscious into the lap of the old woman who sat beside her.

ℰ—1876 AD—ℛ

"Shanarra! Shanarra! Wake up, ma wee one! You're a-dreaming!" Ian MacGregor stood over his ten-year-old daughter, shaking her gently, trying to waken her from her nightmare and silence her screams.

"Shay, darling. Wake up. Wake up now. It's alright." Her mother, Maria, cooed while stroking Shay's hair back from her face.

Shanarra slowly came into consciousness, recognizing her father's strong voice and the soft gentle touch of her mother. She opened her eyes, struggling to focus. "Where … where am I?" she asked in a barely audible voice. "They killed her. My friend. They killed her in front of everyone." Shay's voice began to tremble.

"No, Shay, it was just a dream. You're on the ship with us. We're anchored in the harbor. In a few hours we'll be on our way to visit the ruins of Knossos. Remember?"

"But … it was so real. So … real. I don't understand." Shay looked up at her parents, noticing the look that passed between her mother and father.

"Please, ma wee one, tell us about your dream." Ian's voice was soft and soothing. The sound of his fluid Scottish burr had always brought comfort to Shay. He pulled the blankets up and tucked them under his daughter's chin.

"Yes please, tell us," echoed her mother in an equally comforting voice.

They listened intently as Shay recounted her dream with astonishing clarity. They asked no questions, made no sound until she was finished. "That is quite a remarkable dream, Shanarra. But now it's over and you can go back to sleep and dream about the wonderful day we will have exploring the ruins." Maria smiled sweetly at her daughter, rose from the bed where she had been sitting at Shay's side, and turned to leave the cabin. Ian leaned over to kiss his daughters' forehead and followed Maria out of the cabin.

Shay lay quietly under the covers, trying to make sense of her dream. It wasn't like her other dreams. This one was too real. She physically felt the jubilation, the fear, the horror at seeing her "friend" brutally killed in front of her. Too many questions were swimming around in her head; she wanted answers. Decision made, Shay threw off the covers, sat up, slid her feet into her sheepskin slippers, and headed out of her cabin to find her parents. She walked silently, not wanting to disturb anyone else at this early hour. No more than a minute elapsed and she found herself standing in front of the heavy wooden door of her Da and Dya's cabin. Solemn voices were coming from within.

"Do ye think she has it?" Ian asked, his voice edged with concern.

"At her age it would be unique. However, her earlier episodes do seem to support it."

Episodes? Support? Support what? thought Shay, suddenly uneasy. She could tell someone was pacing back and forth in the room by watching the change in light and shadows underneath the door.

"Can ye prepare her, Maria? We canna let her out into the world with it and nae prepare her."

"Of course not, Ian. I can teach all that I know, while there's time, but she will never fully comprehend it until she's older. That's how it was with me, my mother, my grandmother, with all my female ancestors. It's our special talent. No doubt it's my Rom blood that flows in her veins."

"Aye, she's her mother's daughter, all right. I suppose there is nae much I can do to help." Ian sighed heavily.

"Shanarra is truly special. I had often prayed that healing would be her only Talent. It seems our only daughter has been blessed twice. She is also gifted with the Sight."

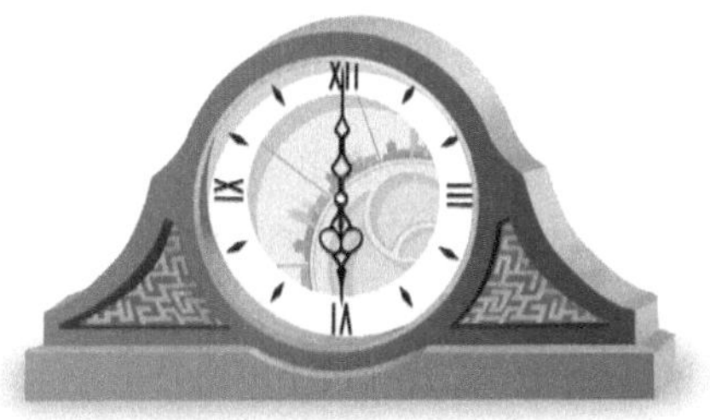

HUNTER

A Tale of Jhrin

By Dover Whitecliff

6:00 AM, Rannport

"We'll be over the drop zone in five. You ready, girl?" That was Kyree's way of asking me to run through the plan. Again.

"Touch down on top of Dalibor Ziggurat. Head east by northeast to the Solstice Arena. Jump the wall in the blind spot between the observation platforms. Leave the exoskeleton. Retrieve the case while their attention is on the match. Strap back in. Exit at the same point. Meet you at Rannport skydock in fifty-five," I recited, and blinked away the sight of the harbor lights winking slowly closer through the occasional flurry of snowflakes.

"And IKAROS?"

"The case with the device is located at 37 degrees 23 minutes North, 115 degrees 81 minutes West in the southeast quadrant of the arena." I felt Kyree seat the battery into the slot on the back of the exoskeleton surrounding me and tighten the straps on the frame.

"You have full aitheric charge. Should get you through to the rendezvous." He paused. Lowered his voice. "Crown can't sanction this. Not on foreign territory. You know that. If you get caught …"

"—Fa knows me not," I finished his sentence. "Not my first walk round the park, Kyree." He grunted and slapped my shoulder. I bent my knees to keep from wobbling as *RAS Tremhor* dropped altitude, and tried to get my bearings.

There. A silver ribbon draping delicately over a dark line that marked the cliff face between the harbor and the highlands. It looked like gossamer, but I could almost hear the waterfall from where I stood. How people in the harbor district slept at night, I couldn't understand. Gaslight and the gold-orange glow of the ziggurat illuminated the crystal bridge that stitched the two halves of Upper Rannport together, and the city lights reflected off the clouds as we descended. Something about the sight twitched the hairs on the back of my neck to stand on end.

"Something's off, Ky. Can't put my finger on it."

"You're jumping at shadows …"

"You're probably right," I conceded unwillingly. I could feel sunrise coming, though it had no grip yet in or below the cloud cover. Had we been flying higher, the brass fittings of the dirigible's gondola would have shone rosy peach in the predawn and the last of the starlight. Keep focused, girl.

One hour. Just one. A year we'd worked to put the pieces together, getting an agent high enough into the good graces of the Five Rings, tracking down leads, passing information, all to get here to the Solstice Games. Slip into the arena while all eyes were on the champions competing to earn their candidate sponsors a seat on the Council of the Five Rings, locate IKAROS and its Jacquard calculations, and get out of Rannport alive with both.

"We're on target. Ready to open the doors. Do me proud, Kenna Wolfesdaughter." Fa's voice boomed out of the squawk box and I started. Kyree smirked; I shrugged in reply.

"I will, Fa." I spoke into the brass tube, picturing him at the helm in my mind's eye, bringing the *Tremhor* down low enough for a drop but not so low as to lose speed. The Black Wolf may not have sired me, but he was my father. Lack of blood would never change that.

"We'll see you at the Slaughtered Lamb."

"Count on it. I'll buy the first round." Kyree fussed over my straps one last time and raised an eyebrow as if to say "I'll hold you to that"—Kyree never could resist Terceran Stout, especially Terceran Stout on the house.

"One more thing, Kenna." This doesn't bode well.

"Yes, Fa?"

"They know you're coming. The ziggurat's lit up like a bonfire."

"That's what's off, should be dark for the changing of the year." Missed the big glowing clue on the horizon didn't you—no reason to keep the lights on unless they expect a thief to drop in and use it as a set of stepping stones to the ground. Best pay more attention, girl, or you'll be a mince pie before you hit dirt, let alone find what you're looking for.

"If they've brought the Archon's Guard in …" Kyree looked as if he were about to tell Fa to pull the plug. Not if I had anything to say about it. I gulped a breath.

"Right then, slight change of plan." Only champions could legally enter the Solstice Arena—or a thief in the night—and since the latter door had slammed in my face—I grinned, pulling the goggles down from my forehead and settling them over my eyes. "If stealth is out, let's give them a penny dreadful entrance and win the prize money …"

"Acknowledged." I could hear approval in Fa's voice. "Changing course to pass over the arena." The squawk box went silent and Kyree let out a sharp bark of laughter.

"Oh, little lupa, you are the Black Wolf's daughter, no doubt about it." He bent down to adjust the leg pistons on my suit to accommodate the extra altitude between the top of the ziggurat and the top of the arch marking the arena entrance, and I sent a silent prayer to the gods of fortune not to end up a splatter of jam in the courtyard—this would be the highest jump I'd made in the suit.

Kyree stood, hooked the safety cable to his belt, and then turned the wheel to open the drop doors. I stepped to the edge. Looked down at the Rannport docks flitting below, then to the sea cliffs, where the waterfall roiled down to skirt through the docklands and out into the bay. The glowing ziggurat passed to port as Fa changed course, and I could make out constabulary steam carriages and security barricades at the base of it. Sure to rights, they were expecting a thief.

Well hopefully they wouldn't be expecting the She-Wolf to come bounding down into their midst. I shrugged into the new persona and changed focus from going unnoticed to swaggering in bold as brass and the center of attention. Scary how bloody easy that was. The head doctors would probably say something about a deprived childhood. If they only knew.

"Watch yourself, girl. You die afore you bring IKAROS back to the skydock and I'll take it out of your hide, come the next life."

"You can try." I looked ahead to the walled arena with its gargantuan iron-barred doors. The arch above them looked like a pitifully tiny target to land on from this angle. "Keep Fa safe."

Three.

Kyree flashed a smile and tossed me a flare.

Two.

I caught it and tugged the cord to light it up.

One.

I leapt out into the nothing with crimson sparks and aither to light my way.

Strange how the wind whipping by settled the nerves. Of course it helped knowing Fa wouldn't drop me out of the sky and into a hornets' nest unless he were certain sure I could get the job done for the Crown with none the wiser.

Icy wind howled past. Spatters of snow numbed my cheeks. I angled myself toward the arena, watching the top of the arch grow from a speck to a pocket handkerchief, rushing up to meet me faster than I would have liked. I toggled one of the switches inside my glove to prime the steam jets and the pistons for touch down. Already I could see the crowd pointing, mouths wide. Well, girl, you wanted to make an entrance. Best not cock it up.

Time to crash the party. I changed angle for the landing, getting my feet under me, resisting the urge to lock my knees. I gauged the speed and distance, and loosed what I hoped would be enough pressure from the tank. Blessed warmth. Steam rushed down the struts around my thighs and calves, bursting out the heels to cushion my landing atop the arch. Not even a dent. Good thing that. Any reparations for damage would have come out of my own pocket. A moment of dead silence as the crowd took it in—wait for it—and threw my arms into the air just as the roar burst out of the lot of them. A single jump trailing the last of the sparks got me to the ground in grandiose style.

This close to sunrise and the candidate sponsors would have already finished choosing champions. I had the right of petition until the sun cleared the horizon, but—who to knock out of the running? I stowed my goggles and looked at the competition. Four stood together, professionals all of them, and all in a heavier weight class. Not a chance that a candidate sponsor would toss any of them over for the likes of a bantam.

And then I saw my ticket. No contest, really. Nigel Norton Scrubbs, right in front of the stands with his armored suit painted candy apple red, flirting with the ladies in the front row, showing off his perfect teeth and swelling biceps, all flash and no substance. I noted whose pennant he carried, walked right up to the barrier between the combatants and the rest of Rannport amidst the furor I'd caused, and leaned over, waving happily at the gent with the gaudiest set of trinkets on his uniform.

"Good morning, Justicar, and Happy Solstice to you! I certainly hope you have room for me to compete in the games."

"All of the candidate sponsors have chosen their champions. The combatant list is closed." His cheeks flushed and he twitched his moustache officiously—by the look of things, he wasn't enamored of the hiccup I'd thrown in to his program.

"Oh surely not, Justicar. You know as well as I that the decision isn't final until sunrise."

"Very well then, make your petition, and be quick about it."

"Thank you most kindly, Justicar." I scanned the faces of the toffs behind him and spotted the one I was looking for. "There you are, Lord Dalibor! If you're looking to impress the Five Rings enough to win your council seat, you can't possibly do it without the three time Terceran bantam-weight champion in your corner—they'd laugh themselves silly. And any of these strapping lads," I gestured to the professionals standing stone still and silent and bowed my head toward them in a gesture of respect, "can tear your pretty boy here to shreds without raising a single bead of sweat."

At the epithet "pretty boy" Nigel swaggered over, leering, doing everything he could to pull attention back in his direction. 'Struth. Poor Dally must have drawn the lot for the last pick if this was what he was left with. The disgusted looks on the faces of the other combatants spoke volumes. "Don't listen to this wench, my lord. I'll win the Solstice for you and bring you the ring. You'll be on the council before your crumpet's toasted. Those 'strapping lads' are all brawn and not a brain among them. And as for this fluff …" He lunged forward and snapped his teeth at me. When I raised an eyebrow rather than react, he changed tactics, reading the brass plate riveted to my pauldron, and yelling loudly to the crowd. "Tell me, what does LUPA stand for? Ludicrously Under-Powered Armor?"

"No periods. Not an acronym." He stared vacantly. Not top of his class this one. A wave of snickers rolled through the stands. I glanced toward the other champions and noted approval, as if to say, we know you—get rid of this idiot so we can get down to the proper business of trying to kill each other. I cocked my head in acknowledgement and smiled, baring teeth. "Lupa. In the Old Tongue, it means She-Wolf." I pitched my voice so that it carried to the toffs and the crowd and squeezed the lever inside my glove. With a hiss of steam, a steel claw slid out of the tip of each metal finger in the hands of the exoskeleton and locked into position.

I turned my back on him, retracted the claws, and addressed the one man who could get me into the arena with all the brash and swagger I possessed. "My esteemed Lord Dalibor, the sun is rising, and the doors will grind open for Nigel, or for me. You know who I am, even if this dandyprat hasn't a notion who he's dealing with. Would you rather have the She-Wolf bring you the ring that will win your seat on the Most Esteemed Council of the Five Rings, or a mewling kitten to lick your boots?" I hoped Nigel would be stupid enough to attack from behind so I could take him down and seal my entrance, but, unfortunately for me, he had some semblance of self-control. He fumed and held his ground, but didn't rise to the bait.

Lord Dalibor's eyes flicked back and forth between the pair of us. I could see the wheels turning. Break contract with the liability he'd been landed with, or lose a chance at a seat on the council of the biggest syndicate on three continents.

"Commander, your military prowess is unmatched." He said over his shoulder to a uniformed gentleman standing a few feet behind with a scarlet-clad, red-headed beauty on his arm. "What say you? Which one will win for me?" Sharp move. Win and he made the right decision. Lose and he could blame it on someone else.

The Commander leaned his head toward his companion as she whispered in his ear. Whatever she said must have tickled his fancy because his eyes twinkled under the brim of his hat. The leather and brass breather-mask rendered his answer into a loud mumble, but he nodded his chin in my direction. Lord Dalibor perused his options silently and the moment lengthened. I held still while Nigel fidgeted behind me.

The first ray of the sun broke free of the clearing clouds and thrust up over the ridge, bathing the top of the arch in gold that crept down toward the doors. "Oh, make your decision, won't you. We have no time for you to dally. Such a bore." The silky voice was followed by a smooth chuckle. I hadn't seen Briar in nearly a year, but I'd know his voice anywhere. I could see him from the corner of my eye, standing at Archon Mynos' right hand. Advisor. Confidant. Spy … Brother. We'd been at the game too long to acknowledge each other, and I kept my attention on Dalibor.

The first ray of sunlight brushed the top of the quincunx design pounded into the doors, and the ground shuddered. Gears far bigger than any man began to turn and steam spilled out toward the crowd. When the ray hit the center pip of the quincunx, there would be no turning back. Lord Dalibor contemplated on.

"Reginald, look at the crowd. They want me." A gasp rippled through the candidate sponsors at the gaff. Nigel, in his impatience, forgot himself and used Lord Dalibor's given name.

I didn't dare twitch, and waited silently as I watched the sunray slide down the door. Lord Dalibor stared daggers at Nigel, then turned to me.

"She-Wolf, bring me the ring."

"My lord." I bowed in respect, and walked toward the doors with the other four champions. I didn't need the intake of breath from the crowd or the chorus of "Look Out!"s to know what was coming. Nigel charged my back louder than a stampeding Angora. I sidestepped and had him on the ground before he knew what hit him, stepped on his arm and wrenched the gold hilted blade away, burying it in the frozen earth. Pity his hand was protected by the struts. I would have loved to have broken his wrist. I took the pennant from his waist and walked on, leaving him sputtering and puce with rage, knowing the Archon's Guard would keep him from charging a second time.

The five of us took our places in front of the outer doors just as they opened, revealing five vestibules, each with the emblem of one of the Five Rings riveted above its entrance: Fire, Water, Earth, Air, Aither. I took my place in the middle vestibule. The Third Ring—a bit of luck if you believe in such things. The Third Ring signified Earth, the ring of armies and battle. Add to that the fortune of getting me into the arena before two of the combatants. I'd take any advantage I could get.

I stepped into the footholds and grabbed hold of the iron bars bolted into the walls on either side of me. The first set of inner doors ground shut, sealing us in to pitch black coffins. I leaned back against the cold iron. Deep Breath. It won't last long. Don't panic. The vestibule creaked and the floor dropped and swayed freely as the outer doors shut and the locks let loose. Here we go ... just a carousel ride in the park. Breathe.

At first the movement was gentle, but that didn't last long. The weight of the spin pinned me back against the inner door. Breathe in. Breathe out. Keep your head. I loved the spin-and-toss rides at the carnival, but that was in the open sky with my friends squealing all around me, each of us sure we would be the last one to lose our breakfast. Here in the dark alone, with nothing to breathe but stale, steam-oiled air was another matter entirely.

After forever, the spin seemed to slow. A clanging clash. A jolting jerk that almost shook me loose of the hand holds. Somewhere a door opened and the First Ring's champion entered the arena. Spin. Clash. Jolt. Another door. Another champion. I tried to breathe shallow; the stench wasn't exactly helping my stomach stay put. Keep it together, girl. Hold tight. Just one more turn of the wheel. I swallowed hard, felt the pressure against my chest lessen as it began to slow. I stepped out of the footholds and braced for the jolt. Fought the dizziness. Squeezed the lever. Extended the claws, knowing that the wheel could spit me out next to a champion or a trap just as easily as it could throw me into the clear.

Steam hissed. The doors split open. I threw myself forward into dazzling, blinding sunlight.

COYOTE

By Kirsten Weiss

7:00 AM, San Francisco

Secret agenting can be dashed inconvenient.

There I was, at the unholy hour of seven in the morning, blinking in the ruddy sun when I should have been tucked in bed. The clatter of construction hammered my head, rattling my teeth. Fog laced with brine edged my mulberry-tweed frock coat with beads of damp.

One gets into the business with fantasies of swanking about Baden-Baden, of being rewarded by grateful Maharajas with winsome daughters, not mucking about in some backwater.

And when I say "mucking," I mean "mucking." The mud in San Francisco was twelve inches deep. I'd already ruined one pair of gaiters and stared down, forlorn, at my new calfskin boots, swallowed whole by my landlady's backyard. Mud clung to the hems of my finest plaid trousers.

Gripping one edge of the water pump, I attempted to pry myself free and sank deeper into the mire.

I was about to beat a melancholy retreat in my socks, when a mangy dog, big eared and golden eyed, slunk around one side of the outhouse. The mongrel was hollowed by hunger, its gray fur matted. That a creature existed in a sorrier state than myself was immensely cheering.

Patting my pockets, I prospected for a bit of dried beef a miner had thrust upon me at the breakfast table. I'd meant to discard the scrap in the yard, but the dog looked like it might appreciate the stinking meat.

With a whistle, I crouched, extending the bit of flesh toward the animal.

It prowled closer, nose twitching, head low. Its yellow eyes met mine, and I felt a flash of recognition.

The dog growled.

There was a feminine shriek. Iron blazed down, thwacking me on the wrist.

Both beast and self yelped. The animal did a sort of leaping twist in the air, spattering pale green skirts with mud. It bounded away.

My wrist throbbed as if smashed between two flaming anvils. I wobbled and fell backward into the yard.

A youngish woman towered over me, glaring with the practiced look of an English governess. She gripped a thick, brown parasol in her hands. "That's a coyote!"

Glancing down, she gasped at the assault on her finery. Her garb was plain, aside from the unusual sartorial choice of a man's leather waistcoat and copper pocket watch. She was shapely, with a British accent tainted by her exposure to the colonies. However, any admiration I might have had for her form was lost in a burning desire to throttle her blue.

I rolled, squelching to my knees in the mud. "I say!"

She brushed at the stains on her gown, leaving a long smear. "You may well say, but that was a coyote and would have taken your hand with that strip of meat. And what are you doing in the mud?"

My hands clenched, sending a sharp throb through my wrist. "How else was I to get to the pump?"

She pointed with the parasol toward her feet. "These wooden planks have been laid for that very purpose."

I grimaced, noticing in the weak light the wooden path leading from the back steps to the pump and outhouse. In my defence, it was covered in mud and barely visible. And I had something of a headache from last night's reconnoitre in one of the local gaming facilities.

A look of sympathy crossed her face. "The territory is quite wild. Little wonder if you are unused to its strange customs."

Unused! I was a professional! With a snarl, I clambered to my feet. Mission or no, there are certain things a secret agent does not tolerate. A particularly cutting remark rose to my lips, when another female, resplendent in blue, glided down the steps. Her mahogany hair was done up in fantastic coils, and she wore a feathered hat at a jaunty angle. Philadelphia tailoring. French perfume. Now this was a woman of interest.

She nodded to the lady and smiled broadly at me. "Good morning."

Flushing, the first lady brushed at her skirts. "Miss Algrave." She looked down, saw the failed result of her efforts, and scowled. "If you will excuse me."

Miss Algrave canted her head, observing her departure. "I see you've met Miss Grey." She glanced down at me. "You're not the first gentlemen she's flattened."

"The inventor?" Miss Grey was famous in the territory, but I had expected someone dour and bespectacled, not a fresh-faced lass.

She cocked a brow. "You know of her?"

"Her mechanicals are quite in demand," I said, recovering.

She looked skyward. "So are umbrellas. I've heard there's a seventy-two percent chance of rain."

My stomach plummeted at the code phrase, but I soldiered on. "And I heard there was a one hundred percent chance of fog."

She extended her hand, gloved in blue leather. "Agent Algrave."

I forced a smile. "I am Doyle." So this was the American agent I'd been sent to meet. But a lady? Employed by the American government? Colonials really were extraordinary.

"Welcome to San Francisco." She eyed my mud-covered trousers, my boots still sunk in the muck. "Need help?"

"No thank ..."

Grasping my hand, she yanked like an Amazon.

I bit back a cry of pain as the tendons in my wrist threatened to snap, but I stood. Bloody parasol. Bloody coyote. Bloody American females.

Rubbing my damaged wrist, I bowed insincerely. "Please pardon my surprise. A lady agent. Is that, er, common?"

"No," she said. "I believe you have some information for my employers?"

"Indeed, but that information would best be conveyed in private, and after I change into clothing which does not reek of Mrs. Watson's laundry yard."

She obliged, waiting in the parlour while I changed and collected my carpetbag. Downstairs, I offered her my arm, and we strolled out the front door into the boomtown. All manner of men jostled us, their clothing worn and bleached and stained from their travel to California.

"I've a place we can speak," she said.

"As do I. This way." I'd made good use of my time in San Francisco, and I'd be dashed if I was going to go to her lair. Anyone could have gotten hold of that code phrase, and this female had a rather nasty glint in her eyes that reminded me of an aunt of mine.

A line appeared between her brows, but she nodded. "What do you think of the territory?"

We reached a series of wood planks crossing the muddy road, and I released her arm so she could precede me across the narrow bridge. In front of a saloon, a miner cursed his mule, burdened with bundles of supplies that obscured all but the animal's feet.

"Charming," I said.

"Really?" Her skirts swayed in front of me. "Most folks consider San Francisco a savagerous mess."

"I live for adventure," I said stoutly.

"Then you must be a master of disguise."

"Yes, I …" What, ho! That was an insult. I stiffened. "Sometimes, it is advantageous to be underestimated."

"Not here. There are plenty of cowboys—and some ladies—who'll take a run at a man who looks soft."

"I have not thus far encountered any."

She sighed, stepping onto a plank sidewalk, and turning to me. "If you're set on being a bully trap, that's your business."

"I assure you, madam …"

"So where's this place of yours?"

Mutinous, I pointed toward the spires of ships' masts rising behind the warehouses. "I've made an office for myself within one of the abandoned ships." And I was rather proud of it too. Usually one ended up in a hotel room. Once, I'd been assigned a space in the basement of a museum. But a deserted ship was by far the most clandestine headquarters of them all.

Her lip curled with disdain. "How—original."

What was wrong with the blooming ship? There was no pleasing this harridan.

"We'd better hurry before someone finds your office," she said, "and decides its contents scavenger-worthy."

In silence, Miss Algrave followed me to the docks. We made our way through the maze of derelict ships. They clotted the harbour and more poured in daily, their crews fleeing their duties for a chance in the gold fields.

Our feet echoed on the floating piers, seagulls wheeling and cawing above us. A sudden gust of wind rippled the water, causing the forgotten halyards to bang and howl like a coyote. Was it my imagination, or did I feel the beast's essence? Foreboding tightened the spot between my shoulder blades. The dock bobbed more vigorously.

Escorting her up a plank to a steamship taller than the others, I led her into the captain's quarters and shut the door behind us. Weak light streamed through open portholes, stripped of their glass and brass fittings. I dropped my carpetbag atop the bare wooden desk with a thud.

"The scavengers couldn't get the desk out the door, I suppose." She drew a long knife—Yemeni, if I was any judge (and I am)—from her sleeve and ran her thumb down the blade. "You were lucky no one thought to chop it up for firewood. I take it you don't get seasick?"

A cold finger touched my spine. "Steady as a rock."

"And the rent is reasonable," she said, "which is more than I can say for any other hidey-hole in San Francisco. Now what have you got?"

"You are, of course, familiar with the occult organization known as The Mark?"

"Ye-es. I've encountered them. We exploded their West Coast operations last year."

"Er, yes. Well." I cleared my throat. "We got word through our agent in The Mark's London office that they were making another attempt for this territory and had developed a new device to assist them with their plan."

"What plan?"

"That, I'm afraid, was unclear. My government sent me here to uncover the plot."

She crossed her arms over her chest. "And did you?"

"With some difficulty, I caught their agent in Virginia City. He was making his way here with a singular device in hand. Before he died …"

Brow wrinkling, she twirled the knife. "You killed him?"

"I am exceedingly deadly when necessary."

"Hmph. So what's the device, and what's the plan?"

"I was getting to that. An assassination made to look like an Indian attack."

She snorted. "Ridiculous. Everyone knows the Indians in this territory are peaceful."

"An arrow through the chest of a certain lady inventor might change their minds."

The woman straightened. "Miss Grey is the target?"

"Two birds with one stone. A conflict with the local savages and the execution of a lady working on aether technology for your government, a lady The Mark finds highly irritating."

"Blast." She gnawed her lower lip.

I steeled myself. "Our intelligence suggests she is planning on selling one of her gold mining devices to a local tribe."

"What?" She frowned. "She didn't mention that to me. But you say you got their agent and the device?"

"Here." I unlatched the carpetbag and drew it from its depths a leather gauntlet with brass fittings. Removing my coat, I rolled up my sleeve. My wrist was red and swollen, but there was nothing for it. Gritting my teeth, I buckled on the contraption. I made a fist of my hand, and there was a soft click.

"That thing fires an arrow?" she asked. "I see an assassin could easily conceal it, but the inventor didn't know much about Indians. The local arrows are longer than a man's forearm."

"True, this requires arrows that are truncated." Pulling one from the bag, I stroked its feathered end. "However, I doubt the average gold miner would make such a distinction after finding it embedded in a lady's chest." I cocked my head, listening.

"No." Her brow furrowed deeper. "I reckon you're right."

"I say, did you hear something?"

"Someone outside?" She went to the door and wrenched it open, stepping onto the deck, leaning over the wooden rail.

I fastened the arrow into place. It was really a most ingenious device. It lacked the heft of a crossbow, yet the gears and pulleys could send an arrow straight through a person. I'd practiced, embedding one deeply within the trunk of a pine.

Miss Algrave stood outside the door, the sun streaming behind her, forming a halo around her figure. "I don't see anyone."

"My mistake. Let me demonstrate how this works." Raising the device, I shot her.

The she-demon must have had some sixth sense. The lady bolted left, too late, the arrow driving deep into her upper torso. She gave a quiet cry, almost a sob, and pitched backwards over the rail.

Racing forward, I peered over the edge. Her crinolines vanished in the murky water. As if to put a final point on the matter, the steamship beside us bobbed closer, grinding against "my" ship. With the weight of her clothing dragging her down, the inability to escape upward, (for the steamship was now attached to mine as if by a magnet), the damage of the arrow, and the unlikelihood of her ability to swim, Miss Algrave was well and truly gone.

I nodded crisply. The Mark hadn't paid me to dispose of the American agent. However, in the time-honoured tradition of double-agents, I was over-billing. I would be adequately compensated.

Grimacing, I referred to my pocket watch. Seven thirty. Just enough time to kill Miss Grey and catch the stage to Sacramento.

The contraption sent arcs of fire up my arm. I reached for one of its straps, thinking to loosen it, then hesitated. I'd barely gotten it on and was unsure I'd be able to gird myself with the blasted weapon again.

There was nothing for it. I'd have to wear it until my work was complete. Jaw clenched, I shrugged into my jacket. The weapon fit neatly beneath my tweed sleeve. It really was a marvel, even if it felt like my arm was being compressed beneath a carriage wheel coated in acid. My heart sang at the prospect of murdering the lady who'd inflicted such agony.

The neighbouring ship had drifted away a foot or so, and I looked over the side one last time. Oil coiled on the water. There was no sign of Miss Algrave, not even a trail of telltale bubbles or bit of floating skirt. But the water was so black, I could not have seen a corpse floating mere inches beneath the surface. It was worse than the Thames.

Looking about without appearing to look about—we spies are trained for such craft—I departed the ship and retraced my steps to the wide street bordering the shore. The assassination would have to be affected from a higher elevation.

I strode through the muck, passing sailors throwing rocks at a mangy dog (the louts), and achieved the opposite side of the warehouse where Miss Grey kept her workshop. Ignoring braying animals and boorish shouts, I made my way to a smithy across from the warehouse. It was a squat one-story, unpainted and crude, with a high false front. From my prior evening's surveillance, I knew that on the alley-side of the smithy was a ladder to the roof.

The alley was cool, dark, and narrow. No one saw me clamber, one-armed, up the ladder. My right hand was swollen and red as an apple, the device squeezing the blood in my arm into my fingers.

Muttering imprecations against the pain, I ducked behind the smithy's false front and looked through the windows of the warehouse, opposite. Miss Grey paced, head bowed. A dark-skinned man wearing long hair and miner's clothing—her savage client, I presumed—stood watching her.

Odd. My contact had informed me the sale to the Indian chief would occur in the evening. No matter. If he was on the spot when she died, all the better.

Miss Grey came to a halt before the window.

I raised my arm and squeezed.

Nothing happened.

I made a fist of my hand, my fingers straining to touch my swollen palm. Bolts of black pain shot to my elbow, but nothing shot from the device.

Rolling up my sleeve, I checked the arrows, the gears, the cables. All appeared in working order. My brawny chest tightened. The only part of the device which was not in working order was myself. My hand and wrist were too swollen for my injured muscles to trigger the device.

Miss Grey moved away from the window and back again, gesticulating. She would not remain such an ideal target for long, and I had a stage to catch.

Right-o, there was nothing for it. I would simply use my left hand. It would be a challenge, but that was why The Mark had hired me. By George, I was a professional!

I clawed at the metal clasps, their straps pulled tight by my engorged arm. It was a real floorer, I tell you. Pulse speeding, I wrestled one-handed with the device. My movements grew jerky, the hooks and cables tearing at the skin on my fingers. It was impossible!

The parasol, the coyote, the entire morning had conspired against me. I fumbled with the latches, aimed, squeezed, to no avail.

Bollocks! I'd need to cut the blasted thing from my body.

I spun toward the stairs.

A dark shape, a ghoul rising from the depths, floated up the ladder. Hair in dank coils about her head, her revolver aimed squarely in my direction, rose Miss Algrave.

Bally Americans.

THE FOREST DEMON

By AJ and BJ Sikes

8:00 AM, Austria

The artist Klimt tramped through the tall, wet grass at the edge of the forest. The early morning light glistened off the dew clinging to the stalks of tall flowers and reedy grass. A shiver coursed his back and he hefted his art case higher onto his shoulder. Klimt pushed on through the high grass and breathed deep of the morning air. With each step, he roved the terrain with his eyes, seeking the dawn light's presence in the landscape.

The still-dark, almost foreboding trees to his left contrasted with the yellowing grass of summer around Klimt's legs and feet. He paused his movement to admire the scene. Something in the separation of tones recalled to him a frieze he'd once seen, the heavy band of the dark trees looking so much like a parade of figures walking above a sea of gold. And there, at the very edge of the wood, he spotted an odd clump of branches and briars across the meadow. As he stared, the vegetation seemed to come alive, taking on the stooped and hunched figure of an old woman

101

at the spinning wheel. Klimt felt sure the figure would move; it seemed almost human, but he saw now it was clearly an illusion.

"Just a trick of the morning light," he said to himself, and then nearly swallowed his words as the cluster of branch and thorn wavered in place and made as if to stand on two legs. Klimt had lifted his foot to step forward, but now stopped, his heart pounding. Thoughts of the locals' stories of forest demons flitted through his head, and for a long moment Klimt held his position, the heel of his forward foot just touching the ground enough to give him balance.

Across the meadow, the forest figure didn't move, save for the swaying of leaves hanging from the upper branches. If it were a demon, the beast appeared to have its back to him. Klimt chided himself a coward, but still could not find the will to set his foot down and continue his walk. Then the morning air cooled in a breeze that pushed through the meadow, lifting Klimt's hair and shaking him from his vigil.

He took a deep, calming breath. "Klimt," he scolded himself, taking slow, measured steps through the grass. "There is no such thing as a forest demon. You are a modern man of the 19th Century. Forest demons are made up to frighten little children." Heartened by his own voice, Klimt veered his course through the meadow and stepped closer to the mysterious tangle of branches. It didn't move. As he drew nearer, he saw that he had cowered before a mere briar bush overgrown with vines.

"Perhaps I will paint you, my botanical apparition," he said. He circled the bush. It was unnerving. It really did resemble the craggy, gnarled figure of an old woman. With a puff of his chest, Klimt stepped back to the edge of the trail and lowered his art case. In a few rapid motions, he set up his easel and had his tools prepared. The sun cast fingers through the tops of the trees now, sending the forest demon's shadow into the meadow like a pot of ink beginning to spill across a pale sheet. Klimt felt himself grow feverish, as always he did when his work consumed him. He sketched the scene, rushing his pencil around the canvas and yet finding his aim true with every stroke.

The sketch done, he set to painting with the same fevered pace, working toward completion before he lost the light. So engrossed was he that he didn't notice a woman from the village until she had passed behind him.

"Good day, Madam," Klimt said as quick as he could and yet still aiming to be polite. The locals had no knowledge of him beyond that he was a painter come to visit their region. Not one of them had greeted him by name, much less spoken to him, since his arrival a week before, and this woman seemed much the same as the others. She gave him such a look, and even crossed herself as her eyes went to his painting. Then she walked on, quick as she was able, muttering to herself and shaking a finger at the air behind her head. Klimt stared after her and nearly called to her for explanation, but the sun glinting off the far edge of the meadow behind him took Klimt back to his work.

Putting brush to canvas, he continued to stroke the pigments into shape and timbre and hue. First dark, then light. Blending here, scraping there. Klimt's vision of the demon in the landscape grew before him until the sun crested the line of trees and spilled into the meadow, scattering the very light Klimt had set out to find that morning. Around the meadow, he heard sheltering rodents skittering away into the deeper shade at the edge of grass.

Klimt sighed. He'd nearly finished.

A shriek pierced the air. He started, dropping a paint tube. It had sounded like a child's voice. Looking around, heart pounding, Klimt spotted a flash of white at the forest's edge. He moved closer and saw that it was a small girl in a white smock. She was crouched down, staring at the briar bush, eyes wide. He called out to her,

"Do not be concerned, child, it is merely a strangely shaped bush." The girl jumped at the sound of his voice and her head whipped around to look at him. He smiled and nodded. "There is nothing here that can hurt you. Come, little one." He held out his hand to her. She looked back at the bush. He could see that she was trembling. Klimt walked slowly toward her, making soft coaxing sounds as he went. She didn't seem to be paying attention to him, instead reacting to the briar bush as the breeze tossed the branches around.

"It is moving. Can you not see that it is moving?" She asked in a soft, tremulous voice. He glanced back at the briar bush. It did appear to be moving but he knew that it was an illusion caused by the wind.

"It is just the wind, child."

She shook her head vigorously, eyes locked on the plant. Klimt finally reached her side and crouched down next to her. She was shaking and he could see tears in her eyes. He placed a gentle hand on her back. At his touch, she leapt to her feet and dashed away, into the woods. The girl crashed headfirst into a tree, fell to the ground, and got up again. Blood was streaming from her forehead. Klimt started forward to help her but she turned and ran into the darkness between the towering trees. He watched her go, perplexed. Why was she so afraid? Did she think that briar bush was really some sort of monster, this forest demon the villagers muttered about? She was young, probably six or seven, so no doubt prone to silly fancies. He thought about following her into the forest but she was already out of sight. He shook his head, ashamed that he let a young child run off into the forest alone. He looked back at his easel set up in the meadow but his desire to paint the bush was gone. The little girl's fear had left a bitter taste in his mouth. He picked his way back through the tall grass to his painting supplies and packed up.

☙❧

Klimt walked into the village of Gablitz and made his way through the narrow streets to his pension. He didn't notice the looks he received from the villagers he passed.

Klimt's stomach growled as he entered the tidy little boardinghouse. He had left too early for breakfast. He placed his art case at the foot of the staircase and wandered into the well-ordered kitchen. Pots and pans stood at the ready or hung from hooks on the wall, all glimmering metal reflecting the light coming through the window.

"Good morning, Frau Huber! Can I beg a bit of nourishment from you?" he said, grinning at the rotund woman peeling potatoes at the sink. She turned to look at him, her face a mask of disapproval, pinched lips and narrowed eyes. Surprised, Klimt asked, "Frau, have I done something to offend you? I apologize for missing your delicious breakfast but the light was so lovely this morning that I had to dash out to paint."

"Men who abuse small children are not welcome in my house, Herr Klimt," she spat out. Klimt gaped in astonishment.

"I beg your pardon? I do not hurt children, why I rarely even switch my own when they misbehave," he said.

"That is not the tale young Lena told her mother," she replied, her face hard.

"Who is Lena?" he asked, deeply puzzled. He did not know any of the village children. Could she be the little girl he had seen in the forest?

"The poor child you attacked in the forest. Her little face was cut and bruised after you hit her. How could you do that, Herr Klimt? I took you to be a gentle man, despite your size." Klimt drew himself up, towering above her.

"Frau, I have not laid a finger on this Lena. I swear this on my son's life."

The woman humphed and turned back to the potatoes. Klimt stood looking at her stiff back. What had really happened out there in the forest? Why was the child saying he'd attacked her? He needed to get to the bottom of this or his painting sabbatical was going to be very awkward. A hammering on the back door startled them both. Frau Huber opened the door. A man that Klimt vaguely recognized from the village stood there, face red and frowning. He spotted Klimt and pointed a pudgy finger at him.

"There you are, you miscreant. You will pay for what you did to my daughter." His voice shook with passion. Klimt stepped onto the threshold and saw that there were at least a dozen villagers standing outside, watching silently. This looks ominous, Klimt thought.

"Herr, I have just explained to Frau Huber that I did not lay a finger on your daughter. I am sorry that she met with some sort of accident out in the forest but I was not the cause. She ran off when I approached her. Perhaps she fell?"

"Ah! So you admit you saw her!" Klimt heard murmurs from the villagers gathered outside. The girl's father grabbed Klimt's arm and tried to yank him over the threshold. Klimt pulled back, his forehead creasing as he frowned.

"Let go of me, Herr! You have no right to manhandle me in this manner!" he cried. The murmurs grew louder as the villagers moved closer. Klimt glanced back and saw Frau Huber standing behind him, arms crossed. She was holding a heavy wooden rolling pin. His heart sank. Thinking quickly, he spun around and grabbed the woman, pushing her at Lena's father. Klimt ran through the house and out the front door. The street was empty. He ran toward the main road, hoping to flag down a carriage but another crowd of villagers loomed at the end of the street, faces hard as they spotted him. He turned down a side street, heart pounding as he ran. The margin of the forest was just ahead. He heard shouts and turned his head. The villagers were pursuing him. He dashed into the trees, the undergrowth tearing at his clothes. His breath was ragged, coming in gasps. He could still hear them behind him. There was no path so he pushed his way through briar bushes, tripping over hidden tree roots as he went. He spared a look back saw his pursuers. A moan escaped his lips and he pushed harder at the hedges. He briefly contemplated hiding but knew they would find him. They had dogs. He could hear them.

He reached a clearing and picked up his speed, changing direction in hopes of confusing the villagers. A small stream crossed his path. He splashed into it. Perhaps it would throw the dogs off his scent. He spotted another of those strange humanoid-shaped bushes but brushed it off as unimportant. He ran on, gasping and sweating. The sounds of pursuit seemed further away now. He burst out of the forest onto a road and stopped, breathing hard. Surely he would be able to flag down a carriage and get out of this insane place. He took his bearings and strode away from the direction of the village.

The sun climbed higher in the sky. A thought occurred to him as he tromped along the seemingly endless road through the forest—what was he going to tell his wife when he showed up at home without his luggage or his art case or, for that matter, any of the paintings he had worked on? He laughed at himself, wondering such a thing when he had narrowly escaped a lynching for a crime he hadn't committed. He sighed with fatigue. He was far enough from Gablitz that no one would know who he was. Now he needed to get out of this wilderness and back home.

The clip clop of horses approaching behind him caught his attention and he turned. A farmer was driving a cart piled high with cabbages up the track toward him. Klimt hailed him.

"Good morning! May I catch a ride with you, Mein Herr?" The man stopped the cart and smiled down, his eyes wide and full of curiosity.

"Of course," he said. Klimt climbed onto the cart and breathed a sigh of relief. The farmer gazed at him from under his broad-brimmed hat.

"Herr, you appear to have met with some trouble. Were you lost in the forest?"

Klimt looked down, noting his mud-speckled, torn trousers. "Lost? No. Not exactly. I was trying to escape the villagers of Gablitz. They thought I had assaulted a child. A ridiculous notion. And I had to leave all of my possessions there when I ran into the forest to get away. My art case." He groaned.

The farmer twitched his nose at Klimt's words. "Ah, Gablitz. Huh. I am Josef Müller. And you?"

"Gustav Klimt, an artist from Vienna, come to Gablitz to experience the serenity of nature. And instead all I encounter is madness."

"Gablitz," the farmer said with a chuckle. "I am sorry to hear you were in this place. A superstitious crowd if ever there was, and bloodthirsty, too."

"You think they would have killed me? I admit my fear told me as much as I ran, but … bloodthirsty?"

"Oh, indeed. A cousin of mine, years ago it was. He wandered into Gablitz with too much wine in his belly. The next morning a young child was found dead in the forest and the villagers, well …" The farmer trailed off and Klimt caught the look that fell over the man's face, a dark mask of regret and anger.

"Now it is I who must express sorrow, Herr Müller. This is terrible. Is nothing done about it all these years? No authority brought to bear upon these madmen and women who chase innocent men about the woods while raving about forest demons?"

The farmer's eyes flashed open and a laugh escaped his mouth. "Forest demons? Oh, Herr Klimt, I am truly sorry you were met with that particular madness in Gablitz. So many of the people there forget we are near the end of this century and all of its favoring of ghosts and spirits. But can you blame them, out here in the serenity of nature, as you call it, surrounded by wilderness as far as the eye can see? A mind must make up stories lest it go mad from not knowing, eh?"

Klimt felt his shoulders settle, the tension falling away at Josef's words.

"I suppose you are right, Herr Müller," Klimt said and swept the nearby tree line with his eyes. Beside the dark stand of oaks he spied another mound of vines, similar to the one he had attempted to paint just an hour earlier. Maybe it was the breeze, but the clump of bramble appeared as if to wave farewell. Klimt thought of Josef's reassuring words again, yet still had to force himself not to raise a hand in reply.

THE POLYCHROME WISHING JAR

By David L. Drake & Katherine L. Morse

9:00 AM, London

Viewed from a distance, the couple strolling in front of the row houses on the west side of Berkeley Square appeared to be a conventional, smartly-dressed pair, just like the other denizens of London. But up close, her shoes were a little too utilitarian, her handbag a little too commodious to be fashionable. He fussed a bit to keep his top hat secure in spite of his continuous, rapid surveillance of the environs. As if by previous agreement, they both snapped open their pocket watches as they reached the bottom steps of a three-story residence in the middle of the block. Both timepieces showed a few seconds before nine in the morning. The woman lifted her foot as if to ascend the first step but paused with her boot hovering.

She whispered over her shoulder, "Wait for it …" When she let her foot alight, the door clicked open to reveal a slight woman wrapped in a vibrant blue-green sari.

"Good morning, Anu," the female visitor said brightly.

The housekeeper replied in a cheerful Indian accent. "Good morning, Dr. McTrowell, Chief Inspector Drake. His lordship is in the sitting room. Please come in."

"Thank you, Anu," the Chief Inspector replied warmly.

Drake and McTrowell shared a secret smile as they trod the well-known path to Jonathan Lord Ashleigh's sitting room. They both took Anu's verbal greeting and colorful attire as a happy sign of her increasing comfort with their frequent visits and her own improved situation.

The parlor was classic Victorian, replete with burgundy and gold wallpaper and wainscoting, and a sprawling royal blue and gold rug. The owner had appointed it with items from northern India and large leather wing chairs. The whiff of cigar smoke added an earthy charm to the chamber. The brightly attired gentleman with warmly tan skin extended his hand in friendship.

"My dear friends, how marvelous of you to join me this morning," Lord Ashleigh boomed. He shook both their hands vigorously and gave Drake a hearty slap on the shoulder. His manservant, Virat, appeared with the silver tea service. He poured "Sparky" McTrowell a cup of chai and handed it to her without question or comment. She took a healthy swallow and smiled blissfully as she savored it.

"And why are we joining you this morning?" Chief Inspector Erasmus Drake asked.

"And why, pray tell, did you request we dress like this?" Sparky added.

"I am invited to a breakfast salon by my neighbor, Lord Frederick Fishburn, and his wife, Lady Beulah. I hesitate to say this out loud, but they are dreadful dullards. She is a socialite whose primary occupation is gossiping at her club. He collects occult artifacts. He is going to unveil his latest acquisition at breakfast this morning. Going alone would be the death of me. I confess, this is a case of 'misery loves company.'"

Drake and McTrowell stood in silent contemplation for a moment before the Chief Inspector spoke up, "I suppose we would not be very good friends if we left you to suffer in solitary. However, I feel some form of recompense might be in order." He grinned teasingly.

"Perhaps one of Anu's home-cooked Indian dinners?" Dr. McTrowell asked hopefully.

Lord Ashleigh chuckled, "You and your husband-to-be have yourselves a bargain. Shall we go?"

Mere moments passed in silence as they walked three doors down to the Fishburn residence. A butler answered the door and announced, "Jonathan Lord Ashleigh, 7th Viscount of Ashleigh, and …" He cast a derisive glance down his nose as the young solicitor's companions.

Lord Ashleigh whispered helpfully, "Chief Inspector Erasmus Drake of Scotland Yard, and Dr. Sparky McTrowell of Western & Transatlantic Airship Lines." He winked conspiratorially over his shoulder at his compatriots. The butler wrinkled his nose and inhaled dismissively, but announced the pair regardless of their lack of titles.

With a bounce in his step, a middle-aged man approached. Sparky noted that his appearance, both his natural looks and his choice of attire, were indistinguishable from those of the kind of men who kept company with her employer, Reginald Wallace. In an instant she measured him up as a self-satisfied, upper class man who had inherited title and money that he thought made him a superior human being. She was quite certain that Lord Ashleigh's assessment of him as a dullard was completely accurate. She groaned internally. She mentally prepared herself for this to be crushingly boring. She wondered if she could surreptitiously ignite the curtains to cover her escape. And then she remembered Erasmus's admonishments about making their own fun under such circumstances. She began formulating plans for some ironic mischief. Unfortunately, her "poker face" must have failed her because she caught her fiancé giving her a stern look. His expression suggested that this was not one of those "making their own fun at the expense of others" occasions. She affected her polite visage.

The middle-aged man closed the distance, his hand extended to shake. He shook Jonathan's hand first.

"Lord Ashleigh, I'm so pleased you were able to join us. As an exotic Indian familiar with the mystical, you will obviously find this morning's proceedings very engaging." Now it was Drake's turn to groan internally. He wondered how Lord Fishburn would react to the truth about his half-Indian friend's personal mission to Her Majesty, Queen Victoria.

Oblivious to his insult to his neighbor, Fishburn turned to Erasmus. "Chief Inspector, I have read about your exploits in the *Times* with considerable interest! Quite the man of action." He pivoted slightly. "And this lovely young lady must be your companion, Miss McTrowell." He took up her hand to kiss it. Drake placed a couple of fingers lightly on the fist formed behind her back to signal her that it would be inappropriate to bloody Lord Fishburn's nose with an off-hand jab the tiresome bore would never see coming. She glanced sideways and made an annoyed face at Erasmus as she allowed her hand to be kissed.

"I am Lord Frederick Fishburn. Please, come in."

The trio followed their host into the dining room. A sumptuous breakfast buffet of eggs, rashers of bacon, bangers, fruit, pastries, and jams was laid on the sideboard. A half dozen other guests had already arrived and were helping themselves to plates. Sparky noted that they were providing themselves generous servings. As surreptitiously as possible, she scurried to the buffet since she had started the morning with nothing more than the cup of chai provided by Virat. She suspected that she would need her strength.

At the platter of ham, she glanced up to see Lord Fishburn shepherding Drake along the exterior of the room, pointing out his various prized supernatural possessions, including an entire case of monkey paws, a giant scarab collection, and a foul-smelling cat mummy burial sarcophagus. She could hear him recounting the details of how he documented, logged, and classified each object, and if its magic could still be triggered. Her beloved cast her a plaintive glance. She heaped more provisions on her plate and dashed to his side, passing the plate to him without comment. She used this maneuver as a ruse to insert herself between Erasmus and his captor. Having relieved her hands of the breakfast plate, she grasped Lord Fishburn's forearm affectionately.

"You have certainly amassed an impressive collection. What amazing new acquisition do you have to share with us today?" she chirped, hoping it would break the tedium.

He perked right up at her supposed interest. He waved his hands for everyone to gather around.

He gushed, "It's a rare South American 'wishing pot.' Made by the Nazca around 150 BC in the Ica Valley on the southern coast of Peru. Their knowledge of colored glazing was beyond belief. This is a classic seven-color polychrome hand-shaped dish pottery with matching lid. But it is much more than that."

A semicircle of guests formed around the three of them as the host continued.

"Some of the glazes are fabled to be mixed with the blood of the great Incan shaman who shaped the pot. When I obtained the artifact, it had three messages sealed inside, written by the shaman himself. The markings on the outside indicate that whosoever extracts the wishes, one per day, will have the wishes bestowed upon them."

While picking at their food, the crowd listened intently, murmuring "Oh, yes" and "How interesting," which told Dr. McTrowell that these were fellow occultists, more friends of the Lord than the Lady.

Between mouthfuls, the Erasmus interjected, "How do you know that?"

Lady Fishburn sniffed, "Yes, how indeed? You would think he would be more interested in our finer possessions." She gestured with her fan at the plate Drake was holding.

"Wedgwood, isn't it?"

"You are a man of discerning taste and a keen eye. I can see why you are a Chief Inspector," the lady of the house cooed. "I suppose you are not one to be bamboozled by this occult nonsense. Pure rubbish!"

A few guests stifled a guttural response out of politeness.

"As I was about to say," her husband interrupted grumpily, "I have also acquired this translation guide." He produced a roughly bound, hand-written pamphlet on yellowing parchment. "The guide is based on the archeologist Dr. Don Juan Diego's study of Peruvian antiquities, which he published as *The Antiguedades Peruanas.*"

The other guests gasped. Sparky just rolled her eyes.

Lady Beulah whispered conspiratorially to Erasmus, "If he keeps up with these acquisitions, I'll have to sell the china to pay for them and to make shelf space for his grimy bric-a-brac." She affected a melodramatic expression of extreme imposition to emphasize her displeasure.

Lord Fishburn motioned to his butler to bring over a multi-colored, lidded glazed pot. He received it ceremoniously into his hands and cleared his throat. With the air of a memorized speech, he announced, "Please gather around closely, everyone. It is now time for a little supernatural fun with my recently acquired Peruvian wishing pot."

It crossed Erasmus' mind that he had heard the words "acquire" and "acquisition" several times, but neither the word "purchase" nor "buy." He focused his attention away from the sausage on his plate and toward the unfolding pageant.

Their host continued, "As you can see, the hieroglyphics on the outside of the pot read, 'whosoever extracts the wishes, one per day, will have the bestowed wishes come true.'"

Not wishing to be pedantic, Sparky didn't point out that the only person in the room who could read the message was the one who was holding the translation guide. Since she considered the whole business nonsense, she chose to play along quietly.

"It originally had three messages sealed inside, written by the maker of the pot, a great shaman of the Peruvian Incas. The first two messages, written on slips of paper, suggest that I am about to experience a great change in my life, perhaps an unexpected windfall," Lord Fishburn continued excitedly.

McTrowell nonchalantly sidled over beside Drake. "Did the Incas have paper?" He twitched his moustache suspiciously in response.

Lord Fishburn intoned sonorously, "Two days ago, I extracted the first message. Transcribed from the pictographs, it states, 'to reap the reward of the pot, the one who has accepted the burden/power/strength of these wishes …' which is to say, broken the seal of the pot, 'must destroy a false icon in cleansing flames within half a day. If not, they will lose the power of the pot.'"

He looked around at the faces of his guests for emphasis. "In my early years as a collector, I bought a carpet in a market in Turkey. Although it was advertised as handmade with mystical powers to answer the prayers of the owner, I later learned to identify it as a cheap fake made in a factory. Yesterday, I set fire to it and burned it to ashes."

One of the other guests asked, "How do you know if it worked? Did anything happen?"

Lady Fishburn practically giggled her disdain, "What a silly wish. I often light a candle in church as a prayer for the poor, but I never *really* mean it." This admission was met with polite, strained laughter at her callousness.

Her husband chose to ignore her and continue, addressing the more thoughtful question from the crowd. "Well, Admiral Weatherly, I don't know for certain. I concluded I would never know if I didn't continue with the wishes. Yesterday I drew the second wish. It stated, 'to reap the reward of the pot, the one who has accepted the burden/power/strength of these wishes must tell their best friend a hidden truth of their past within half a day. If not, they will lose the power of the pot.' Last night at our club, I told my friend Harry," he paused to gesture at another of member of the assemblage, "of a teenage adventure I took. I stowed away on a cargo boat to the west coast of Africa to seek out shrunken heads. Ironically, I never saw one of the totems, thank goodness, but I did get a bundle of divining sticks from which I have never parted."

Harry smiled awkwardly, clearly embarrassed to become part of the presentation. Standing next to the hostess, Erasmus thought Lady Beulah looked like she would faint from her exasperation at the proceedings.

"That's not much of a wish," she sniffed. "I confessed my disdain for the lower classes to Lady Emily just yesterday afternoon at tea." Considering the fact that Erasmus had been in her presence for only slightly more than half an hour, and her disdain for the lower classes was already quite clear to him, the Chief Inspector suspected this truth was not particularly hidden from Lady Emily.

Sparky was beginning to feel a tad sorry for Lord Fishburn. He seemed a little diminished by his wife's ridicule. Even if the wishing pot was nothing more than a cheap fake like the Turkish factory rug, this gathering was intended to be fun. She could tell by the looks on the faces of the other guests that the mirth was draining away. She tried to encourage him, "So what comes next?"

He brightened up at the positive attention. "I thought this was all great fun, so I wanted to have others around to see if the last drawn wish gets fulfilled. We shall see if the occult is truly as powerful as I believe."

With great ceremony, Lord Fishburn extracted the third message on a piece of paper. He fumbled with the translation pamphlet. Sparky had done enough translation in her life to recognize that he was doubling back and rechecking his translation of the early part of the message. The more he translated and checked, the more agitated he became. Beads of sweat formed on his brow.

"Is something wrong?" the adventuress enquired.

"It says …"

"Yes?" the airship pilot prodded.

"It says …" he squeaked, "to reap the reward of the pot, the one who has accepted the burden/power/strength of these wishes must … must … publicly confess their past crimes within half a day and they shall get their just reward. If not, they shall breathe their last." Now he seemed closer to fainting than his wife.

Sparky tried to calm him down, "As Admiral Weatherly has keenly observed, there is no way to tell if the first two wishes had any affect, so maybe this one doesn't either." Out of the corner of her eye she caught her fiancé shaking his head almost imperceptibly. She had known him long enough to know his instincts about such situations were sound, so she desisted.

She waited along with everyone else in the room. For once, Lady Fishburn held her tongue. Seconds stretched into moments that stretched into a minute. Sparky realized she'd been holding her breath. Just as she prepared to exhale, Lord Fishburn blurted out in terror, "I've paid Harry to steal hundreds of artifacts for me from various collectors, museums, foreign churches, and holy places. Look!" He dashed around the room, opening hidden cabinets and pulling out dusty artifacts, books, and stuffed creatures. He continued into the hall where he slid aside wood panels to reveal more concealed storage. Every compartment was jam packed with hordes of mystical artifacts.

He returned to the dining room. "Most importantly," he sobbed, "I directed him to steal relics for me just last week!"

Erasmus stepped up to the host, proclaiming, "Lord Fishburn, you're under arrest."

Sparky smiled at the Chief Inspector, whispering quietly, "You knew?"

He whispered back, "I suspected. There was a recent break-in at the British Museum occult collection which is not open to the public."

McTrowell caught sight of Harry trying to slip out unnoticed. When he realized he'd captured her unwanted attention, he bolted. "Why do I always have to run when I'm wearing one of these blasted obstructions?" she growled. She grabbed the tops of the ribbons that ruched the sides of her voluminous skirt and yanked upward with force. The sections of the skirt disconnected along the ribbons, revealing a garment similar to Indian pajamas, but of heavier fabric. She sprinted after the fleeing criminal, the heels of her ankle boots echoing off the dining room floor.

Once he regained some semblance of composure after the kerfuffle, Admiral Weatherly commented to Lady Beulah, "Amazing! Your husband was a true believer to the end, even willing to face incarceration instead of simply ignoring the third wish." Her only response was a puckish smile. "Perhaps the shaman made the pot as a gift to an enemy; it could have been Lord Fishburn's confession that saved him."

Jonathan Lord Ashleigh held the door for Drake to escort their erstwhile host out. The Chief Inspector chuckled at his friend, "You know. Harry is not going to be happy he ran when Sparky catches and subdues him."

Lord Ashleigh laughed as he pulled the door closed behind them, "Thank you for making the last hour so unexpectedly entertaining."

Ten O'Clock

A Dark Victorian Story

By Elizabeth Watasin

10:00 AM, London

On the South Bank of Westminster Bridge, red-cheeked boys with long curls caught the morning sunlight through paper pinholes, making tiny suns on the embankment. Their well-to-do mothers watched and walked as a man in a hansom cab rode past, the bold headline of his paper reading: SOLAR ECLIPSE. Near them, a well-dressed woman waited, tall and broad-shouldered, her walking stick set to the walk. From hat to toe, her body gave an eldritch glow, and in her hand sat a white skull wearing a black top hat.

Artifice stood holding Jim Dastard, her partner, and smiled at the women. The little boys approached and stared at Jim's eye sockets, their pinholes forgotten.

"How prospers truth in thy parts, little ones?" Art greeted gently.

The mothers took hold of their children and hurried away.

"Art, such Quaker flirtations," Jim said. "You've a fetching smile, but it is a ghost's."

"An artificial ghost's. And thee has the toothier grin."

"Indeed! One well-admired by women."

"Friend, though we are here to witness the eclipse, I've yet to see the significance of our viewing position."

"As our Secret Commission has informed me, an astronomical occurrence is an excellent opportunity for devilish manipulations, and Her Majesty's England is replete with such ambitious occultists. If the Commission's prognosticators say this spot is likely for mischief, then verily, we shall stand upon it."

Art dutifully did so and spoke no more to passersby. But all present soon turned their gaze to the sky. A black disc grew and gradually ate away the sun. To Art, the lessening light was unlike clouded sky or the fade to dusk. The land fell sway to the moon's umbra. Art watched the Houses of Parliament and the dials of Great Westminster Clock shadow while the River Thames' sparkle died. Birds silenced, and people and carriages grew still on the bridge.

"Hm!" Jim said. "There's a wrinkle, somewhere. Can't place it, though I can taste it. Feels—vaguely over there. I'd gesture helpfully with a hand, had I one."

"I understand, Friend. 'Tis in the air, toward Middlesex bank. The celestial movement of our moon o'er the sun should not cause such a 'wrinkle.'"

"Scientific Quaker! A more evangelical nature would protest that our gobbled sun was a sign from on high," Jim said lightly.

"Of God's wrath? Nay. 'Tis a practical matter, Friend."

"Then we shall find the practical cause of our eldritch wrinkle. Let us alight and traverse further."

Art took translucent form and floated across the walk for Westminster Bridge. She could stroll, but she thought that the sound of her heels and the tap of her walking stick would only disturb the uneasy hush that befell the bridge and city. The edging eclipse robbed the sky of more light, and the greying land took on a lifeless hue. As the last bright sliver of sun winked out, Art and Jim looked upon a shadowed London.

"This cold! This silence. We are in our true light, the twilight," Jim said. "We've lost our good mother and her living world."

He activated his eldritch glow. Art glided along the bridge and between the still carriages, carts, and pedestrians who gaped at the sky. She saw a young, pregnant wife shrink in the darkness of her carriage while her curious husband stepped out. She looked at the weak shadows around them in the queer twilight and thought how flimsily the shapes lay, like the grey gauze of ghosts.

"Is this akin to your Fourth Dimensional existence, Art? Will it be the nearest I can approximate to your elusive ghost state?" Jim asked.

"Nay, Friend. In my ghost state I've yet to view our world like this."

"If this eclipse never ends, mayhap you and I will view the point of crossover once again, whether into hell or where dwell our dead friends. Look at this abandoned world!" he said in a hushed voice. "All are a pale semblance. It's death, hanging."

An old woman in a cart pointed at them.

"Evil!" she quavered. "They rise!"

"Oh come now!" Jim said. "We've been in the papers, madam! We are Ghost and Skull, your spectres!"

"They walk! Evil walks when the Lord forsakes us!" she yelled as Art glided away.

"Bah!" Jim twisted in Art's hand to look back at the old woman. "Blow upon your conch shell, then, harridan, and drive we demons away!"

"Hush," Art soothed. "We are nearly halfway."

Jim swiveled back in her hand.

"Hag. See if I give back her sun," Jim muttered.

"Friend." Art pointed her stick to Great Westminster Clock across the river. It sat as grey as the other buildings, yet its faces gave an itch to her eldritch senses. "There. Does it not seem … wrinkled?"

"Indeed!" Jim said. "Tally-ho!"

Art hefted her stick and leapt off the bridge for the clock tower.

Big Ben sounded.

"Ten o'clock!" Jim said.

Art looked around, startled. She was back on the bridge, as if she'd never leapt.

"Well, I'll be!" Jim said.

Art leapt off the bridge again. Her skirts flapped in the wind as she crossed the water.

Big Ben sounded.

"Ten o'clock!" Jim said.

Art looked around again. She was back on the bridge, gliding among the vehicles and onlookers.

"Friend! We lived this moment before!"

"Don't I know it! Something's changing time! Unless the fault lies with our own perceptions. Are we dreaming, Art? Are you a figment, or am I?"

"Bite my pinkie, Jim."

He chomped on the gloved pinkie Art offered him.

"Ouch! Thy teeth are sharp!" Art waved the injured little finger.

"Not certain that helped, Art, I could be the one dreaming," Jim said.

Big Ben sounded.

"Ten o'clock!" Jim said.

Art found herself at the start of the bridge. She leapt and took off flying, Jim whooping in her hand. She sped for the nearest-facing dial of Great Westminster Clock. In the half-light of the eclipse, she spied the shadows of creatures, formed vaguely like men. They skittered across the dials.

"Hell's bells! What's that?" Jim said. "Phantasmagoria of the Fourth Dimension?"

Big Ben sounded.

"Ten o'…"

Art threw Jim at the tower. His bony pate and top hat passed through an unseen veil that rippled. Jim hit the hour hand of the closest dial and nearly tumbled off the edge. He bit hard upon the hand and righted himself.

Art found herself returned to the bridge again, no Jim in hand. Her gaze faced Great Westminster Clock while the clock struck ten. A tiny fire flared bright on the hour hand of the dial. Art ghosted and barreled through the air.

"Take that! And that! Eat hellfire!" she heard Jim shout. He sat on the clock's hour hand, spitting flames. Shadows flitted close. Art hit the unseen veil and shimmered through, her ghost matter squeezing like whey. She popped out the other side, her flight a tumbling trajectory. She smelled sulphur and solidified, smacking into the numeral twelve.

"Art! What are you doing? The fiends are down here!" Jim cried. He spat more fire.

Art fell feet-first upon the hour hand and saw strange, shadow symbols waver on the clock surface. She faced the flitting shadows and ghosted. In the roar of the Fourth Dimension, the shadows solidified into twisted, demon-faced men. Jagged lines of silver and black tore the sky while the Thames roiled red, the city melted. Jim was a small shadow near her feet, and Art breathed sulphur. She hooked the dial's second hand with her stick and seized the nearest demon by the throat, her ghost fingers clenching solid flesh.

Big Ben gonged, the sound reverberating backwards.

"Thee shall release this clock, now!" Art cried.

The demon in her grip stretched its face. A hole broke open in its visage.

"Release my city, now!"

She slammed the demon into the dial, shattering the glass. The fiery numerals were unknown to her. A giant, golden engine burned above, with flaming mechanical limbs that pierced the clock dial.

What machine is this? she thought.

The demon's feet rose and gripped her. It willed her body back into solidity, and she shuddered, fighting the change. She ripped the demon from the shattered glass as she lost her ghost state.

"Art …" she heard Jim shout when she reentered their world.

She tottered on the hour hand, gripping the demon shadow. She ghosted back into the Fourth Dimension and breathed sulphur. The solid demon screamed and shifted Art into solidity once more.

"… are …" Jim said.

Art changed back into a ghost. The demon shifted her a third time.

"… dancing?" Jim said as Art solidified.

Art ghosted and flung the demon off the clock. She took up her stick and swung, smashing the gold limbs sunk in the glass. The pieces flew. Demons piled upon her and she threw them off. She launched away from the dial and flew around the four faces, thrashing every mechanical limb. Demons leapt for her, and she careened up into the great, gold engine above. She struck it with her body, sending it toppling. Her stick and arm erupted in flames.

The clock tower warped before her, melting, and she felt the world closing. Art landed on the twisting, burning dial she'd left Jim on and solidified.

"Art!" Jim cried as Art fought for footing on the hour hand. "Where in the Fourth Dimension did you go to? 'Bout time you came back! I've been spewing flame at this funny shadow-symbol, and I believe by eradicating it I broke the spell!"

"'Spell'? Friend," Art said, breathing. She stared at grey London and the glimmering Thames.

"Well, shadow-numbers, Art! That says 'sorcery' to me."

"Aye … most recondite sorcery, if that," she answered. She took a deep breath and ghosted. In the Fourth Dimension, the world remained the same to her vision; it was her London. She looked for signs of hell on Earth.

"Eh?" Jim said when she reappeared again.

"Friend, did thee not see me grapple with a demon?"

"A—? Art, I briefly saw you choking a most unfortunately ugly fellow, and a naked one at that! These sorcerers, it takes all kinds. Look at that burn he gave you! Since I see him nowhere, did you conclude the matter?"

She picked Jim up and directed him to take in the dial with her. No strange shadows marred the glass, and there was no trace of the golden machine. She looked at her hand that clenched her stick. Her glove and sleeve were burnt black.

"Art?" Jim said.

"The matter is done," she answered.

"Ten o' one! Light cometh, and our work is done!" Jim said.

Art turned for Westminster Bridge and the River Thames. A growing crescent sun warmed the sky. She watched the ghost shadows fade upon their world.

"Demons, begone!" Jim said.

SEEKER

By Dover Whitecliff

11:00 AM, Valley of the Kings

Elle crouched down in the dust. "Allow me to help you, sir," she whispered, gently using her outstretched finger to roll the ball of dung around the rock on which its caretaker had gotten it stuck. "There you go, Mr. Beetle. All better." The beetle turned, twitching his antennae, then turned back once more and began to roll the ball onward with its back feet. Elle reached out again to guide the ball around another pebble. "Wait, Mr. Beetle, you'll get stuck aga—"

"Elle Quartermaine!" Elle jumped to her feet at the shout, startled. "Leave that beetle alone. You know exactly where he's been."

Elle hastily wiped her hand on her knickers. "Yes, Aunty Clarissa. Sorry, Aunty Clarissa."

"Really, child, dung beetles have been doing their work for thousands of years." Aunty Clarissa took Elle's hand and pulled her along the rocky path between the cliffs. "They're quite capable of getting around pebbles without your assistance."

131

"Thousands, really?"

"Yes, thousands."

"How do you know?"

"Well, if you'll hurry along, you'll find out. Kilima and the *reis* are ready to breach the tomb. There's bound to be at least one hieroglyph of Khepri in there somewhere."

"But, Aunty, isn't Khepri a scarab?"

"I can see we need to add biology and Egyptian lore to your lessons. Tomorrow morning, you will be able to explain the significance of Khepri and his relation to the dung beetle." Elle groaned at this pronouncement.

"Yes, Aunty Clarissa ..." Elle scuffed her boots in the dust, wishing she hadn't asked that last question, "*Ma'alesh,*" she muttered. It can't be helped.

"Well that's something ... your Arabic is coming along nicely. You'll be ready for a new language soon ..."

Elle bit her tongue rather than get herself more lessons, but cheered as they rounded a bend and saw the dig site buzzing with activity. Elle loved the sights and smells, the sounds, the amazement of walking in a place thousands of years old. But there was something else. Since she had arrived, she had felt something calling to her, something that wanted to be found. She kept within earshot of Aunty Clarissa as she studied the rock strata of the valley around her, waiting for her daily lessons. Up one side of the cliffs, a dark shadow caught her eye. She cocked her head, listening. There it was, the low rumble of purring. Coming from her cave. My own discovery. I'll uncover it all by myself. Today's the day. She was sure she could sneak away when the workers were busy checking for traps and Kilima and Aunty Clarissa were less hawk-like in overseeing her every move.

In the meantime, Elle reveled in the music of the ongoing work: the *reis*, Mahmoud, instructing the workers on some of the beams to be used in the tunnel they'd unearthed, Aunty Clarissa's lecture on traps and engineering. And then there was Kilima N'Jaro, their guide here in the valley, who told the most wonderful stories of her adventures in tomb raiding. To Elle's young ears, it was a symphony of adventure swelling around her.

Not much time passed before Aunty Clarissa and Kilima walked away with Mahmoud to inspect the shoring of the tunnel … soon they and the workers were inside and nowhere in sight. They'll be in there a bit. Now's my chance. Elle sidled away cautiously in case one of the workers emerged, and then, when she was out of the line of sight from the tunnel, she sprinted toward the cliff and started her climb.

Loose rocks slipping under her boots gave her a turn once or twice, but she kept going, certain she could still hear something like purring. She was breathing hard by the time she pulled herself over the ledge, and she lay on her back a moment to catch her breath. When she rolled over, she could see that the cleft was shallow, but even through the shadows, she could see there was a slit in the rock face at the rear of the cave near the floor.

Elle crouched down to peer through the hole. It wasn't pitch black, but it was dark enough. Only then did she realize she had forgotten her lantern. But then fainter and further down the cave, the low rumble of a jungle cat … a deep purring growl called her onward. *Ma'alesh.* I can't go back now. She crawled on her hands and knees, but had to slide forward on her belly for the last bit until she passed through the crack in the rock. The floor inside the cave was thick with guano. Elle crinkled her nose. Aunty Clarissa will smell me a mile away. I'd best lose my waistcoat on the way out. At least now I know where the bats are coming from every night.

"I'm here, Kitty Cat. I'll bring you home. Where are you?" Elle whispered into the shadows. She closed her eyes and listened. At first, all she could hear was the sound of her own breathing and heartbeat. Then the rustling of the bats hanging overhead. "There you are. I hear you. I'm coming." She followed the sound, quietly stopping still to listen when the cave branched in two directions and always following the rumbling purr.

The cave took on a gentle slope, making it easier for her to navigate in the dark. Elle kept her hand on one wall as she continued down. It was certainly not like any other cave she'd seen here in the valley. As she went on, she began to think that this cave had been crafted rather than formed, and crafted by someone other than the pharaohs. Then there was the purring. Was the cat lost, or had someone taken it? And if the people that made the cave had taken it, were they still here? Elle tried her best to step lightly lest her stomping echo round the cave.

Either I've eaten way too many carrots, or it's getting lighter in here. Elle thought. But if I'm under the ground and going downhill, why would it be getting lighter? A hole up on top of the cliff wouldn't light up the whole way, even this close to lunch time. Would it? Her hand ran over something other than plain rock. Smooth, regular grooves. She squinted at the wall in the dim light. They were carvings. Spirals. Swirls. In rows. Almost like writing. Elle ran her fingers around one of the grooves, wondering who could have made them. They weren't hieroglyphs, or hieratic, or Greek, or even Chinese. They almost looked like drawings of snakes—snakes with arms.

Elle gulped. She remembered the stories Mama and Papa had told her of the Naga. The giant snake people that ate all creatures, devouring everything in their path. Oh don't be silly. The Naga live in China and India and that's an awful long way away from here. You're just scaring yourself. Keep going and find the cat before Aunty Clarissa figures out you're gone, or you're not going to be able to sit for a month.

The thought of getting her backside tanned by Aunty Clarissa being infinitely more probable than being eaten by a bedtime story helped Elle take the first step down the slope. The purring pulling her onward helped with the second, and the third, and the fourth, until she was back on course down the cave, and getting closer to her goal. Almost there. *Then we can go see the tomb and have some lunch. I'm sure Kitty Cat's probably hungry after being stuck down here.*

Elle's thoughts wandered to what the cat might like for lunch, goat's milk or camel's milk, until she curved round a bend and froze. Something huge blocked nearly the entire path. It was mostly still, but shivered slightly with every three or four beats of her heart. The purr rumbled and shifted into a hiss. Light flickered behind the shape. Light and shadow. A shadow growing, approaching, looming toward her from the cave below. Rearing up. Lunging.

Primal fear took over. Elle turned and sprinted back up the path as fast as she could, trailing one hand against the wall to keep her bearings. The hissing filled her ears as she pounded back up the path, terror at her heels. Something scraped on stone behind her. *Run Faster. Run Faster. Don't look back. There. The entrance!* She dove forward as bats, thrown into a frenzy by her sudden appearance, flapped and squeaked above her head. She slid through, pushed up to crawl forward until she could stand in the cleft. *Stop! You can't climb down with something chasing you!* Elle made herself stop, wrenched off her boot, and held it high, ready to smash down on anything that followed, breathing hard, heart pounding.

Nothing. Nothing at all. No, wait. The scraping. The hissing. A flickering light, like a torch on the other side of the rock reflecting out of the cave. Elle lifted her boot higher … but the light and sounds diminished, as if heading back down the cave.

"Elle!" Aunty Clarissa's voice echoed up the wadi. *Uh Oh. That's not good.*

Elle laced her boot back on and took off her waistcoat, hoping Aunty Clarissa wouldn't notice the guano on her knickers. She peered over the edge. No one in sight. She lay on her stomach, scooted her legs over and felt for the first foothold. Her head had just ducked below the entrance when she heard it … It was a slippery voice, and one full of menace.

"An intruder. We cannot delay until the equinox. Prepare the ritual. Tonight we feed on Bassssst."

What have I done? Elle scrambled down the rock face, berating herself for not facing her fear. I've made it worse. They'll eat him if I don't do something. Elle stumbled round the bend in the canyon only to run into Aunty Clarissa.

"Elle! There you are. Hurry up. I want to show you the hieroglyphs of Khepri before we stop for lunch." Aunty Clarissa sniffed and shooed Elle back to the dig site. "What's that smell?"

Elle ran ahead to avoid answering, and found Kilima standing in front of the tomb entrance. Kilima looked up to the cave and then down at Elle. Silent. Measuring. Then finally beckoned her toward the tomb and turned to enter. Elle chanced a look over her shoulder at the cave. I'm so sorry I got caught, but don't worry, Kitty Cat. I won't let them eat you. I'll come back for you. I promise.

Twelve Hours Later

A Demon in the Noonday Sun

By Lillian Csernica

12:00 PM, Kyoto

Dr. William Harrington stood on the famous veranda of the Kiyomizu Temple in Kyoto, Japan. Between exhaustion and the biting chill of the winter breeze, he longed for his greatcoat and a muffler. Even at noon, the gray wool of his tailcoat, waistcoat, and trousers were not enough. The Japanese had a custom of carrying their outer coats during important events. That explained a great deal about all the layering of kimono. He shivered. The study of medicine had left him unscathed, but the art of diplomacy might kill him yet.

Two of the monks of the Kiyomizu Temple helped their aged abbot cross the cypress planks one slow step at a time. All three wore what looked like a white kimono, a black kimono over that, and a golden garment wound around their torsos. The wheelchair sat waiting, its brass and copper fittings gleaming in the late December sun. Davis, the naval engineer who'd built the chair, stood behind it. The seat itself was a modified wingback, not quite as broad nor quite so high, yet well-upholstered in fine tapestry fabric. Harrington had wondered at the strange pairing of cranes and turtles until his interpreter had explained the folklore about both creatures representing longevity.

"The chair will work?" asked Alexander Thompson, Undersecretary for Technological Exchange. One could scarcely believe he was a diplomat or an engineer. Short, stout, and balding, Thompson looked like a banker facing an audit.

"Yes, Undersecretary," Harrington said with dutiful patience.

"There's some family connection between the Emperor and the Abbot. That makes this situation twice as delicate, twice as critical!"

"I understand, sir." Harrington understood he was about to collapse. First Madelaine's fever had left him in an agony of frustration and fatigue. Then came her sudden recovery, which nothing in any modern medical text could possibly explain. Now Thompson held Harrington responsible for the health and well-being of the abbot of Kiyomizudera. It was an honor, and quite a feather in his cap, but only if he succeeded in keeping the eighty-nine-year-old abbot healthy. Otherwise he'd be plucked cleaner than a Christmas goose.

"Be sure you do understand, Doctor. The New Year's celebration is the biggest event of the Japanese year. Everything must be clean and in good working order. No dirt, no stain, and above all, no sickness." Thompson scowled. "The Abbot must be able to preside over today's events. Any sign of poor health would be a bad omen for the coming year."

Harrington had been relieved to discover the Abbot was in excellent health for a man of his advanced years. Japan was full of surprises. Since the Shogunate had fallen and the old caste system had been abolished, there were so many possibilities. Japan wanted to catch up to the rest of the world. That meant good luck and prosperity for everyone. Now Harrington was on the front line of maintaining good relations between Japan and Great Britain. Any bad omens today spelled disaster for Harrington's career as well. That in turn would cast a serious pall over Madelaine's opportunities for making a good marriage.

"I say! Doctor! You look like you're asleep on your feet!"

Harrington straightened up. "I do beg your pardon, Undersecretary. My daughter's recent illness was quite an ordeal for the entire family."

Thompson's scowl mellowed a trifle. "Yes. Well. Terrible things, fevers. Good to know the little girl is on the mend."

"Thank you, sir." At the far end of the veranda, Madelaine sat at one of the dainty tables in the tea garden, her dark hair shining in the winter sun. Her mother sat at her right and Nurse Danforth at her left. It was so good to see that pretty little face smiling. Madelaine waved to him. Harrington smiled and gave her a discreet nod.

The monks had reached the wheelchair. They lowered the Abbot into it and helped him arrange his robes. Harrington's interpreter, a slim young Japanese man named Fujita, now stood at Davis's elbow to translate his explanations of the steering and the brake. The Abbot pushed the control stick forward. The hissing and sputtering of the machinery sped up. The wheelchair rolled ahead a few feet with the two monks keeping just behind it. The Abbot pulled up on the brake. The wheelchair slowed to a smooth stop. The Abbot spoke to one of the monks, who passed on his comments to Fujita. There was much bowing. Fujita turned to shake Davis's hand.

"Harrington-*sensei*." Fujita hurried over to him. "The Abbot is quite pleased. He praises the builders for making such a comfortable chair move so well."

Thompson let out a gusty sigh of relief. "Thank God. Let's hope the Emperor shares the Abbot's opinion." Fujita turned back to Davis. Harrington watched the two of them explain the finer points of turning and backing up. Thompson strode off to confer with a cluster of his subordinates, who scattered to fulfill their assigned tasks. Harrington wanted nothing so much as a cup of tea and somewhere to sit down.

"Oi! *Gaijin*!"

Harrington flinched. A man's voice, deep, harsh, and angry. Behind him stood a samurai in full formal attire, gray *hakama* topped by a black *kimono* with the full-shouldered vest over that, tied by the big white knot hanging down over the chest. No top-knot tamed the heavy mass of black hair that spilled down the man's back. Behind the man's left shoulder, Harrington could see the hilt of what had to be a very large sword.

"You are Harrington-*sensei*, father of the little *gaijin* girl?"

"You have me at a disadvantage, sir," Harrington said. "You know my name but I have not yet had the pleasure of learning yours."

"I have not come to bring you pleasure, *gaijin*. No, quite the opposite!"

Harrington realized the samurai was speaking Japanese, and yet Harrington understood him. Something was wrong here, very wrong.

"One moment, sir, while I fetch my interpreter. I believe there is some misunderstanding."

"There is no misunderstanding. Your child's nurse called down the power of your Christian god against me. She turned the *kami* of this temple against me!"

The samurai drew his huge sword. As long and as broad as a claymore, the blade curved and rippled like a stream of frozen metal. Japanese swordsmiths were world-famous. While Harrington could appreciate the science of metallurgy, a deeper part of him knew no human skill created the black flames flickering along the sword's keen edge.

"I will destroy your little machine, *gaijin*. Then I will see you shamed and driven from this place like a criminal!"

Harrington leaped aside as the sword came down. The wheelchair jerked around to face the samurai. Steam hissed out of the joints. It began to rattle all over then jerked backward, scattering the monks, Davis, and Fujita. The Abbot called out, clinging to the wheelchair's arms. One of the monks bowed and dashed into the temple.

"Stop that this instant!" Harrington threw his weight against the samurai's left side. Pain exploded in his shoulder. The samurai might have been a brick wall. "The Abbot is my patient! Smash the chair if you must, but have pity on the old man!"

"Harrington!" Thompson came charging over. "What the bloody hell is going on here? You said it worked!"

"Sir," Harrington said. "Call the guards. This man is clearly a danger to the Abbot!"

Thompson looked to either side, then behind him. "What man?"

"He's standing right there!" Harrington pointed. "Can't you see that bloody great sword?"

"Harrington, have you been drinking?"

"Only you can see me, *gaijin*." The samurai looked Thompson over. "This fat fool expects you to take the blame for the machine's failure so he will not lose face. Are all *gaijin* such cowards?"

The monk came rushing out of the temple carrying a wide strip of paper in his hands. On the paper were kanji painted in large black brushstrokes.

"Hah!" The samurai whirled and brought the sword down again, hurling black fire at the monk. It struck the monk and threw him sprawling. The paper fluttered away on the wind.

"Harrington!" Thompson barked. "The festival is about to begin! Do something!"

The samurai let out a roar of laughter. Another burst of black fire ruptured something on the wheelchair, sending up a plume of steam.

"Sir, I am a physician," Harrington said, "not a mechanic or an exorcist. If you have any suggestions, I'm all ears!"

"Papa?"

"Madelaine?" Harrington turned to see Madelaine running toward him. "Go back! Go back to your mother at once!"

"Papa!" Madelaine flung her arms around his waist. "I see him! I see the man with the sword!"

"You do?"

"She does?" Thompson looked around again.

"He's bad, Papa! Call the lady who lives in this temple. She'll make him go away!"

"Fujita-*san*!" Harrington shouted. His interpreter came running.

"Harrington-*sensei*, Mr. Davis has no idea what's wrong! If the chair was human, I'd say it has gone mad!"

"Fujita-*san*, listen to me. Who is the lady who lives in this temple?"

"Kannon, the Goddess of Mercy."

Harrington crouched down to look into Madelaine's big blue eyes. "Maddy, what makes you think the lady of this temple will answer me?"

"Papa, this is her home. Today is her big New Year's party. She won't let the bad man stay here and hurt the Abbot."

Etiquette. Good manners. The Japanese were famous for it. Surely their gods shared such a deeply rooted element of their culture?

"Maddy, how do you know all of this?"

"I've been reading Japanese fairy stories, Papa. Did you know the Emperor is part magic? Way back in time, his grandmother was the Sun Goddess herself!"

"I had no idea." Keeping Madelaine with him, Harrington hurried up to the very door of the temple. "Madam, I'm a Christian man who is far from home. I beg you, come and make that fiend with the sword leave this place! I fear for the health and safety of your abbot!"

Nothing. Not even a breeze stirred the temple chimes. Harrington kissed the top of Madelaine's head.

"Stay right here, darling." Whatever the samurai was, demon or hallucination or common gate crasher, William Harrington had a duty to protect his patient. He stood up and stormed past the wheelchair that still chugged in demented spirals all over the veranda. The samurai stood there, both hands on the hilt of the huge sword, holding it drawn back beside his ear.

"It's time for you to leave," Harrington said. "Will you go quietly? Or shall I call St. Michael the Archangel, Commander of the Armies of God, to crush you beneath his heel as he did the Devil himself?"

"You turn to a child for counsel, a girl child?" The samurai spat at Harrington's feet. "Your manhood must have shriveled like an earthworm dying in the sun!"

"Amatsu Mikaboshi."

A woman, no, a Lady, stood at the edge of the veranda. All the natural majesty of the forest spread out behind her. The sight of her made Harrington's fatigue fall away. Anxiety and fear and anger faded before the beauty of the Lady's smile. She was beyond beautiful, garbed in a kimono resplendent with chrysanthemums and cranes and so much gold thread Harrington had the urge to shield his eyes from the Lady's glory. A small hand slipped into his.

"See, Papa?"

"I do see, darling."

The Lady walked toward the samurai. The wheelchair spun around and trundled toward her. One glance brought the wheelchair to a gentle stop. The two monks rushed over to lift the Abbot out of the seat and lower him to his knees. All three bowed down before the Lady. She bent to touch the Abbot's shoulder, speaking softly. He answered her, keeping his head down. The Lady straightened up.

"Amatsu Mikaboshi." The Lady studied the samurai. Her smile faded. "You draw your blade here, in my temple? You bring evil to the monks who tend my shrine?"

"Lady Kannon." The samurai bowed. "I am here for the *gaijin*. He has cost me face, and I will see the debt paid."

"Harrington-*sensei* is my guest."

The Lady spoke in a tone of great gentleness, but behind that tone lay authority far more powerful than the samurai's huge sword. Harrington knew the value of hospitality in a British home. The Japanese probably made an art of it, as they did with so many other aspects of daily life.

"The Emperor himself has appointed Harrington-*sensei* as personal physician to the abbot of Kiyomizudera," the Lady said. "Harrington-*sensei* holds the respect of the son of Amaterasu Omikami. Would you dare to do him harm?"

The samurai leveled a blistering scowl at Harrington. With much reluctance, he sheathed his sword. "No, Lady Kannon. I would not anger Amaterasu Omikami."

The Lady smiled, brighter than ever.

"Arigato gozaimasu, Amatsu Mikaboshi. Please, stay and join us for the festival. There will be dancing and drinking and young people trying to walk between the pillars with their eyes closed. Surely there will be enough happy chaos to satisfy you?"

The samurai bowed. "You are most gracious, Lady Kannon. I accept your kind invitation."

"I must speak to Harrington-*sensei*. The festival is about to begin."

The samurai bowed again, and then vanished.

The monks hoisted the Abbot to his feet. Davis ran to the chair, some tool already in hand. Madelaine took a step forward.

"Doh-mo ah-ree-gah-toh, Miss Kannon." She bowed.

"What a courteous child." The Lady beckoned Madelaine. That same delicate hand stroked Madelaine's cheek. The Lady looked up at Harrington. "You are her father, Harrington-*sensei*?"

"Yes, Madam."

"I am happy to see she is well enough to attend the festival."

Harrington clenched his jaw to keep it from falling open. How did these—these "people" know about his private household matters?

"We—we are honored to be allowed to attend, Madam."

"Jizo-*sama* and Chimata-no-Kami would have been most disappointed if your lovely daughter had not joined us."

"I'm sorry, Madam. I—I'm afraid I don't know who those people are."

"Child, have you not told your father of your nurse's courage?"

"No, Miss Kannon. Papa is a scientist. He doesn't have much use for legends and folklore."

Harrington winced. That was a direct quote. He took Madelaine's hand in his. "I would be most interested to hear this story, darling. Perhaps you can tell me later, after we go home?"

"Of course, Papa. But only if you promise to believe me."

Harrington looked at the Goddess of Mercy standing before him in all her splendor. "Darling, I give you my word."

LORD OF DEATH, PART II

By Steve DeWinter

1:00 PM, London

Nick jolted awake and bolted upright in bed.

"Airship," he said out loud and looked around him. He was in a private hospital room overlooking the River Thames.

Jack woke up suddenly from the chair in the corner and rushed forward, blinking away the sleep from his bloodshot eyes. "Nick! I thought I had lost you. The doctor said you might never wake up again."

Nick blinked at the bright sunlight spilling in through the open window. He pointed at it, his hand shaking in terror. "Close that window!"

Jack looked at the window and then back at Nick. "What?"

Nick stood up and nearly collapsed to the floor. "He can come in through the windows. Close it!"

"Okay, I'll close it. But you have to lie down."

Jack guided Nick back into bed and then went over to close the window. Before he did, he looked out and up into the sky. He locked the window and turned back to Nick. "The police came by earlier this morning and told me you were here. I think they confiscated the breather because the doctor said you weren't wearing anything when they brought you in. What happened?"

Nick stared at the closed window. "How long have I been out?"

As if in answer to his question, Big Ben rang out a single chime as Jack answered. "Nearly twelve hours."

Nick looked at his hands. "Where's the mask?"

"What mask?"

"I took the ghost's mask. I ripped it off his face, scratching him with my fingernails."

Nick swung his feet over the edge of the bed and set them on the floor. "I hurt him. If we act quickly, we can get to him before he heals."

Nick stood up and wavered on his feet. Jack grabbed his arm to steady him. "Easy, Nick. Why don't you rest?"

Nick shot a hard look at Jack. "I know how he can fly."

Jack's forehead wrinkled in confusion. "How who can fly?"

"The Lord of Death. He was tied to an airship. The fog and darkness obscured the rope. But I saw the ship before I passed out." Nick looked at him, and the smile returned despite the throbbing pain in his head. "He's not a ghost."

Nick tried to stand, but the room spun around him and he fell back to the bed. Jack tucked him back into bed. "You need to rest. We can find him later."

ℝ℞

A faint knock on the door was followed by the head of a gentleman in a frock and top hat poking into Nick's hospital room. "I don't mean to intrude ..." the man said.

Jack looked over at him. "Can I help you?"

The man came fully into the room. "I wanted to thank your friend for saving my life last night."

Nick sat up in the bed. "Was that your house I barreled through?"

The man nodded. "The name's Allister Blomquist, and I am forever in your debt."

Nick leaned against the headboard. "You're welcome. I was just doing my duty to keep London safe."

Allister smiled. "You've done more than just keep London safe, my boy. You have secured the employment of nearly a thousand workers at my company."

Nick frowned. "I'm sorry?"

Allister cleared his throat. "I was scheduled to sign a contract with the city this morning that would create jobs for a thousand unemployed workers. If I had died last night at the hands of that ghost—well, there's no telling what would have happened to my company. It probably would have gone belly up like all the others."

Jack sat up straighter at that comment. "What others?"

Allister looked at Jack. "I'm part of a clandestine coalition of business owners whose purpose is to get people back to work in the various industries. We are fighting the mechanization of several types of jobs. The types that have been putting able bodied men out of work and leaving their families to starve in the street."

Jack stood up. "Are you saying that the men who killed themselves these past months were part of your coalition?"

Allister nodded. "I'm sad to report that there are only a few of us left."

Jack was nodding, but stared at the floor deep in thought as he spoke slowly. "And you say this was a secret coalition."

"Oh yes. This was not something we could advertise publicly."

"Did you tell the police that all the suicide victims were part of your coalition?"

"I wanted to, but the one who started it said we had to remain silent if we wanted to achieve our goals."

Nick leaned forward in the bed. "And after everyone started dying, you still remained silent."

Allister nodded sadly. "I don't think, after what happened last night, that I can remain silent any longer. I was just on my way to the police to tell them everything I know. But I wanted to stop by and thank you for saving me, first."

Allister turned to leave when Jack rushed forward, stopping him. "Mr. Blomquist. I would like you to stay silent for just a while longer."

Allister's forehead wrinkled in confusion. "Why?"

"I think we can catch who's doing this, but we're going to need your help."

Allister smiled slightly. "Of course."

ℬℭ

It took a little convincing to get the doctors to release Nick. Actually, it took more than a little convincing. It took Allister to grease the wheels of the administration with money to get Nick out of the hospital. Allister then took them in his private carriage back to his house. Once there, he opened the front door and Jack's mouth fell open when he saw the breather leaning against the wall in the parlor.

Allister noticed Jack's attention. "I took it off of your friend before the police arrived. I knew they would try to keep it, but I thought you might want it back."

Jack rushed in and inspected it before looking at Allister. "Thank you, Mr. Blomquist. Both of our life savings are in this thing."

Allister stood next to Jack. "I looked it over and saw some improvements that could be made."

Jack nodded. "We've already poured everything we had into it just to get it this far. We can't afford to do any more."

Allister smiled. "There is one thing I know, Mr. Flint. If money is your only problem, you don't have a problem."

Jack shook his head. "You wouldn't be saying that if you didn't have any money."

"That is true. I have plenty of money, and access to manufacturing facilities. I think we can improve your suit and do some good for this city. That is if you and Mr. Steele are interested."

Nick and Jack looked at each other and then back to Allister as they replied in unison. "We are interested."

Allister smiled. "Excellent. I think we can form a partnership that will benefit everyone."

A knock at the door interrupted them. Allister looked toward the clock on the mantle. "That would be one of my coalition partners. We had a meeting set for this morning. I'm afraid that you two will have to stay in here. You can imagine that the rest of the coalition would want to remain anonymous, for various reasons, the first being someone trying to kill them."

Nick nodded. "Of course. We'll stay in here."

Allister nodded and left the parlor, closing the sliding doors behind him. From the muffled sounds echoing through the walls, Nick could hear Allister greeting his guest. "How nice of you to meet with me privately this morning. I was surprised to get your call."

Nick didn't recognize the other voice. "Yes, well, these are troubled times for the coalition, and I wanted to meet with everyone to ensure that we take the necessary precautions to remain safe."

"May I take your cloak?"

"Thank you."

"Oh, dear. What happened to your face?"

"My wife allowed a stray cat into the house, and I'm afraid it scratched me while I slept."

Nick's heart rate increased. The man who had just come into Allister's house had been scratched on the face. He rushed over to Jack, who was still kneeling next to the breather. "Jack. I scratched the ghost's face."

"I know. You keep telling me."

"The man who just called on Allister. His face is scratched. Do you think he could be our man?"

Jack stopped inspecting the breather and looked at Nick in alarm. "But he's part of the coalition. Allister knows him. Why would he be killing the coalition members?"

"I don't know. Do you think he's getting the contracts after the others are dead?"

"Nick. You can't keep thinking everyone you meet is a suspect in nefarious dealings."

"I don't think that."

Jack gave Nick a grimace forcing Nick to hold his hands up in surrender. "Okay, so I think people generally do more than they are willing to admit. They just shouldn't act so suspicious all the time if they aren't doing anything."

"We need more evidence if you want to accuse Allister's partner of being the Lord of Death."

Nick jabbed a finger in the air. "You're right. I need proof."

Jack gave him a wary look. "What is going through that crazy head of yours, Nick?"

Nick stood up and grabbed the damaged breather. "I'm going to get proof."

₧₨

Nick pulled open the sliding doors to the study and strode into the room. Allister and the other man immediately stopped talking and both regarded the man who looked half-man and half-automaton as he sauntered in.

The other man's eyes widened and he shot up out of his chair, pointing at Nick. "It's the killer!" he shouted.

Nick looked at the man and then at Allister, his voice muffled by the faceplate. "What?"

The man backed away, pointing at Nick in terror. "Allister! Do something! He's here to kill us!"

Nick rushed forward and slammed the man into the wall. Nick grabbed his face and turned it to the side, inspecting the scratches. They didn't look like human fingernail scratches. They were too thin and closely spaced. In fact, they looked exactly like the thin scratches from a cat's claws.

Allister was immediately at Nick's side. "What are you doing!?" he demanded.

Nick looked at him and then lifted his faceplate. "I'm sorry. I thought this was the guy."

"And what made you think that?"

"I heard you mention the scratches on the side of his face. I scratched the guy who tried to kill you when I ripped off his mask."

Nick looked back at the terrified man. "I'm really sorry. I thought you were someone else."

Nick backed away, but the man stayed pressed against the wall, his face pale.

Allister moved in between them and faced Nick. "If you'll please leave, I will work to repair the damage you have caused by frightening the life out of my associate."

"I really am sorry," Nick said as he backed out of the parlor and slid the doors shut.

℘℘

In the hallway, Nick leaned his back against the closed doors. Jack was standing in the doorway to the parlor, shaking his head. "I told you. You can't keep rushing in like that."

"Like what?"

"With guns a-blazing. It's going to get you into trouble."

"I was so sure," Nick said.

Jack led him back into the parlor and shut the doors. As they removed the breather, a barker, no more than eight years old, was yelling outside the window as he walked holding a newspaper over his head. "Mayor holding press conference to discuss unemployment concerns."

The kid continued to yell the same thing as he walked down the street, his voice fading to the distance.

The doors opened and Allister rushed in, cornering Nick. "What the devil did you think you were doing in there?"

Nick held his hands up in supplication. "I said I was sorry."

"Do you have any idea who that man is?"

"I thought the whole point was that I didn't?"

Allister shook his head. "If we are to work together, there are a few things you need to get straight. First, I am in charge."

Jack held his hands up. "Whoa. We agreed to let you help us, but being rich doesn't automatically make you the leader."

Allister turned on Jack. "Maybe in your fantasy world it doesn't. But in the real world, money is power. And I have a lot of power. I want to use my power for good and not just for my own advantage. I can help you make a difference in the world. But we have to do this my way."

Jack puffed out his chest and inched closer, his fists forming tight balls. "And if we refuse your help?"

Nick moved between them before they started swinging at each other. "Jack. We need his help."

"No, we don't."

"Yes, we do. You said so yourself just last week. We have enough funds for a couple of months at best. After that, we have to go back to America. Neither of us wants that, right? He is giving us access to his money, and more importantly, access to his machinery. You can build the suit better and we can finally do some good in the world."

Jack shook his head. "We don't need his money. We can do this on our own."

Allister lowered his head. "I was hoping I could convince you otherwise. But, I will not force you."

Jack picked up the breather. "Come on Nick."

Nick shrugged his shoulders.

Allister held the door as they left. "If you ever change your mind, you know where to find me."

"We won't be changing our minds," Jack shot over his shoulder as they walked away down the street.

∞ℝ

The crowds were getting thicker as they approached the center of the city. Nick pushed his way through the milling throngs as they made their way back to their humble flat. Jack stayed behind him and followed in the path Nick cut through the mass of people. Nick glanced over at the raised stage where the mayor of the city was settling into the chair after having finished his big speech. Men of high standing were settled into the other chairs on either side of him.

Nick stopped short and Jack collided into his back.

"Why'd you stop?" Jack asked.

Nick focused on the bodyguard standing behind the mayor and pointed. "Look. The man behind the mayor."

Jack stood on his toes to see above the crowd and then dropped down. "I can barely see. What about him?"

Nick spoke just barely above a whisper as he glared through the masses at the man on the stage standing behind the mayor. "He has scratches on the side of his face. Fingernail scratches."

Nick ripped the hoses from the faceplate, separating it from the rest of the breastplate armor, and strapped it to his face.

"What are you doing?!" Jack stammered as he inspected the torn hoses.

Nick looked at him, the illuminated eyes glowing brightly. "I'm just going to have a little talk with the mayor's bodyguard."

Nick slipped into a back-alley and made his way over to the rear of the podium. Everyone was paying full attention to the current speaker and Nick was able to work his way closer to the side of the stage. He peered over the edge and his heart skipped a beat.

The mayor and his bodyguard were gone.

Spinning around, he spotted them heading down another alley, walking briskly away.

Nick ran full speed down a parallel alley and moved ahead of them.

He pressed himself against the corner and waited for them to pass. Then he stepped out quickly to hit the bodyguard over the head. The bodyguard slumped to the ground without as much as a muted grunt. Nick grabbed his legs and quickly pulled him backward through the alley. Just as he pulled him into a door and slammed it shut, he heard the mayor calling for his bodyguard.

Nick watched as the mayor disappeared around the far corner, still calling out.

When he knew they weren't going to be disturbed for a while, Nick tied up the bodyguard and propped him against the wall, splashing cold water on his face.

The bodyguard woke with a start. He spotted Nick and struggled against the ropes. When he realized he wasn't going to escape, he gave Nick a good hard stare. "You better let me go."

Nick leaned in close, letting the metal mask he had kept on do all the intimidating for him. "Not until you tell me why you are killing leaders of industry."

The bodyguard laughed. "You fool. You don't know what you're getting yourself into."

Nick leaned in closer. "Then tell me what I'm getting myself into."

The bodyguard grinned at Nick. "You can kill me, but you can't stop what's happening. I'm just a puppet. Easily discarded. Five minutes after you took me, I was replaced."

"Who is pulling your strings, puppet?"

"The mayor."

Nick stared at him for a moment and then rushed out the door, the bodyguard calling after him.

"Good luck getting to him. You got lucky when you took me. We are like the hydra. Every time you take one of us away, we add two more."

ഔഝ

Allister hurried down the hallway to answer the incessant banging at his door. "I'm coming!"

He opened it to see Nick and Jack standing there, breathing heavily as if they had been running.

Nick and Jack looked at each other before Nick stepped forward and held out his hand.

"We have decided to accept your offer."

Allister smiled and took Nick's hand. "What made you change your minds?"

Nick smiled. "Jack finally convinced me that we can't do this alone."

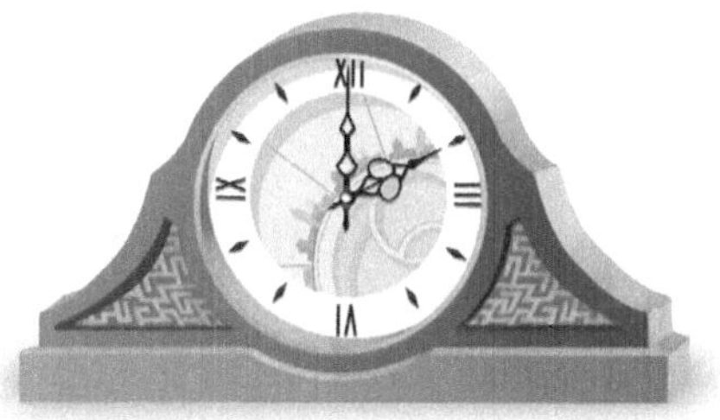

Nous Sommes Quatorze Heures

By Sharon E. Cathcart

2:00 PM, Paris

Lucien Dubois awoke in his own bed. He wore a nightshirt of fine linen instead of his usual red wool flannel. On the bench at the foot of his bed rested his shoes, cleaned and polished, and a shirt and trousers of better quality than any he had ever owned.

On top of the clothes was a sealed letter; the deckled edge was the black of mourning stationery.

His head muzzy, Lucien reached for the letter and broke the red wax seal. The handwriting inside was spidery and almost childlike.

"Monsieur Dubois,

"I hope you will accept these replacements for the garments that were damaged by your foolish exploits.

"When you return to the scenery shop tomorrow, you will find that you have been promoted to journeyman.

"Your skills are such that you have long deserved this. However, the price of this promotion is your silence. Should I learn that you have bruited certain information around the opera house, I cannot but feel sorry for you … and the family that needs your income."

There was no signature, but Lucien had no doubt of who had written it.

The black-edged letters were infamous in the opera house; Lucien had been in the presence of the so-called Opera Ghost himself! He thought back to the scarred body of the man who had—there was no denying it—saved his life. The man who was Claire Delacroix's lover.

Lucien could still smell the sandalwood soap on his skin, as well as the lavender that had been kept in the clothespress with the nightshirt he wore.

Even if he did decide to tell someone, who would believe him? Everyone told tales of the Opera Ghost and his mysterious notes—and just about everyone thought them silly phantasmagorias good for nothing but frightening the chorines.

Lucien put the note on the highest shelf of his own clothespress, far out of sight. No one could know of it. He folded the night shirt, resolving to put lavender in with his own garments so that they would carry the sophisticated scent, and donned the new clothing.

On his way out of the opera house yard to visit his family for church, and to tell them of his good fortune, he passed Claire Delacroix. She was riding her Friesian mare, Josephine; they had just come from a brief turn around the nearby Parc Monceau.

"Bonjour, Mademoiselle Delacroix!" He turned on his heel, tipped his cap, and then took the horse's reins so that Claire could dismount.

Lucien's gaze was frank and admiring; Claire wore a green and black riding habit that suited her perfectly. The gleaming black sidesaddle from which she extricated herself could only have come from Hermès. Claire's lover was a generous, and fortunate, man.

"I want to thank you," he began, only to be stopped by a black-gloved finger laid gently across his lips.

"No thanks are necessary," she replied.

"But …"

She held up her hand.

"I know what he has done for you, and what was asked of you in return. Keep your end of the bargain, *mon ami*."

She reclaimed Josephine's reins and walked toward the stables without a backward glance.

Lucien watched her go, a slightly wistful smile crossing his face. Then, he turned toward Saint Sulpice, and home.

THE TIME OF GHOSTS

By Anthony Francis

3:00 PM, Edinburgh

ဆ–1847 AD, 3:03 PM–03

Half a mile under Edinburgh Castle, lost in a damp warren of ancient masonry lit only by his guttering candle, Navid Singhal-Croft, Dean of Applied Philosophy at Liberation Academy, wished he'd paid more attention to the ghost stories his cadets whispered about the tunnels.

Of course, that was his own fault: he led the college of sciences at the premiere military academy in the Liberated Territories of Victoriana, and he'd always thought it his duty to drum ghost stories out of the young men and women who were his charges, not to memorize them.

Now was the time, but where was the place? A scream echoed in the dark, very close—and eerily familiar. Shielding his candle with one hand, Navid ran through crumbling brick and flickering light, desperate to find his father before the "ghost" claimed another victim.

If he couldn't rescue his father … Navid might never be born.

℘—1897 AD, 3:05 PM—℆

"A student lies wounded, and a professor dead," Navid said, fixing the coldest gaze he could muster upon his most promising yet troublesome charge. "Clearly a matter of life and death; it was your duty to at least *attempt* to recruit a faculty member—*Cadet*."

Without ever breaking her perfect attention, Cadet Jeremiah Willstone seemed to wilt. Her spine remained ramrod straight, her clear blue eyes never strayed from forward—but her lids widened, fractionally; and her golden curls shivered at the ends, as if she'd trembled.

Hardly a violation, even of parade attention, but given her battered state, it was a miracle Jeremiah stood at all: temple cut deep enough to leave a scar, cadet's blue vest-coat bloodied, its flared tails drooping with dried mud—all in all, trivial wear and tear for saving the world.

Briefly Navid thought of commending Jeremiah's valor: she, a third-year at Liberation Academy, had detected, intercepted and *thwarted* an Incursion of a Foreign monster, virtually singlehandedly—but his eyes were drawn back to that cut on her forehead.

On his mantel, Navid displayed memorials to the reckless: a broken Falconer's wing, an unknown alumnus's lost ring—and finger—and a daguerreotype of a cadet with round-rimmed glasses, a man he'd never met. Navid hated to do it—but he had to twist the knife.

"I am *particularly* angry," Navid said, quite calmly, "that, given the rapport I *thought* we had developed, you felt you could not confide in me until *after* the fact." Her eyes widened further, and he said, "Was I mistaken in believing I had won your trust?"

"Sir, no, sir," Jeremiah said, in that lovely soprano that turned the heads of all the men and half the women—and then, as she began to trip over her words, Navid began to suspect there were other reasons she'd likely kept quiet. "Sir, I … I simply had no time—"

One hand subtly pressed at her rumpled cadet's blues, and Navid noted the tails of the vestcoat didn't just droop—they were buckled improperly. Cadet's blues could be swapped, woman to man—and Navid realized how her adventure had likely started.

"No, you feared being caught in your *dalliance*," Navid snapped. Her face sagged: at last, he'd gotten through to her. "Yes, you stopped an Incursion—leaving a professor dead, a cadet in hospital, and every honor rule broken. A disciplinary hearing will be called. Dismissed."

The cadet clicked her muddied heels, staring straight ahead; then she whirled and marched out of Navid's small study. When the bell rang in the outer chamber, he went to the window to watch his most promising cadet go.

"Ah, Jeremiah," Navid said, sadly. "What am I going to do with you?"

"Well, don't drum me out just yet, sir," came that familiar soprano, not quavering, but confident, amused, even sympathetic—and right behind him. "No matter how bad this turn of events looks, I have it on good authority that I have a glowing future ahead of me."

Navid spun on his heel to face Jeremiah, now wearing the field garb of a commissioned Expeditionary: gold tailcoat, black mesh vest, both cut odd to his eyes—but the strangeness of her kit was nothing compared to her bomber goggles—and her great brass dragonfly wings.

ⅆ—1847 AD, 3:07 PM—ⅇ

Navid shot around the corner and before him lay his father, as he'd always imagined him: a young, slender Indian, wearing round gold-rimmed glasses, just like his Academy picture on Navid's mantel—but in living color—bloodied in the dirt beneath a fallen beam.

Then the eyes behind those gold-rimmed glasses opened and saw him.

"Look sharp, fellows!" the young man who was Navid's father said. "A blackcoat!"

Navid froze, then straightened, one quick glance taking in his father, the fallen beam, the dust shifting out of the masonry overhead, the trio of standing cadets looking in shock at Navid's black professorial cassock. Navid threw on his drill sargeant's face—and scowled.

All the cadets recoiled, and Navid's eyes were drawn by the rustling of their cadet's blues: a similar cut, but older, when Liberation Academy was still a new institution under the old British Empire. Navid was an anachronism; he would have to tread carefully.

These young men and women stood merely embarrassed, not fearful; they had clearly not been attacked by the mechanical monster the Jeremiah from the future had sent him back here to hunt. No, this was far simpler: even in 1847, cadets risked their lives for a lark.

And, on Halloween, cadets lost their lives in the tunnels—as had his father.

∮—1897 AD, 3:09 pm—∯

Navid stared at Jeremiah half a second, then whirled and looked out the window, where he spotted her again on the path—bruised, in her borrowed cadet's blues, staring back at his study window, her lower lip trembling, eyes near tears—and her face visibly younger.

Navid turned back to the older Jeremiah, who'd lifted her bomber goggles to reveal glowing eyes—then the brass dragonfly wings flipped back, revealing four diaphonous membranes that slowly unfurled into glowing faery wings.

"Cadet," Navid began, astounded.

"Commander," the elder Jeremiah corrected, not unkindly, but with such authority Navid both believed the title and felt his confidence in her ability to lead immediately confirmed. "Forgive the light show, sir, but we are on the clock, and I wanted to save time."

"Older, weirder—yet the same," Navid said, eyes tracing the scar on her temple—then the antennae erupting from her forehead: brass, filigreed, and clearly not of Earth. "I—must surmise time travel. My word … Was Professor Dyson right? Do the Foreigners come?"

"Like the rain, sir—though not all bad; on that I'm an expert," Jeremiah said, glancing at her faery wings; then she unbuckled something from her wrist. "But that mechanical vampire I thwarted last night, it's one of the worst, sir, and it's why I've come to you for help."

"What's this?" Navid asked, inspecting the strange bracer she handed him.

"It's how I traveled through time, sir," she said. Her eyes glinted. "Now it's your turn."

℘—1847, 3:12 PM—℘

"What are you doing in the Castle tunnels, Cadets?" Navid asked sternly. "They're not off limits for history's sake, but danger's. Cadets have died. I lost my fa—we lost an alumnus once; all we have left is a ring and finger on my mantel. Was it worth it, chasing legends?"

"Sir?" asked his father. "Sir, I don't know what legends you mean—"

"The legend of the time of the ghosts, son," Navid said. "At three in the afternoon on Halloween, the tunnels swarm with the ghosts of cadets who died before graduating. Bring a light, or when they find you—*they'll take you with them!*"

All three cadets leapt back, and even his father twitched, then groaned. But he was not mortally wounded, merely pinned by the great beam that lay across his chest. That chest with its strangely cut uniform, too small for him, but oddly large in breast and hip—

Navid looked up in shock to see that the younger female cadet had his *mother's* face, poking out of oversized cadet's blues that likely belonged to his father—and Navid smiled, as he realized how their afternoon's adventures had likely started. Cadets never changed.

"Well, Cadets, your fellow is in quite a pickle, but he'll survive," Navid said, standing, bracing the beam. "One of you lend a shoulder, the other two pull him free—then take him straight to hospital. No delays! On three, ladies and gentlemen; one; two—three!"

Navid and the taller cadet lifted the beam to creaks and groans; the other female cadet and Navid's young mother slid his father out as dust fell. But the taller cadet didn't quite mirror Navid, the beam twisted under uneven pressure, then cracked—and the roof caved in, raining stones down upon Navid's bracer—and his father's chest.

With a cry, his father died—and Navid was ripped from time.

ဢ—1897, 3:19 PM—ဢ

"The monster is ruthless, parasitic—and self-replicating," Jeremiah said, adjusting the bracer on Navid's wrist. "By 1954 it had infested the whole of the Liberated Territories with inroads on the Austrian Empire. I traveled back to stop it before it started—but it's gone."

"Gone?" Navid said, staring at the jury-rigged bracer she called a springback: odd key punches, glass thermionic tube, and the sharp teeth of meshed brass gears. He tried a further surmise: "Gone—back in time? But why do you need me to fight it?"

"Leapfrogging, sir," Jeremiah said, dialing coordinates on the bracer. "You can't meddle with your own past—unless you step outside of time. We've a time machine parked outside this reality, and are using this temporal springback to punch backward on my own timeline."

"Sounds … hazardous," Navid said—but inside his mind, gears were turning. This preposterous wristwatch granted its wearer the power of time travel—and she was giving it to him! "But why leapfrog, then? Is there a limit to how much travel you can take?"

"No, I'm a hardy sort—but this is as far as I go," Jeremiah said. "This springback uses its passenger as its anchor—and can send you only back near your own worldline. I started at Liberation Academy just three years ago, so my trail swerves away from here—"

"But mine does not. My parents went to the Academy," Navid said, possibilities opening up in his mind: that picture on the mantel, of the man he'd never met—what if he could? Then another linkage closed in his mind. "Wait—so did the monster? It traveled to my own past?"

"Near to it. I thought my younger self destroyed the monster last night, but it apparently escaped backwards through time. We've tracked weak signals back as far as fifty years, but only at regular intervals—correcting for leap years, around 3 pm on the day of Halloween."

"The legendary time of the ghosts," Navid said. "But *just* that time?"

"Yes, as if skipping back through the years," Jeremiah said. "Perhaps seeking an earlier, less advanced, more vulnerable time, in which to establish a beachhead." She scowled. "It must be stopped, but I warn you: it is self-replicating. The smallest component could be hostile."

"I am prepared," Navid said, drawing his deranger and checking the charge. Then he realized he'd not yet looked at the envelope Jeremiah's younger self had given him. "One moment, Commander. What am I looking for, and how will I find it?"

"The core is a circuit: sparkling, ornate, and foreign to anything of Earth," Jeremiah said. "It's a temporally parallel processor, leaving ripples in time. The springback is calibrated to home in as best it can—but it's dodgy. You're likely to get closer in space than time."

"But you think I'll find it," Navid said, peering at the locator, "at the time of ghosts?"

"Yes. This springback is also calibrated to skip back yearly," she said, stepping back. "It has safeguards—if you materialize in matter, it might skip a year—but it's a harrowing method of travel. And you must act quickly: time progresses within the hour. You have forty minutes."

"I welcome the challenge," Navid said, reviewing the springback's controls. Yes, he could use it to fulfill a childhood dream—and from there, or rather *then*, methodically fulfill Jeremiah's mission, starting back to front. "Any further words of wisdom?"

"You trained me, sir—but this is time travel," Jeremiah said. "Avoid disturbing the past. Don't dawdle, don't meddle, don't babble—and especially *don't tell me about my future self*. I was quite xenophobic as a youth; it could cause—I think the phrase is heterodyning."

"I shall do my best to avoid it," Navid said. "Wish me luck."

Without waiting, Navid pushed the controls to their furthest extent, and was immediately ripped through time. Flashing light and color ripped at him, his ears popped, and all the air whooshed out of his lungs. Then, moments later, he was down—in the darkness.

Damnit! He should have brought a gas torch! He reached out into the dark—and felt the familiar walls of the tunnels under Edinburgh Castle, no doubt beneath David's Tower. He checked the time on the springback's dial: 3:00 PM, October 31st 1847.

Farther back than he'd expected: the Halloween before his birth. If Jeremiah was right, this was as about as far back as

Navid could go. But, with horror, Navid realized there was more: the springback's locator pointer indicated he was right atop the monster. It was *here*.

The thing was meddling in time. Navid realized it could do more than meddle in history: it could erase him, personally. Navid slipped a nightcandle out of his pocket and struck it against the damp stone; it flared to life, revealing, with yellow light, a cramped tunnel.

Navid raced forward: he had only minutes to save his father.

ↄ—18?? AD, 3:30 PM—ↄ

Navid screamed, immediately realizing his mistake: he had not gone back before his birth, but *to* his *conception*. It was impossible to alter the past to save his father: Jeremiah had even warned him of it. If only he'd listened, rather than thinking himself so damn clever!

Navid understood why Jeremiah had called it hetero-dyning: the live wires of alternative pasts rippled through him, their resonating frequencies scrambling time and memory. Navid felt strangely lightweight and gripped his chest. Then the locator engaged: the monster had moved to a new position—and the springback began drawing him forward through the changing years.

The tunnel swam before him, first just a hallucinatory haze, and then real flickering light, as years upon years of wayward cadets carrying torches through the tunnels seeking cheap thrills encountered his temporal echoes, a glowing form hovering in the tunnels.

Navid realized *he* had been the ghost—then suddenly rematerialized in his own study.

Or was it? The room swam around him. Desks moved; papers shifted; chairs transformed. Navid struggled to match the shifting office to his memory. Yes, it was his—but the nameplate on the desk shimmered between NAVID SINGHAL-CROFT and NAVID SINGHAL.

As the name resolved to SINGHAL, a terrible weight settled onto Navid's soul: he hadn't saved his father; he'd killed him before he and his mother had time to marry.

Then, with horror, Navid looked up at the figure behind the desk.

It was him, without a doubt. And freshly dead, without a doubt. And, as Navid noticed at last the decrepit state of the shattered office—as Navid briefly looked out the window to find a shattered world covered in gears—a metal *thing* began crawling out of his corpse's mouth.

Navid engaged the springback and hurled himself desperately back in time. First he'd gone to his conception; then to his death, where the monster had taken first the world, then him. But why had the springback thought the monster had always been so near *before* he meddled?

Then Navid again clutched his strangely light chest—and realized Jeremiah had never delivered that envelope to him; she'd probably been afraid to, if the orphaned, angry Navid Singhal hadn't drummed her out of the Academy entirely.

He had to make it right—by finding her before they first met.

Even as the springback shuddered him through the years, Navid raised the bracer to his face. Even through the shimmering miasma, he managed to set a date. Even as the gears twanged, he engaged the lever. The device leapt again, to a new destination.

Navid materialized, shimmering, half embedded, almost up to his knees in an angled pile of rock. The bracer screeched and twisted, the emergency rematerializer trying to shift him to safety—but Navid clamped his hand down on its gears before it could shift him again.

"Cadet!" he barked, staring straight ahead in the tunnel, as phantom miscreants swarmed around him. Then despite his strength, the gear slipped a notch, the device bit into his hand, he glowered—and overlapping faces of cadets quailed and turned to run. "Cadet, *stand firm!*"

An impossibly young cadet with gold curls clicked her heels to attention.

Navid stood before first-year Jeremiah, his hands folded before him—his right clamped tight on the gear that was chewing into him like scissors. Navid knew he glowed, perhaps was even transparent—but she held a flickering torch. She'd never see through him.

"I—I—Sir, forgive my retreat, sir!" Jeremiah said. "I thought you a ghost!"

"'Sir, I thought you were a ghost, *sir,*'" Navid corrected, and Jeremiah's eyes widened. "What are you doing in the Castle tunnels, Cadet? They're not just historical ruins; they're literally ruined, unsafe. Cadets have died. I lost my father here, you know—"

"Sir," Jeremiah cried, immediate regret spreading over her face. "I'm sorry—"

"And one alumnus," Navid said, as if he had not been interrupted, "lost a finger." As she blanched, and the device tightened on his hand, Navid guessed whose finger it was. "But these tunnels aren't just unsafe; they're off limits—which makes this an honor code violation."

"S-sir, just out for a little bit of fun, sir," Jeremiah said. Behind her came a cry and a clatter, followed by a vicious snap and a pained yell—and Navid then knew he had nailed the date. Jeremiah's head turned fractionally. "Sir, begging your pardon, sir, that sounded like—"

"Your companion has broken her leg," Navid said calmly, recalling Jeremiah's first adventure: a cave-in, a break—and heroism from a young cadet, which had brought her to his attention. "No need to complicate an injury with a disciplinary offense. Help your fellow cadet get to safety, and I'll overlook this—if you do me a favor, Cadet. Take Dyson's class."

"Sir?" Jeremiah said. "I am trying out for the Falconry—"

"Cadet." Navid leaned forward, tightening his grip on the gear as much as possible, even as it shuddered in his hand. "Few believe that Foreigners are coming, but they're coming like the rain. Take Dyson's class. Educate yourself. You have the gift; don't be afraid to use it."

"Sir?" Jeremiah said, confused.

"One day," Navid said, "you may find yourself facing a Foreign monster, without time to call for help. Do not be afraid: instead, act with extreme boldness. Do what needs to be done— but if you're still in my charge, *bring the matter to me at your earliest convenience.*"

He smiled. "Even if you've been caught having a little fun."

The cadet stared at him, blinked and then clicked her heels. "Sir, yes, sir!"

"Go tend to your friend," Navid said. "Get her to the surface safely. Dismissed."

Jeremiah turned and left. Navid watched her go—until the bracer exploded in his hand.

‽—1897, 3:47 PM—⁐

"Aaargh!" Navid Singhal cried, falling to one knee. The bracer's gears had sprung apart, the sawtoothed gears chewing outward, slicing off his middle finger of his right hand—but he was back in his study, with the dragonfly-winged Jeremiah leaning over him. "God damnit!"

"Sir," Jeremiah said. "You've lost your finger—"

"No, I know where it is," Navid said, nodding at his mantelpiece—where in a glass jar sat a wizened finger, complete with what he now recognized as his *own* class ring. "I found it when

I was a cadet, recall? Must have flipped backward through time when I sprang forward."

"A … forceful Italian salute, sir," Jeremiah said. "But what about the monster—"

"Never traveled back in time," Navid said, letting Jeremiah tourniquet the stump with a scarf. "Not under its own power. Your readings were—detecting one of my mistakes. I went back to the beginning of my timeline, trying to save my own father from death …"

"But sir!" Jeremiah reproved. "I warned you—"

"You did, and you were right," Navid said. "But have no fear: you can't edit your own timeline. Events righted themselves to course—but after the cave-in, I was sent skipping forward through time. The signals of the monster you detected? They were simply echoes of this."

He pulled out a thick, sealed, lumpy envelope. Jeremiah stared at it in shock—then her eyes glowed, and she snatched it from his hand and tore it open. Punch cards fell as she extracted a tiny circuit board—elaborate, glittering, Foreign—which she quickly broke in half.

"I recovered from my error most capably," Navid said, with some satisfaction. "Managed to catch the monster before it started, by delivering a message to my best agent. I had to finesse the wording, of course, but still—you delivered that envelope to me an hour ago."

Navid watched as Jeremiah quickly repaired the spring-back. He'd thought it hopelessly ruined, but what he'd taken to be a belt of copper chains about her waist proved to be six spindly limbs sprouting from her spine, with which she deftly reassembled the sprung device.

"Well, sir," Jeremiah said, checking readings on a flat piece of black glass even while her insect arms worked in tune to her waving antennae, "it appears we've set the infestation back at least a decade, but we haven't cleared it. There may be more material left—"

"I shall institute a hunt," Navid said, "and put my best agent on it."

Jeremiah looked at him, and her eyes glinted. "I thought you might."

"Till next time, Commander," Navid said, as she strapped on the bracer.

"Till next," Jeremiah responded—and disappeared in a flash of light.

Navid stood there, staring, sitting down heavily on the edge of his desk, holding his throbbing hand. No matter; a quick trip to the infirmary, and they'd bolt on a prosthetic. But there was no time for that right now; he had an invasion to stop.

Navid walked down to the river, where Jeremiah sat on the bank, crying.

"Cadet!" Navid cried. "In the mud in your blues? On your feet!"

"Sir," Jeremiah said, standing, quickly wiping her eyes. "Your hand …"

"Never mind that, a bit of rear guard action in a war that hasn't happened yet," Navid said, watching wonder pass over her face. He smiled. "Quit your moping, Cadet, you don't get expelled for saving the world. Follow me; we have a lot of work to do."

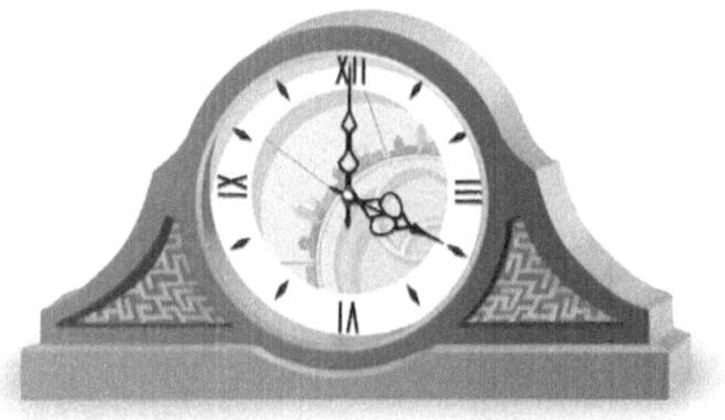

Afternoon Tea and a Little Murder

A Miranda Gray Mystery

By T.E. MacArthur

4:00 PM, Bath

The Pump Room, overlooking the Roman Baths, was stuffed from wall to wall with British patrons. Four in the afternoon was the most ideal time for Traditional Tea, and anyone of fashion or good sense was seated for one of Bath's finest experiences.

Fashion, in 1892, seemed to be rather in transition. There were a few small bustles still being worn by ladies. Men's clothing was changing too; trending toward a more casual and colorful look for an average fellow. That did not stop the majority of men from wearing typical black coats with tall black hats; the dignified gentleman's attire had not changed in forty years.

Miranda Gray, who had been seated at a medium sized table near the back, where her being a woman dining alone would not interfere with the proper atmosphere of the restaurant, embraced the newer look for women because she wore it well: a tailored jacket of brown Harris Tweed, over a waistcoat of mauve silk with a matching tie wrapped around a high, starched collar. Her skirt had no bustle whatsoever and fell in a soft "A" shape to the floor. Her hair was piled up to support a small straw boater with a pink ribbon. Feminine but not silly. Formal enough for tea but not fussy. Young, without looking foolish on a woman of some practical years.

Being "hidden" by staff was fine with her today. She still had not slept and her temper was on the verge of demonstrating that fact. A night to forget, she thought grumpily. She was disinclined to remove her gloves as it would reveal the bandage around her hand. After all, ladies do not get into knife fights. At her feet rested a leather satchel with several books, papers, and pencils inside.

The waiter, with a nondescript expression on his face, arrived with a glass of the pump water; Bath's so-called "healing waters." She'd had it before and it was vile. She'd not ordered it, but before she could complain, the waiter put down two more place settings.

Ah. The Ministry is here. The Pump Room seemed a tad public for a discussion of the events last night. Well, shall we get it over with? There was enough of a dull roar in the room to cover any sensitive discussions and certainly she was seated far away from the crowd.

"Have you slept at all, my dear?"

She hated it when he called her "my dear." From him, it was dismissive not endearing. She could have replied, "Why no, darling, I haven't, and you know exactly why since it was you who bloody well nearly got me killed by giving me this assignment." She didn't. She merely replied, "Not as much as I should have liked, sir."

The large man in his dour black suit, black tie, and black hat made himself comfortable in the chair across from her. No one sat at the third place.

"As I understand it, your mark was killed before he could provide you with vital information?" He began to look over the menu without really taking notice of her.

Miranda smiled. "Oh, it's not much of a cut on my hand. Surprisingly superficial. A little ointment, a bandage, and it seems to be already on the mend. It doesn't actually hurt at this point, if you don't mind my anticipating your inquiry."

The man scowled. "This is why I hate using female agents."

"I'm sure I could find better ways to spend my time than wasting yours."

He made a slight humming sound. "Then again, perhaps not. As to this mission, we are still where we were before."

"And this is why I am not fond of working for self-proclaimed geniuses who are sure they know exactly what is what." Before he could express his indignation at her insubordination, she added, "We are far beyond where we were. Allow me to bring you up to date. I have in fact completed my mission, despite poor intelligence and a source of protection that only bothered to show up at the last possible moment to kill my one and only resource. Happily, his tardiness did not impair my success."

The voice that replied had a medium pitch, a soldier's accent, and little annoyance at the accusation thrust at it. "I was there the entire time. I was just waiting to see what you might be up to, as it wasn't entirely clear." The Colonel sat down at the third place setting. He was not quite the same man she'd met a day or so before. The swelling on his face and hands had diminished somewhat. His beard was now neatly cut, as was his clean hair. He smelled of barber's lotion. His suit was stylish and possibly quite expensive. There was a lingering scent of exotic tobacco to him and yet his hat was outrageously shabby, not to mention out of fashion. "He was about to kill you."

"I had things in hand."

"No, ma'am, he had your neck in hand, and he was ready to break it."

The large man thumped his hand on the table. "Suffice it to say, Colonel, your quarry is dead and Miss Gray is not." He gestured slightly, silencing them as the waiter arrived with a pot of tea and a plate of sandwiches. The Colonel wrinkled his nose slightly and made no effort to partake in the meal. Once the waiter was out of hearing, the large man gestured for Miranda to continue.

Miranda drew in a deep breath. "The quarry, as you call him, was a second-hand thief with little understanding of policies, politics, or cryptic codes. We should be aware—if you are not already, sir—that despite all the secret codes and clues being utilized, there is another, very clever party involved here beyond the man you are tracking. My quarry mentioned 'his boss.' Unfortunately, this means you have more players than agents in the field."

"Hence, my dear, the urgency of the matter."

"Hence my lack of sleep while I worked through this problem." She waited for a sign of impression from either the large man or the Colonel. Neither provided it. "The entire matter is in the stars. At first I was annoyed at the possibility that this was just another ridiculous search for treasures, resplendent with clues and directions—like a child's scavenger hunt. But then, that would hardly bring you out of your club, would it, sir?" She stared at the large man. "The cartouches are the key. They are false, meaning they do not provide names of kings or gods as cartouches normally do. They are keys to deciphering mathematical clues. Oh, do fortify yourself, Colonel, this might take a while."

With some amusement, the Colonel accepted a cup of tea but kept his eyes on Miranda.

"The first cartouche you found indicated in a rather primitive manner the location of the next clue. Once that led us to the rubbing, I discovered the next set of cartouches were purely mathematical. The problem was never with numbers. Those could be ascertained rather easily once they were found," she continued.

"You and your colleagues at New College worked out the cryptic formulas," the large man said, sipping.

"Yes, we did. We had no difficulty working the code, but had no place to apply them. They were meaningless, until I looked again at the stars." Miranda unfolded a small section of the paper rubbing, taken from her quarry the night before. "The Egyptians adored symmetry, but none of these stars are symmetrical. I spent far too much time trying to see if they were perhaps constellations."

"I gather they were not?"

"No, sir, they were not. I did notice that a few of them created a gentle, snake-like shape, but that too made little sense. Until I looked at ..."

"... a map of London," the Colonel finished for her. "That's the Thames."

She caught herself smiling slightly. "Precisely. The numbers from the decryption dictated scale. Once I could copy the stars onto a map, using an accurate scale, I found that each corresponds to a building, connected by similar sewage lines."

The large man never looked over his cup as he replied, "Why does everyone feel the need to use the sewage system?"

"Because Parliament is not available. It is already overrun with the refuse of humanity."

"Miss Gray, your sarcasm is not appreciated."

"It never is," she said, looking at the Colonel, who grinned sympathetically. "Whatever you are looking for can be found in these locations." She reached into her satchel and handed an envelope to the large man. He didn't take it but allowed her to set it near him. "I have no interest in knowing what it is you are looking for, thus I shall wish you good luck and good day."

After a moment, the large man set down his cup. "We are always looking for something, as you well know Miss Gray. In this case we are looking for the parts of a larger device, which when assembled, could achieve God only knows what. What we rarely have is someone so uniquely qualified to find whatever it is we're looking for, hence our request for your assistance."

"A weapon?" The Colonel asked. "Might be individual bombs set to go off. Or stolen secrets?"

"Perhaps." The man leaned on his arms. "You may wish to know and to care, Miss Gray. We're dealing with a man whose reputation is to achieve as much death and destruction as he can sell. Such elaborate schemes could be a perfect way to protect his plans from being found casually. Until now, it has been carefully concealed and cloaked in an odd set of clues built upon what appeared to be Egyptian hieroglyphs. It was all incredibly convoluted and complex; almost like an obscene treasure hunt. We don't know who this man is, but we do know he is dangerous, and whatever he is doing is being done right under our noses. We did have individuals who could discern his identity and draw him out, but qualified persons are not in abundance these days. And we're slowly losing those few who are so qualified." His last sentence was punctuated with a deeply held anger and pointed directly at the Colonel. The Colonel, to his credit, did not take the bait to react in any way. "I should like to be able to call on you again, Miss Gray. We are in need of your continued assistance, I'm embarrassed to say, most especially now that you have proven there are other interested parties. It's almost too much, if you ask me. The world has lost its mind. You are needed, Miss Gray."

Somehow, his statement was not unexpected. It had slipped into Miranda's thoughts several times as she had been completing the map for him. "Why me? There are thousands of soldiers, sailors, spies, and various persons who are expert in these covert matters."

"But none that I trust."

"Do you trust anyone?"

He did not reply, but rose to leave. "Every Ministry seems to have their special services, except ours. Congratulations. You are our first."

"Doesn't she get to say no?" the Colonel asked casually.

"As much as you do, but under far better, more honorable circumstances."

As the large man mentioned "honorable circumstances," the Colonel's face showed his discomfort for the first time. He quickly found another expression.

"Miss Gray. Colonel. You may want to get to know one another better. I fear you will need to cooperate often in the future." He collected his hat and the envelope. "Miss Gray, he is a better shot than you. Colonel, nature has bestowed on this woman a mind that might make your former employer appear imbecilic. Or not. She appears determined to use some understanding of crime to better study mummies, a pursuit I say I do not understand. In the meantime, Miss Gray will continue with her expertise in mathematics and Egyptology to help us understand what is to be found at those locations. Colonel, you will use every skill Her Majesty's Army taught you to keep this woman alive to do her work. I, for one, am tired of someone staying so far ahead of us."

The Colonel leaned back in his seat. "I would have thought in the last few years you might have gotten used to it."

The large man frowned. "I'm glad to see my assessment of you both is that you are two sides of one sarcastic, odd little coin. Congratulations again."

"I'll need a few of my belongings back." The Colonel waited as the large man hesitated.

"Such as?"

"My own rifle. That outdated elephant gun you gave me is loud, clumsy, and cumbersome. I doubt anyone has even sighted it in. I want my rifle."

"Fine," he said with disgust, never turning to look at the Colonel.

Miranda and the Colonel were left staring at one another. For several long minutes, each waited for the other to speak.

"I didn't study for years, suffering the displeasure of Academia, to become a treasure hunter." She stood up and began to walk away.

The Colonel caught her damaged hand, causing her to wince. "I didn't kill his damn brother, though I probably should have. He doesn't have anyone else to blame, so he turns it on me." His whisper was more like a hiss.

"I don't care. I don't care about any of this. I'm not a puppet."

Jerking her hand free of his grip, she walked out of the room, down a few steps to a hallway, and out onto a short balcony overlooking one of the Roman Baths. A mist of steam hovered over the green, sulfuric waters. She took a deep breath, refraining from comment about the rotten egg stench. Standing there, no one could see her face and the frustration that played out on it. Everyone was having tea. Damn them. I won't be trapped. I won't be used.

A man came up behind her. Too many bloody tourists, she thought, deciding that she would ask him to step back to a more gentlemanly distance. It was probably the Colonel anyway.

The man grasped her arm, as if escorting her. His other hand laid a long, thin blade near her neck. "Apologies. This is as private as we may be."

Prussian? His accent is thick enough, northern but not German. "Not private enough to commit murder and still get away."

He stifled a laugh. "I think, Miss Gray, I do not wish to kill you. Let us agree that this," he adjusted the knife, "assures me it is your attention I have."

"I think I can agree to that. Why don't you put it away?"

He didn't change his stance. "You would prefer to be in a museum, not chasing foolish men who sell things to high bidders, *ja*? Good. I think that would be best."

"Are you the seller in question?"

"No." He leaned in until his breath was on her collar. "You gave the map with the locations to the Ministry?"

Miranda hesitated. If his breath was on her collar, but he was not pressed entirely against her, he was bending slightly; that placed him around five feet nine inches or taller. No more than six feet as he would not lean over so awkwardly. His hands were gloved, but she could see his wrist partially; thick with strong veins. Athletic? Military? There was fur on the cuff of his coat, making it an expensive garment. He spoke English clearly and quite elegantly.

"Answer please."

"Yes. I gave it to the Ministry."

"Excellent. Now you can walk away freely and not look back. I recommend doing so."

"I was thinking the very thing. Now I'm not so sure." She grasped the blade with her bandaged, gloved hand, and rammed her elbow into his ribs. Her right heel stomped down on his foot. She turned, pushing away the knife. He seized her collar and threw her as hard as he could into the balcony rail.

Miranda nearly tumbled over. She pushed herself back and landed on her knees, facing the hallway. A couple stared at her and alternately at the man fleeing down the hall, out of the building. Instead of helping her stand up, they whispered to one another and fled as quickly as possible.

So much for chivalry.

She managed to stand up ungracefully. The Colonel looked at her oddly as she returned to the table, holding her arm over her stomach. "Did you see that …?"

"What?"

"Never mind." Miranda sat down quickly and lifted a cup to her lips in the hope of appearing nonchalant.

"You're back now? I thought you didn't care, Miss Gray."

"I do now." She set her cup down. "You're a gun aficionado? You want your favorite toy back? Is there something more powerful than an elephant gun?"

"I would call a Von Herder .455 caliber air rifle 'something more powerful.'"

"Good. I think you're going to need it. We'll need it."

At first, they stopped looking at one another, uncomfortably aware that circumstances had changed. The Colonel finally reached out to take up the glass of Bath's Healing Waters.

"I wouldn't drink that …" She watched him drink it down in a single, ungentlemanly gulp.

"It's not too bad." He set the cup down. "As you said, I should fortify myself … this is definitely going to take a while. And it would appear we're partners now. Does that bother you?"

Miranda Gray chose not to reply.

MONSTERS

By Vicki Rorke

5:00 PM, Crete

ଛ—1876 AD—ଔ

The ground shook beneath her feet, a low, steady trembling from deep in the earth. Shay lost her balance and landed on her backside amongst the stone ruins with a distinct thud and a loud "ouch." She chided herself for letting a little thing like a small earthquake cause her to lose her balance. I must still be tired from my nightmare, she thought. A giggle from behind startled her. She had thought she was alone. Shay bolted to her feet and turned to see a girl about her age, standing a short distance up the hill.

"Very graceful, I must say." The girl laughed again at Shay's expense. She looked about ten, with long dark hair and blue eyes. She had light brown skin, tanned from the Mediterranean sun. Her smile was warm and friendly, and Shay found herself smiling back. The girl came down the hill and stood before her. "Glad to meet you," she said.

Shay was surprised to hear the girl speaking English. She was expecting Greek. "Glad to meet you, too. My name is Shanarra," she replied, hoping to get the girl's name.

"Would you like to see a secret place in the palace? I found it a while ago when an earthquake tumbled some rocks from a pile. It's just down the hill, there." Shay's green eyes followed the girl's outstretched arm across and down the ruins to a spot that looked like nothing but a large pile of rocks.

Devastated by time and earthquakes, the palace and its surrounding buildings had been reduced to ruins. There were still plenty of artifacts and painted stones lying around, an occasional column or wall still standing, so that she could get a small sense of the peoples and culture that once thrived on this tiny island. But to have a local guide show her around, to delve further into the ruins, was just too good an offer to pass up.

The hill the girl pointed out was several hundred yards down and west of Kephala Hill, away from the rubble that was the Great Court. Or at least what historians of the day thought was the Great Court.

Shay hesitated for a moment, not sure what to make of this girl or her sudden appearance. But Shay's fascination with ancient history propelled her forward into the unknown. No, she couldn't resist.

"All right, let's go!"

The two young girls picked their way through the stones and rocks and the occasional patch of colorful, fragrant flowers. Like honeysuckle, light with an earthy scent, the flowers reminded Shay of the Highland heather when it bloomed in late summer.

They reached what looked like the outer walls of the palace, now crumbled, and a pathway leading out and down the hill. The local Cretan girl skipped her way down the stone path, giggling all the way, while Shay trailed warily behind. When the path came to a fork, they veered to their left and continued downward toward the pile of rocks. The girls stopped and stared at the mound of rubble, weeds and grasses growing through the cracks in the stones.

"Now what?" asked Shay. She didn't see any visible openings. Well, I suppose if I could see them it would no longer be a secret.

Her new friend moved toward the right side of the pile and pushed on a large boulder. "Come help me," she said. The two girls managed to move the boulder away from the mound and sure enough, there was a hole big enough for them to crawl through. Shay crouched down, looking first into the hole, then to the boulder, and wondered how the girl had managed to move the large rock away from the hole and to cover it up again all by herself. Had she really found it or was there someone else here that knew of the "secret place"?

"See? I told you! You want to go first?" the girl offered.

"No, you go. You've been here before. I don't want to trip and break my leg or something."

"Okay, have it your way." The girl dropped down on all fours and maneuvered her way through the opening. Shay pulled out the mini-torch from her sporran, pointed it into the hole and switched it on. The gears began whirring and moments later the gas sparked and the flame lit, producing light and showing her the way in. She got down on her hands and knees and crawled inside. There was room enough for the two of them, but their way forward was partially blocked. A heavy bronze gate, twisted and rusted with hinges partially torn away from the wall, barred their way.

"Come on this side. We can make it through with no problem." The girl indicated the side of the gate that was falling away. They were able to squeeze through, with little room to spare. Once past the gate, the passageway opened out and the girls could easily stand up. Shay estimated the ceilings were twelve feet above and the passageway widened out to fifteen feet across.

They could easily make their way around. Shay moved her torch up and down, side to side, looking at the walls and the corridor in front of them.

"This is amazing!" Shay said, her voiced drenched with awe. The walls were filled with brightly colored paintings. Sea motifs dominated, just as she would have expected.

Bright blue dolphins, yellow fish, and red octopi were numerous. Monkeys, birds, and young men and women were also depicted.

"Come, there's a lot more to show you." The young girl walked ahead in the dark and stopped. Shay caught up, with her torch illuminating a set of stairs that led downward. The girl began descending the stairs but Shay hesitated.

"Wait. How will we find our way back?" she wondered aloud.

"Don't worry. I told you I've been down here lots of times." She smiled widely, but Shay still wasn't sure if she should completely trust her just yet.

"Shine your light down here, along the bottom of the wall. See that?" The girl was pointing to a string of colored fabric lying on the ground. "That's how we will find our way back."

"You're kidding right? A length of colored fabric." Shay raised her eyebrows but the girl just nodded and giggled.

"And I suppose Daedalus himself gave you the ball of fabric?" Shay asked sarcastically.

"No, but I did steal the idea from him. It saved Theseus, didn't it? I gathered scraps of fabrics from the ladies in my village and tied them together until I had enough to come down here."

"Smart, I guess. This is not a place I would want to get lost in. No one would find you here. Lead on." Shay pointed her torch down the stairs as they descended and continued down the next corridor, all the while checking to see if the fabric lifeline was still in place.

After hiking along corridors and down several more flights of stairs, passing by the upstairs routes, Shay realized she was having the time of her life. She had seen so many amazing paintings and carvings on the walls. Pictures of celebrations, daily life, and even murals paying homage to the Gods, lined every passageway. Shay was particularly intrigued by the painting of King Poseidon with his trident, God of the Sea and the Shaker of the Earth. No wonder they had so many earthquakes on this island, she thought. One level down, she recognized the myth of Daedalus and Icarus. Looking at the paintings, Shay couldn't help but wonder if this place was the mythological Labyrinth designed by Daedalus.

"Here, look at this one." said her new friend, pointing to a painting of a distraught woman with a snake wrapped around her arm and waist. "Do you know this one?"

"Yes, it looks like a depiction of the woman whose children were killed by the Goddess Hera. She went mad and ate other people's children in her grief." Shay shivered at the thought of being eaten. She was glad it was just a myth. "I can't remember her name though. I should know it. It's right on the tip of my tongue. Oh well, I'll think of it later."

The next painting brought Shay to an abrupt halt. She walked up close to the wall, studying the depiction intently. It showed three young people and a bull. Shay knitted her brows together. There was something about this one. She brought her hand up and touched the bull, and froze. Her mind could actually see what was happening. A young man, holding a rope around the bulls' neck, another man running and jumping over the bulls' head, his side being torn open by a horn, the blood splattering everywhere. The crowd screaming in horror. Cheering as the young man stood up holding his hands triumphantly over his head. A man with a red and gold robe standing on an altar. A woman lying down on that altar. The man in the robe holding a large knife, thrusting it into the woman's heart. Blood. There was so much blood. A woman screamed. Shay gasped and pulled her hand back from the wall. What just happened? she wondered. The vision was so real in her mind. She shook her head to clear the images away, took several deep breaths and stepped back from the wall. She turned down the corridor where her friend was waiting for her.

They started down the next set of steps when Shay stopped abruptly. She had heard a noise. "Did you hear that?"

"Hear what? Come on." The girl urged her forward. They started down the next passageway. Shay heard the noise again. She stopped and concentrated on what she heard. It didn't seem human, or animal, but if it was being filtered down from a pasture above, through a shaft, then the noise would be a bit distorted.

Shay took a few more steps and halted. She cocked her head to the left, listening, willing herself to hear the sound that was now replaying in her mind, familiar yet sinister. She was sure she heard something. What on earth could be down here? she thought. Her imagination was starting to run wild. Shay took three more steps down the dark passageway, and heard it again, this time more clearly: the unmistakable whirr of gears and the soft hissing sounds of steam being released. She could smell the faint scent of hot machine oil in the musty air.

Mechanical. Definitely mechanical. The realization made her shiver. What on earth could be down here, this far underground? She tried to remember what she had seen of Kephala Hill on the airship flight up from the harbor. There was nothing above ground that needed power that she could recollect. Shay hesitated, not sure whether to proceed further. Her torch had started to lose its luminosity, preventing her from seeing too far ahead. The sound came again, echoing off the stones walls—unmistakably a footstep.

Shay looked at her friend, who nonchalantly shrugged her shoulders and smiled. The girl took a few steps forward then turned to wave Shay onward. Shay was adamant this time and forcefully shook her head and mouthed, "NO!" afraid to speak for fear that the—the thing—would hear her.

"But there's nothing down here. I swear. I've been here lots of time and I often hear strange noises. It's nothing. Wind through the stones." Her companion shrugged with indifference. A soft glowing light came from around the corner.

"We need to go and we need to go now!" Shay whispered urgently. A movement down the passage caught her eye. Too late.

Shay saw the shadow high up on the wall, where the passageway made a curve to the left. It was unmistakable—the outline of a head, a chin, a nose—and a huge horn. Her heart jumped into her throat and panic began to set in.

Shay looked over at the other girl. Her friend's face turned stone cold; her eyes became dark and menacing; her mouth twitched at the corners like some evil spirit in an illustrated book Shay once read. A chill ran down her spine. Every part of her being told her to run, run now, it's my only chance.

Before she could get her limbs moving, the thing stepped out of the shadows and looked straight into Shay's eyes. Dear God, she thought. This is a nightmare. I'm having a horrible nightmare! The Minotaur is not real! It's a myth! An allegory! But there it was, standing not more than 30 feet in front of her. The little light left in her torch allowed her to assess the thing standing before her. Tall, almost nine feet, and broad, its left hand holding a large double axe; it was a sight Shay never expected to see.

In the Greek books that she had read, the Minotaur was human, a man with a bull's head. But this monster was made of metal. Gears showed at its knees and elbows. The hands were large, the head massive with large, steely-red eyes, and horns that protruded from either side. Horns with razor-sharp tips. The Clockwork Minotaur raised its arm with a loud whirr and pointed straight at Shay. Steam hissed out its nose as it opened its mouth to speak the words she never wished to hear again in her life—"You. Are. Mine."

Shay turned and ran as fast as she could. She looked to the floor to follow the fabric trail that her friend had laid down to show them the way out. Where was it? Had the Minotaur seen their trail and taken it up? How am I to get out and back to the surface?

Questions ran through her mind simultaneously: How on earth do I escape? Did my friend lure me down here on purpose? Am I to be prey for the Minotaur by design? She didn't know and, at that moment in time, she didn't care. She only knew the way out was up. Just keep climbing.

The failing light of her torch caught the glint of a painting on the wall just in front of her in the hallway. It was the one that portrayed the woman who descended into madness when her children all perished. Shay thanked the Gods that she had taken the time to stop and examine the paintings on her descent into the Labyrinth. Those murals would guide her out.

She bypassed the first set of steps she encountered, and kept running. She swung her torch side to side out in front of her, looking at the walls for familiar murals. Boom! Crash! Boom! The sound of metal footsteps pounding on the stone floor was getting louder. The Minotaur was getting closer. But how could it run? Was it more agile than it appeared? It looked heavy, slow. Shay thought it was gaining on her; the steam hiss of its mechanisms seemed nearer, but was it really, or was it her mind playing tricks on her? She turned once to gauge her lead and noticed that her friend wasn't following behind.

After running along the corridors and climbing several flights of stairs, Shay gasped for air. Coupled with the panic, she had expended her energy. Her muscles were starting to revolt from the unexpected strain of the climb. She stopped and flattened herself up against the side of the passageway, trying to keep a low profile since she couldn't find anything to actually hide behind. She had to keep an eye out for her friend as well as her pursuer. She breathed heavily, rejuvenating her lungs, trying to calm herself so she could think clearly.

No time! This monster, this half-man half-bull, this—Minotaur, was faster on its feet than she had gauged. It came around the corner, and threw an arm forward. She screamed and ducked, as the double axe head slammed into the wall just above her head. She ducked under its arm and began to run. It turned and grabbed at her, catching the edge of her shawl and pulling her backwards. She lost her footing as it dragged her.

Shay fumbled to unpin the clasp that kept the shawl around her shoulders. She leaned forward, straining against being pulled, regained her balance, and—there—the pin pulled away from the cloth. Shay darted forward as the shawl fell away from her body. The Minotaur roared, having lost its prey twice in just a few seconds.

Shay bolted down the passageway. Up the stairs. Down the hall. To the right. Bypass those stairs. Up the next stairs. To the left. Up once again. Her torch went out and she realized the monster was still behind her. Her anxiety level rose again as she struggled in the darkness to see the paintings to guide her out. Down the hall. Up once more. Down the length of the corridor. Just keep running.

After an eternity of running, Shay saw a light ahead of her, dust glowing in a sunbeam. The gate! It must be from the hole they had come through. The ray of light has to come from above ground. Please be so, she thought. I've got to escape. Da and

Dya would never find my body down here. It will kill them not knowing what happened to me.

Shay squeezed through the open side of the ruined gate, and threw herself on the ground, landing on all fours. She crawled through the hole in the pile of rocks where she and the Cretan girl had entered. She made her way over the rocky uneven ground a few yards away from the opening, and rolled over, flat on her back.

Shay lay there, gasping for air, silently sending a prayer to the Gods thanking them, for she had safely made it out of the Labyrinth. She had made it … but was it real? Doubt flowed into her mind. How could it have been real? Who could have made such a beast? Why? For what purpose?

As she lay there, regaining her strength as well as her composure, she could have sworn she heard the Minotaur roar once more and thought about her the Cretan girl. Had she made it out of there? Had the beast killed her? A shadow fell across Shay's face. She turned her head and looked up. There stood her friend, frowning at her.

"You made it out?" Shay asked with a mixture of relief and skepticism.

"Well, yes," the girl replied sarcastically.

"But you were behind me. As was that … thing!"

"Well, you should have come with me. I know shortcuts. I've been exploring the maze for years, you know." Something about the look on her friend's face and her story didn't make sense. Years? She's only ten. How many years could she have been here? She doubted the girl's parents would let her come up here alone, much less explore the ruins, at such a young age. That thought was quickly pushed away as Shay heard a familiar voice calling out to her from over the hill, halting their conversation.

"Shanarra! Shanarra! Come on back, lass! Your ma's put out supper for us. We only have an hour before the airship flies us back to the harbor."

"Coming, Da!" Shay yelled in response, hoping the anxiety of the afternoon's experience didn't resonate in her voice. She stood up, wiping the dirt and debris off her kilt and knees, and repacked her torch in her sporran. She looked back at her friend to say goodbye. Shay was startled by the sight of her. She looked much older, grey streaks emerging from her long dark hair. Wrinkles had sprouted around her eyes, which had turned grey. She was also half again as tall, almost as tall as Shay's mother. The person standing there wasn't the young girl she had spent the last hour with. This was a woman who looked old, haggard, worn out from life. Shay couldn't comprehend what she was seeing before her.

"Uh, thank you for showing me around, but I need to go. My parents are waiting for me. Thank you again." Shay started backing up the hill in the direction of her parents, not wanting to turn her back on this—stranger.

"Please don't go." The girl-woman pleaded and reached out a hand to Shay. She took a step toward her, and said more forcefully, "Please. Don't go!" There was an edge to her voice that frightened Shay.

"No, really, I must. Thank you for everything, but I really must go." Shay turned and started up the hill, wanting to get back to the safety of her da's side as quick as possible.

"Wait. Shay. Please," the girl-woman pleaded.

Shay stopped, whipping her head around to face the person she had first thought was a friend. How did she know my nickname was Shay? I never told her that! She thought. Goosebumps sprung up along her arms. "You never told me your name." Shay tried to smile at her, still hoping this was all just a strange dream, that she had misunderstood her friend's actions and there really was no mechanical beast below ground.

"I didn't?" The smile that spread across her face made Shay's blood turn ice cold. "It's Ari!"

HUNTED

A Tale of Jhrin

By Dover Whitecliff

6:00 PM, Rannport

Dark. Fuzzy light. Drums beating. No. Hammers pounding on my skull. Hangover? Think, girl, think. This ent your bed. Voices nearby. Indistinct. Then, "… at the Slaughtered Lamb …" Now that rings a bell—Kyree and his Terceran Stout. One too many pints at the pub? I didn't remember even getting to the skydock, let alone drinking enough to feel this wretched.

Focus, girl. First things first. Where are you? I took in the sounds. Footsteps. Two pairs. One in boots, and the other in dress shoes. A tea kettle whistling, and then being taken from the stove in another room. Someone's house? No, the smells were wrong. Blood. My blood? Alcohol, and not the drinking kind. Infirmary? More sounds. Chirping. Claws scrabbling on a window sill. Wings flapping. Gut wrenching panic. Wings. IKAROS. Where was the case? Did I get it out of the arena? Did I fail?

Open your eyes, girl. Crusty, blurry, pain-stabbing even in the dim light, but I opened my eyes. Eye. Eye? What the hell happened? I reached up. Found thick bandages wrapped round the right side of my head. Something's not right. I rolled to the left, toward the blur I could see. The world upended and I found myself on my knees, with everything in me trying to get out at once. I felt a bucket rushed in between my hands and heaved. A voice came from somewhere over my head. A man's voice. Baritone.

"Aithogram coming in from Wolfesson, Doctor." From Briar. Right then. These must be allies of a sort.

"Read it, would you please?" Another man, his voice slightly higher than the first, but not by much.

"In your debt, Nathaniel. Consider projects funded through next Solstice." The first voice read, saying STOP in place of each period like some aithercast of a penny dreadful. "First deposit in untraceable funds in usual account. Best close up shop for the day."

"Not exactly unexpected. Certainly not the best time or place to spirit away a suspected anarchist. Anything else?"

"Yes, Doctor. A message for her. Lupa, the game's afoot and you're the game. Get off your sweet arse and take wing. I can't put them off the scent for long." The baritone laughed. "Hugs STOP" His voice sounded familiar and yet not, almost as if I had heard it through a wall or some other … other … breather-mask?

"Well he does have a sense of humor. I'll give him that. And poetic. Take wing. I like that. Let's get her up. Not much time to dither." Several hands hauled me up to stand and kept me upright when I listed sideways. One of them wrapped my hand around a shot glass shaped blur. "Down the hatch, dearie. You'll need all your wits to get to the skydock ahead of the hounds. This will clear the cobwebs." I sniffed. It burned my nostrils and I gagged. Do it, girl. Not the time to be squeamish. Briar wouldn't leave you with poisoners.

I tossed it down. Nearly heaved it right back up. I swallowed hard. The whatever-it-was took hold with a vengeance. Shards of lightning shot down my arms, leaving gooseflesh in their wake and every hair standing tall. A roaring filled my ears, a whirlwind scouring through the fog and pain until I could feel each little drop of blood scooting here and there to the thunder of my heart. I yelped. Covered my ears. Slammed my eyelid shut. Gasped at the overload of senses and thoughts. Questions. Every last one of them tripping over themselves to make themselves noticed. Think, girl. Ask the right questions before you run out of time.

"Why?" I choked, cracking my eyelid, and tearing up at the knife-sharp edges on everything in my sight. I gestured to the bandages.

"Not to worry. You'll be able to see again. I replaced it with the newest model."

"It?" I wasn't sure I wanted the answer. The gentleman stripped gloves off and turned to take something from a drawer in the roll-top desk behind him before turning back to me. The pin on his waistcoat glowed red around a carved piece of onyx. A black heart.

"Your eye. Not enough of it left to repair after the bomb." Wait. What? Bomb? What bomb? "In your line of work, it should be quite useful. All the latest enhancements built in to the ring of the iris."

The ring of the iris. Ring. A quicksilver jolt of memory. I'd handed someone a ring. A ring. A shiny ring. I turned all my concentration to the ring. Anything to keep the rest of what he was saying from sinking in and leaving me a gibbering mess. What ring? Big. Near a foot across, and heavy. Metal. What kind of metal would be heavy? Think, girl. Gold is heavy and shiny. A gold ring. No, that's not quite right. Another image. My hand smeared with paint. A gold ring that wasn't gold? I almost had it. Almost. What happened? Think. Remember.

"Don't lose these." Mr. Black Heart Pin tucked something in my shirt pocket and I lost the thread, sparks of memory scattering like dandelion seeds on a summer breeze. "Keep it dry and covered for at least a week. Four drops from the bottle when you change bandages … every two or three hours, assuming you make it out of the city alive … the instructions are with the bottle." He pulled on a frock coat and set a homburg on his head. Why's he leaving in such a hurry? Briar's words came back to me. Close up shop … You're the game.

"Where is this place? What happened? How long?" I threw out as many questions as I could, knowing I wouldn't get all the answers, but hoping for something. Anything.

"Sorry. Can't stay to chat," he said, then turned and called down the hall, "Clara, I think an afternoon at the shops is in order." He shook my hand. "Pleasure meeting you. I'll send your exoskeleton along once I've had a chance to untangle the parts and tinker a bit."

"Shall I come with you, Doctor?" The Commander from the arena. Minus the breather-mask.

"That won't be necessary, Commander. We'll be taking the blue door. See to our guest and lock up, would you?"

"Of course." He nodded and clicked his heels. His eyes followed the doctor down the hall. I heard a door shut and a few odd noises. The Commander proffered an elbow in my direction to lead me out of the—the what? Mad Scientist's Laboratory? More like a back-alley surgery.

Being treated as a lady felt decidedly odd considering the circumstances, let alone after not being at court for over a year, but I took his arm and played along. When we reached the door, we were greeted by the lady in scarlet. A bright aitheric streetlamp shone behind her, turning her hair to flame under an intricately feathered fascinator.

Streetlamp. Night then. But which night? How much time did I lose? Somehow I doubted the Commander would be any more forthcoming with information than the doctor. Miss Scarlet tied a scarf around my head to hide the bandages and then pulled a slouch hat down over the top of it. Good stuff that whatever-it-was. That should have hurt like the dickens. She passed a bundle to the Commander.

"They're setting up barricades—you'll need to blend in and move quickly." Her breath steamed in the icy night air. The Commander shook out the bundle, and handed me into a sheepskin coat that hung a little past my knees. "It's not the height of fashion, but it will keep you warm." She continued as I pulled the collar up against the chill. "I ducked in and checked the dockmaster's books. You have a little less than an hour until moonrise. The *Tremhor* only has docking privileges until it clears the horizon. The Five Rings have closed the upper tram. The only way up is the Lift, and they're checking papers for every traveler." Shouts and boot heels on cobbles. Maybe a street or two away.

"Knife and knuckle dusters to fend off the hunters. More your style, and less conspicuous in the city than a pistol or a rifle if you have to duck in somewhere." The Commander paused while I cinched the belt with the knife on my hip and slid the knuckle dusters into the coat pocket, then he nodded toward the shouts. "That will be the hounds. They can't stop the Lower Tram. The longshoremen would riot if anyone tried to keep them from going home for Solstice Night. I'd suggest heading toward the Crystal Bridge once you get to Highland Station. The Archon's Guard wouldn't dream you'd be brazen enough to try it, even considering your flashy entrance this morning."

I snatched at the scrap of information. This morning. It was the same day. And moonrise was near seven tonight. Just twelve hours later.

"Pleasure meeting you, Lupa. I saw your match against Inarion Blue last spring. Impressive." The Commander smiled before pulling the breather-mask back into place.

"Off you get. We'll get together for supper next time you're in town." Miss Scarlet hugged me quickly and straightened my hat and coat one last time before turning to the Commander. "Shall we, Darling?" She paused for him to lock the door behind us. I turned left, away from the shouts; they turned right, easily just a couple out for a twilight stroll.

I took a few exploratory steps with my hand on the wall and managed to keep myself upright. The shouts and boots seemed to be running parallel to my course. I rolled the doctor's words over and over in my head as I found my feet, trying to picture Briar as a poet and failing miserably. Take wing. Seriously? Let go the wall, girl. One step. Two. Get to the docks. Blend with the longshoremen and get to the tram. Good plan, girl, but where in bloody Rannport are you? And where's IKAROS? Wait. You know damn well that Briar's no poet. Take wing. Opening a case. An empty case. Someone got to IKAROS before you, girl—can't go back without it, can you? Need to find it and take it back. Take it back from who?

I slammed into the wall on my blind side. Pay attention, girl. They pull you in for public drunkenness, it's not going to help you in the slightest. Don't go off at half cock. What you need is information, not speed. Best place for information is the last pint before going home. The smell of the cannery and the bay told me I was in the docklands, but I could have been anywhere in the maze of alleys that had been old before the Sundering. I listened past the shouts and hubbub for the overarching roar of Kinship Falls. Behind. To the right. That put the dockland tram station in front and to the left—with a fair portion of the constabulary between me and it.

I kept to the darker alleys for stealth and less pain on the one eye I had left, veering toward the bay by sound and smell. Not exactly the best course, by my reckoning. Nowhere to run on the docks, and too easy to get cut off by the guard with my back to the bay. But Miss Scarlet had a point. Better to blend with the longshoremen on the way to Highland Station than take the tram alone, and to join them I needed to go to the docks. The sounds of people talking and of water slapping up against the sides of ships grew closer and closer until I stumbled out onto the docks about halfway between the River Rann and the tram station.

I headed right. Kept my head up and the brim pulled down. Walked liked I belonged, as the longshoreman who volunteered to work the Solstice collected their bonus packets and meandered toward the nearest watering hole for a bottle to celebrate before heading for the highlands. Some here might have had bets on the arena, and be looking to get news so they'd know whether to collect or pay up. I slipped in with a group coming off of unloading a three-masted paddle steamer from Qin-To and followed them through a set of swinging doors to a driving beat just in time to avoid a patrol stepping on to the docks. I slipped into a shadow to watch and listen.

The band rendered any sound from the aithercast unintelligible, but I could see that the images reflected onto the crystal screen were just adverts. Conversations swirled around me, mostly about this boss with fish for brains, or that idiot who slipped off for a kip on shift and left his mates to do all his work on top of their own. A gaggle of cannery girls danced or draped themselves on the tables up front, swooning over the boys in the band, without much to say but the occasional scream or squeal. Nothing that would help me. I kept my one eye on the door, thinking to find a better pub, but could see the patrols roaming by and decided not to risk ducking out just yet. It wasn't long before the music died and the cannery girls hooted and screamed their approval.

"Thank you, ladies and gents, you missed a spectacle this morning and that's no lie." The singer, a handsome lad if you go for fresh-faced pups not too far out of short pants, addressed the crowd. "The Dreadfulle Show's up next and bound to have highlights. So we'll take a short break—now ladies, ladies, never you worry, we'll be back in a bit." He blew a kiss to the cannery girls and followed his mates to the green room as the barkeep raised the volume in time for—

"Welcome, lads and lasses, to the Solstice edition of the Dreadfulle Show," the off-screen voice announced, and I focused on the flickering images in the crystal. "This special aithercast is brought to you by the Blackfriars Courant, promoting literacy, one sensational story at a time, and by Cor Kuro Industries, bringing you the Heart of the Future Today." I blinked when the CKI logo flashed by, though I must have seen it a hundred times—a black heart limned in crimson. Mr. Black Heart Pin was the man behind CKI? I replaced it with the latest model. Hah. Well that explained a few things. I barely stopped myself reaching up to my face. "And now, your host, Penelope Dreadfulle!"

"Greetings, My Darlings, and Welcome! I'll dispense with the usual pleasantries. I just know you're all chomping at the bit to find out if the rumors are true. Let me assure you they are. Well, the one about Archon Mynos' tattoo isn't. It's a bull, not a hamster. And it's on his other cheek if you take my meaning. But I digress—"

"I love this show. Mind if I sit here?" The singer had come up on my blind side. I turned to look at him. Younger than I thought. Not yet twenty if he was a day. Not even a decent bit of peach fuzz on his chin. I pulled the skirt of the coat over my lap so he wouldn't sit on it. "Peri. Peri Stephansson."

"Kenna." I shook the hand he held out. "Band's not half bad. You could play the Sword Dance in Istavara if you keep that up."

"Don't know if I'd go that far, but thanks. I'd love to see the Sword Dance someday—oy. Would you look at that tosser? Can't believe he would even think of petitioning." I looked back at the screen to see Nigel working the crowd, and taking the pennant from his patron's hand. Then, out of nowhere, the view went shaky and the image shifted to the pre-dawn sky. Run out now, girl, before he recognizes you. The doors swung open and a patrolman stepped in, blocking my exit. Wonderful. Don't tense. You belong here. Don't call attention to yourself. Wait for it. Soon as he moves in. Slip out. Get ready. G–

"Bloody hell, she's still gorgeous!" Peri raised his voice to be heard over the catcalls from the longshoremen. "Even better the second time."

What? I flicked a glance back at the screen and blinked. Closed my eye, opened it, and looked again. No the image didn't change. Fractured memories slipped and slid to overlay what I was seeing, but the face staring back at me from the screen— I recognized LUPA. She was my second skin. But the woman wearing that skin was—I couldn't help it. I looked down. No. No change there. Still flat chested or near enough. Bunchy. Muscular. No heaving bosom that I could see. No gold hair streaming in a wind that, by some miracle, was only blowing her hair and not whipping the pennants on top to the arch. Her smile was dazzling enough to blind someone a mile away. Briar would never have teased that woman and called her a bulldog, nor would he have fought back to back with her in a pub brawl.

I watched carefully as she/I leapt to the ground to petition the Justicar, disconcerted. It took a moment, but once I knew what to look for, I could see it. A slight flicker, the barest of shadows—the footage from the games was being overlaid. By the Doctor? It would make sense if CKI was sponsoring the 'cast. I breathed a little easier, but didn't relax. All this meant was that the entire population of Rannport wouldn't be after me, but I'm sure the Archon's Guard would know exactly who they were after, and they were much more dangerous.

"Don't you think so?" I realized Peri had been talking.

"Sorry. Noisy in here. What was that?" I asked, and Peri leaned closer to speak near my ear.

"The Archon's advisor. The man with the white hair and the black braids. Don't you think he fancies her? There's something in his eyes." When I looked up and saw that he was referring to Briar, I nearly laughed outright. The boy certainly had a romantic view of the world if Briar's "what in the name of Fa's left buttock are you doing here and what happened to the plan we worked on for a whole bloody year?" glare could be seen in any possible way as a look of undying passion.

"Can't tell. She's certainly pretty enough to turn a man's—" I heard my voice trail off as I saw it. Nigel, you clever son of a— The hilt of his knife was black a second ago, where it lay strapped to the leg strut of his exoskeleton, but when I stepped on his wrist and took the blade, it was gold. Gold like the palm of his hand. Gold like the paint on my own hand after touching the ring. The ring that was the bomb. The bomb that took my eye.

Memories and speculation scraped together like the montage of snippets of the Solstice Games flashing by on the crystal screen, at first a kaleidoscope, tumbling, shifting out of focus, and then falling in beside one another. A mosaic rather than a complete story. The cement between the pieces was still missing, but I began to make sense of the picture the shards created. Peri hit the nail true. Nigel was a tosser. How could he even petition? Where were the other professionals? Tercera was rampant with fighters who could wipe Nigel off the pavement if he didn't poison them first.

"Don't see Inarion Blue. Not in the line up?"

"No, nor Feng-Tan or any of the middleweights neither. One of the bookmakers was in for the closing show last night. Mad as an Angora in shearing season that they got themselves sick before the match. Something in the chowder, he said. Good thing Nigel signed with the Duoros circuit after the She-Wolf handed his arse to him, or we'd be stuck watching him for the season."

The chatter in the room grew louder and I looked back at the screen. The me that wasn't me was approaching Lord Dalibor with the Solstice Ring, smiling and waving, with naught to show she'd been in the arena but a few strategically placed dirt smudges and a rip in her shirt showing a bit of cleavage, and amazingly not a single drop of blood. She walked LUPA up to the dais, rear assets swaying in a way that I knew wasn't remotely possible in an exoskeleton and laid the ring on the pedestal. She turned to leave. Looked at her hand—here there was a close up of the gold paint—and then started to turn back toward the dais, shouting. The image shook and went black. I'd seen enough. Nigel poisoned the other fighters so he could petition to enter the arena and take IKAROS. Signed for the Duoros Circuit to leave Tercera before he got caught. Time to find him and take it back.

"See you at the Sword Dance, kid." I shook Peri's hand. "Remember the little people when you get there." He laughed and bumped fists with me.

"Happy Solstice to you." The last I heard as I slipped out of the pub was Penelope Dreadfulle's voice.

"Rumors that the Archons themselves replaced the Solstice ring to assassinate Lord Dalibor have not been confirmed. Now, right after this advert from CKI, we have an exclusive interview with—" I breathed in the frosty air and made my way to the Lower Tram, being sure not to swing my non-existent, bunchy assets as I crunched the dusting of snow into the cobbles.

I made the tram ride to Highland Station, camouflaged by the folk from the docks, without so much as a backward glance just as Miss Scarlet predicted. I skirted round the Ziggurat with my luck still holding and making good time. The outer lights had been extinguished and a black drape cascaded down from the roof down to the front entrance of the building—Dalibor had been a bit of a prig, but he hadn't deserved that. I paused a moment to blow on my hands and look ahead.

The bridge itself took my breath away each time I saw it and tonight was no different. It had survived war, fire, flood, quake, and dragons, and still looked like nothing more than glowing gossamer threads of crystal ice. Threads that could hold the weight of an army and defy all rational thought at the same time. Guards stood at either side of the entrance, both of them stamping their feet to keep warm and watching the toffs, with their servants carrying their purchases, crossing over to the Estates with bored but polite expressions. The Commander had the right of it; they weren't expecting me. Stop dawdling and keep your head, girl. The clock's ticking. I looked back toward the current of people streaming up.

There. That's your ticket. Large retinue, and the servants' coats aren't too far off yours. One of the girls at the back balanced three or four packages. Not so much heavy, but odd-shaped and bulky. I slipped in beside her and grabbed at what looked to be a wrapped painting before it squirted out from under her arm. "Here, mate, let me help you."

"You shouldn't." She whispered back, but I held on to it when she tried to take it back.

"Of course I should. Besides, I ent done my Solstice Kindness for a stranger yet, and moon's near to rising. Don't want the Old One to toss me into the Void, do you?"

"Well, we can't have that, not tonight." She smiled. "Thank you." I nodded as we walked past the guard, made my gait tired but happy, to match my benefactor, and acting for all the world as if I belonged. We chatted softly about this and that until we reached the Estates, and I left her with her packages and melted into the shadows.

The Doctor's whatever-it-was started to lose its edge about halfway to the Customs House beneath the skydocks. A dull ache started to crawl up over the back of my head to settle in under the bandages. Not exactly helpful when trying to figure a way to find Nigel and take IKAROS back without ending up at the wrong end of a firing squad. Oy. Girl. Stop Whining. IKAROS is priority one. Prototype or no, at least with the wings I had a chance of getting up to the *Tremhor* before the moon cleared the horizon. I sent a silent prayer to anyone listening and made my way into a whole different arena.

I found Nigel some minutes later straddling a chair and cheating at cards. The gambling den was cleaner than most—being in Five Rings territory did have its benefits. He looked hunched, and for a moment I wondered if he had been injured in the explosion, until I realized that the idiot had actually dumped the case and was wearing IKAROS under his travelling cloak. No time for subtlety. I slipped on the knuckle dusters and waded in to grab his wrist. Twisted it until he squealed. Threw the hidden aces on the table. Pushed the money toward the other players.

"If you'll excuse me, this gentleman stole my pack." I punched Nigel before he could raise the alarm and heard the satisfying crack as the dusters connected with Nigel's jaw. "What you do with him for cheating on the Five Rings is your business." I unhitched the straps and pulled IKAROS from his back, maneuvering it to keep it wrapped in the cloak. I tipped my hat to the bouncer and left the room to the sound of just desserts.

My head was spinning by the time I threw open the door to the roof, climbed through, and closed it behind me. Aitheric lamps beneath the skydock left no shadows from here to the Lift. The Guard would have a clear field of fire as soon as they heard IKAROS. The drone of airship engines far above pounded in time with my heart. I looked up to see the *Tremhor* among those warming up to leave. The top edge of the full moon peeked above the horizon. Now or never, girl. I flung off the slouch hat, flipped the switch, deployed the wings, and primed the aither, then ran and jumped from the edge.

Between one breath and the next, IKAROS caught air, and I soared. I held my breath for the splang of bullets off the wings, but none came. I could see them clear as day. Why weren't they shooting? Gauging the distance upward with no depth perception took all of my concentration, and I let the mystery go. Splattering into the bottom of the skydock wouldn't help the situation in the slightest. Twice I had to veer off and back before I alighted on an empty skydock to see the *Tremhor* already in flight. The word trap sprang to mind.

"Thank you for testing them, Wolfesdaughter."

"Archon Mynos." I turned around to face him and stare down his pistol, flipping the switch to fold in the wings before the wind caught me up and blew me off the dock. "Let me guess. Rumors that the Archons themselves replaced the Solstice Ring to assassinate Lord Dalibor have finally been confirmed."

He laughed. "I do love that show. And now I am the only Archon left. Slide IKAROS over to me, please, and I'll call your ride back to the dock. No harm done. Consider it your tribute to the Five Rings."

"I can fly before you get a shot off." I held my finger above the switch.

"Now really, Lupa, you don't want to do that." I felt the barrel of Briar's gun at my back. "That's it, take them off." I undid the straps and shrugged out of IKAROS, laying it on the dock and sliding it away from me. Archon Mynos walked over to pick them up and then stroked the wings like a kitten.

"Such a beautiful night. I can't resist." Mynos strapped them on over his crimson tailcoat. "I must thank you, Briar, for bringing IKAROS to me."

"I live to serve." I heard the mocking in Briar's voice; pretty sure Mynos didn't.

"It is sad, Wolfesdaughter, that all you endured to get back the wings for your Crown came to nothing." Mynos smiled a condescending smile and opened his mouth to elaborate. The shot came from behind me and the Archon died, a look of surprise on his face.

"I'm sorry, Archon. Did you think this was about the wings?" Briar pulled IKAROS from the Archon's body and helped me strap it on. He peeked under the scarf to check the doctor's handiwork. "Well worth the price to have you alive. They'll be here any minute. Go quickly, before we're seen together. Tell Fa the Five Rings is in our control." He squeezed my shoulders brusquely and shoved me off the edge of the skydock to fly.

SENSIBILITY AND THE STRANGER

By Kirsten Weiss

7: 00 PM, San Francisco

Sebastian stood in the doorway to the laboratory, waiting to be noticed, for her startled glance. He enjoyed the taste of apprehension.

But Miss Grey bent her head to a collection of metal parts. An outré set of goggles was strapped to her eyes, mussing her thick, mahogany hair.

"The key," she muttered, "What on earth could it be? My aether machines work. Their aether machines work. This is correct to the last detail. I'd swear I got everything and yet this doesn't work. Could it be the entry point?"

Which was all fascinating, but—Sebastian yawned. No, it was not fascinating to Sebastian. Ennui had long been his bane. The tinkerer's prattle was as dull as it was incomprehensible.

He cleared his throat.

"It's as if it has a mind of its own and just won't cooperate," she said beneath her breath.

Feeling for his cold, empty center, he pushed a wave of chill outward.

She shivered and looked up, her green eyes comically large through the lenses of her goggles. "Oh!" She whipped the goggles from her head, strands of hair tearing. "Mr. Fitzsimmons." Rising from her stool, she smoothed the leather apron she wore over her narrow, brown skirts. The tinkerer unhooked a copper pocket watch from her leather waistcoat and opened it. The click rang in his ears. "You are early."

He bowed. Time had little meaning anymore. "Have I discommoded you?"

"No, not at all." She glanced about the laboratory, at the shining alembics and coils of copper wire and barrels of scrap and ore, as if she'd forgotten why he had come.

His sigh was the crackling of dried leaves skittering across a lonely road. The game must be played. It would be his last, and the lady's as well, but perhaps this time he would be surprised. The odds of that were low, but the game existed for a reason.

"I am afraid I am a bit out of sorts," she said. "A friend, Miss Algrave, was supposed to visit my laboratory but sent a message that she was delayed by an assassin."

He raised a brow, and she colored.

"I know how that must sound." She made a face. "Assassins! What must you think of this territory? But it's all right. The assassin has been captured and is being taken into custody by the Army."

He said nothing, and she hurried on to fill the void.

"I attended your lecture on your Egyptian explorations," she said. "The ancient Egyptians are quite fascinating."

He nodded. He had seen her, of course, sitting near the door, ready to bolt should the lecture prove dull. His might have been, but people never left. He did not know how much of that was due to the quality of his content or his natural magnetism. But the lady had taken copious notes.

"A terrible tragedy about Miss Brown," he said.

"What? Oh. Yes. She seemed quite well at your lecture, though I confess, I did not speak with her." She frowned, a faint line appearing between her dark slash of brows. "The doctor said she must have been disguising the signs of her consumption until the end."

A sudden onset of consumption, indeed. It was remarkable how the human mind twisted and turned upon itself to concoct an explanation for the inexplicable. "I understand her fiancée was devastated."

Her chin dipped, the lines deepening. "Yes, the poor man took his own life." She shook herself. "But I wished to ask you about the Egyptian priests. You said they used magic to summon a demon from another world into this one?"

He glided toward her. "And do you believe in magic, Miss Grey?"

"I believe that magic only exists until science finds a way to explain the phenomena. Then we shall see it as firmly rooted in the natural world."

"So science is the enemy of magic?"

"Some might say it is the enemy of wonder, but the more I learn, the more fascinated I grow. The priests …"

"And the vampire they summoned." He was close now; close enough to feel her heat, to see the pulse fluttering in the hollow of her neck. "That is what you wished to ask me of, is it not?"

"No, I wished to ask about the other world. Could the ancient Egyptian priests have known of aether?"

He halted. "Aether?"

"An invisible energy. Its web is everywhere and nowhere, but the energy appears to originate from somewhere not of this world." She put her hands to her cheeks, wincing. "I know that sounds like utter nonsense."

He cocked his head, thoughtful. She had tickled his memory, and that was no mean feat. There was something …

"I just wondered if the ancient Egyptians were opening doors to other worlds," she said, "if perhaps that was the so-called magic they let in?"

A net. Perhaps he could satisfy her curiosity. She had a mind, he would grant her that. She deserved a final gift before that light was extinguished. "There was a mystery school in Egypt," he said. "Its adherents called themselves masters of an invisible web of energy. You can find carvings depicting the god, Thoth, pulling a single thread seemingly from nothing, from the other world, and bringing it into this one."

"Aether? I know it flows from another world to ours." She frowned. "But I wonder if the energy moves in both directions?" She shook her head. "Thoth's invisible web of energy sounds much like aether, but I see I shall need to learn more about the ancient Egyptians. This Thoth, was he the jackal-headed god?"

Sebastian flinched. "No, the jackal is—another." He could not bring himself to say the name, Anubis, Lord of Death. Thinking it was bad enough. "Thoth is the god of magic and writing, and has the head of an ibis." Thoth was safer territory.

The lady's eyes glittered. "Where can I learn more?"

His gaze flicked to the darkened windows, the moonless night. Time was winging away, and he did not wish to await another lunar cycle for the end. "First, the package I left in your keeping?"

She colored again, a delightful rush of blood to her flesh. "Of course. How thoughtless of me." She strode to the tall iron safe in the corner, reached into her apron pocket, then into one skirt pocket, into the other. She turned to him, eyes wide. "Oh, dear. I'm terribly sorry. The key, I must have left it …"

In one leap he was before her, his nostrils flared. "My package, if you please."

"You don't understand. I changed my skirts this morning after encountering a coyote, and the key to the safe was in my other skirt. The coyote …"

"A coyote?"

"A local carnivore much like a jackal."

Her heart beat in his ears, mixed with his own internal thunder, his ancient enemy's footfalls echoing in his memory. A jackal? Anubis? Was she toying with him? But he had no need to fear death now. On the contrary, he embraced it. Just—not the sharp teeth of that fearsome deity. "Yours is the best safe in San Francisco. You said you would keep my package safe."

"The animal splattered mud on my skirt," she prattled, "and …"

He grasped her forearms, lifting her up on her toes.

She gasped, eyes widening, and he sank his will into those green pools. Her expression slackened.

"You will get the key and open the door."

"The key," she said, her voice a monotone.

He released her.

She dug about in her pockets and turned toward the door.

"The key," he commanded. "Think where you left it."

She went rigid. Like a sleepwalker (and that was all humans were), she returned to her table and looked down.

He followed her. So the key was in the laboratory after all and her silly tale of a jackal a fiction.

Standing before the litter of brass and wire, she placed one finger on the table, glided it through the pile of scrap. Of course. She had hidden the brass key in a pile of brass, much like Poe's Purloined Letter.

Clever girl. Too clever to live, but her death would be quick. Lightly, he placed one broad hand across the back of her warm neck.

She pried open a bit of metal and turned it upside down. A crystal fell into her hand.

What the devil was that? No key, to be sure.

She turned beneath his hand and now his palm pressed against her clavicle.

Holding the crystal between two fingers, she raised it to his eye. "The key will open the door."

The crystal blazed.

Searing pain engulfed him. He stumbled back with a cry, shielding his face with his hands, but it did not matter where he looked, or if he did not look at all. The light, the pain, were everywhere and nowhere, and he was heavy, so heavy.

There was a terrible screaming, and vaguely, he understood the cries to be his own. His bones folded in on themselves, excruciating, his body telescoping to a line. He had become part of the web, flowing like a thread back to the other …

Sensibility shook her head and looked about. She stood facing the back of her laboratory. Why was she facing the back of her laboratory? And the crystal in her hand—she did not remember picking it up.

She turned. The door to the laboratory was open, for anyone to enter. Had someone come? Good gad, she was turning into her father, an absent-minded scientist.

The crystal warmed her hand. Odd. She must have been holding it for some time for her body temperature to heat it. But the crystal was warmer than she. Why could she remember nothing?

Quartz crystals were the key to aether technology. Perhaps her mechanical problem with aether lay in the shape of the crystal? There was so much she did not understand.

She checked her pocket watch. Mr. Fitzsimmons was late.

Idly, she wondered what was inside the package he had given her for safekeeping. An Egyptian artifact? A personal item? Ah well, that was for him to know and for her to keep her nose well out of. Certain mysteries a lady did not explore.

THE DEMON FOREST

By AJ and BJ Sikes

8:00 PM, Yamanashi Prefecture

The diplomat Klimt, Austria-Hungary's envoy, gathered up the package he'd prepared earlier in the day. The set of brushes and inks would make a fine gift for his cousin, poor Gustav the artist, a man without a penny's worth of political sense. As if painting landscapes could help secure the empire's position atop the heap of nations. At least he, Jurgen, was doing his part to advance the Archduke's purpose and prestige, and so far afield, too. Yamanashi Prefecture had risen in prominence with the success of its silk trade. Jurgen's addition of military contracts to the local economy would ensure his name would be remembered well after that of his cousin.

"Oh, Gustav," Jurgen said to himself as he wrapped the art case. "I'm afraid these brushes will travel farther than any of your paintings. But Japan is a land of gifts, I have learned, and so, here is yours."

The package wrapped and bound, Jurgen marched away from the provincial lord's compound and down the quiet lantern-lit

225

street to the carriage depot. The empire's embassy in Tokyo would send a postmaster around in the morning to collect packages on his trip through the province, and Jurgen hoped to remain asleep well after the man had come and gone. The lord had left him a bottle of the sweet wine they drank, and Jurgen's lips had been dry the whole day through.

At the depot, he set the bundle by the other packages that had been stacked beside the door and marveled, not for the first time, at the Japanese sense of propriety and honor.

"In Vienna, a stack of goods like this would attract thieves like it were all the gold in the treasury," Jurgen said to himself with a shake of his head.

For a brief moment, Jurgen thought about collecting the package and waiting until he returned to the embassy himself, but he didn't need the extra burden of a painter's tools on the long trip to Tokyo.

Returning down the street, a clatter and hiss came to Jurgen's ears, signaling the presence of a steam carriage, not an uncommon sight in Japan, but Jurgen knew them to be normally reserved for daylight travel. As he rounded a bend in the roadway, he spied the vehicle by the lord's gate. No one stood attending the carriage as the steam engine coughed and shook, sending white puffs of smoke out its chimney and vibrating the machine as though it might fly from its wheels at any moment.

Jurgen had seen rickety carriages before, but this one bore signs of the worst maintenance. Approaching with a sense of wonder lifting his brow, Jurgen sought for some sign of a driver or passenger, but he saw no person near the rattling machine. The driver's bench felt warm to the touch, so certainly someone must be nearby.

With a quick step around the noisy machine, Jurgen entered the gate and made his way to his quarters, a small pavilion off the main house. Sliding the door aside, Jurgen came face to face with three men who gave no indication of their purpose, neither word nor movement. Jurgen felt the beginnings of a smile crease his lips but he quickly remembered himself and gave the customary bow instead.

The visitors were unexpected, but he had learned not to assume knowledge of Japanese custom. Still, his chest tightened with the need to put matters at ease. The middle of the three men was a familiar face, and one Jurgen thought he had seen the last of.

"*Konbanwa*, Takeshi-*san*," Jurgen said, letting the words fall from his tongue like droplets of honey. Takeshi was a minor lord from a neighboring province. He and his family had been guests at the provincial lord's manor the night before, and he had left in good spirits that morning.

What has him here now, and in my quarters? Is he rethinking the contract? But it is already signed—

"Takeshi-*san*, if this is about our business of last night, I am sorry, but—"

"No, Yoo-urgen-*san*," Takeshi said. "This is about a gift. To you, from me and my ..." Takeshi seemed to search for a word. "My advisors," he said, motioning to the two men flanking him.

All three men, Jurgen now noticed, were armed. They gave a slight bow and Takeshi made a meek grunting sound. Despite the oddity of their presence at this hour, and with weapons in their belts, Jurgen couldn't help but take Takeshi's grunt to reflect the man's sense of failure.

How could Takeshi feel anything but failure—Jurgen had, after their dinner, secured the man's commitment to purchasing a fleet of airships to be built by Austria-Hungary's finest mechanics and engineers, and if the carriage outside was any indication, the fleet would be bought at a price much higher than the fledgling lord could afford. Perhaps this gift Takeshi spoke of was meant to sway Jurgen's mind, lure him from his better senses so the contracts could be somehow altered before he delivered them to the embassy.

"Takeshi-*san*, in my country, it is not … customary to offer gifts at this hour. Though I am grateful for your gesture. May we—"

"Yoo-urgen-*san*," the lord said. "I have a rare treat for you. This night we shall visit the beautiful forest, Aokigaha-ra, where you shall receive your gift. We are in my country, and I must insist that you follow our customs."

With that, the two men either side of Takeshi placed hands upon the hilts of their swords, and stepped closer to Jurgen, framing him and putting him of a mind to comply with whatever it was they intended. All thoughts of securing the contracts for delivery had vanished when the men before him touched their weapons. Memories of the demonstration from the night before were fresh in Jurgen's mind. The blades seemed to dance against each other and had sliced so cleanly through logs as thick as a man's neck.

Jurgen allowed himself to be led from his quarters and through the compound. Takeshi walked at his side but said nothing as they followed the stone trail between the wispy leaves of maple trees.

At the gate, one of Takeshi's men mounted the carriage and took the driver's bench while Takeshi and the other man stood by and gestured for Jurgen to take the rearmost seat, facing forward. Takeshi climbed in after him and took the seat opposite, and was soon joined by his other bodyguard. What else could these men be, Jurgen thought to himself, his heart beating a cadence in his chest.

Steady on, Jurgen. The Japanese are decent folk, not brigands.

He kept reassuring thoughts in his mind as the machine rumbled under the labor of moving four grown men to some unknown destination in the darkness of night.

ℬↄℭ

Their path took them clattering past towering forests of bamboo and evergreen along a winding track that led deeper into the valley at the base of Mount Fuji. The mountain seemed poised to topple on them, and hold them fast, Jurgen felt, as though his journey were less about gift-giving and more simply one of abduction. But he wouldn't let himself fall to thoughts of panic, not yet at any rate.

Again he reminded himself that the Japanese were a people of honor and propriety; they followed rules and were not the sort to engage in skullduggery or kidnapping. It had to be Jurgen's meagre understanding of the language that led to his feeling something was amiss.

By the time they arrived at the entrance to a vast and deep wood, he had found a sense of calm replaced the temptation to fear that had grown in his heart. The moon cast reaching fingers of light through trees, dotting the ground with a dappled glow and puddles of silver amidst the dark undergrowth.

"This is a lovely place, Takeshi-*san*. Thank you for showing it to me."

"I am glad you approve, Yoo-urgen-*san*," Takeshi said, gesturing with his hand for Jurgen to dismount. "Please, precede us from the machine."

Jurgen climbed down and felt the others following close behind him. "I feel unprepared for a hike, Takeshi-*san*. How long shall we stay?" he asked as he turned around. Jurgen couldn't help but ask about the other man's plans, as he was in no way ready to remain out of doors for very long. Jurgen had only his shirt against the weather—the humidity reigned, still, but it would not be long before the air turned chill.

When he had turned fully, he saw Takeshi removing his blade, still in its scabbard, from where it had rested in his belt. Takeshi held the sheathed weapon across the palms of both hands and extended it to Jurgen, bowing only enough to make a showing of it.

"But, but … Takeshi-*san*, what is this gift? A sword? Offered at the edge of a wood, and at this hour? I—"

"A gift, Yoo-urgen-*san*, yes. Redemption, with honor, is a gift to you now, and I shall even offer you a choice." Takeshi stood upright and held the sword by its scabbard in his right hand. Sweeping his left hand through the air, he indicated the two men standing beside the steam carriage. "You may fight Isamu-*san* or Yuudai-*san* in single combat. This will bring you honor." The driver of the steam carriage came forward one step and gripped his sword where it was tucked into his belt. His companion did the same but remained a pace behind Takeshi.

Jurgen had heard of the custom of single combat, but the samurai and their barbaric manners had been outlawed years before his arrival. Now this country noble would presume to threaten him with a duel, and over what?

"A little jest, Takeshi-*san*. I see," Jurgen said, his voice only just holding in the fear that he had presumed wrongly about the Japanese and their sense of honor.

"It is no jest, *gaijin*," Takeshi said, the venom clear and thick in his voice. "You defiled my daughter in your room last night. His lordship rightly suspects I will usurp his position with the airships I bought from you, so he seeks to shame me into obeisance by sending my daughter to be your whore."

Takeshi pulled a scroll of parchment from his shirt and unrolled it, showing Jurgen a series of hastily scrawled kanji. Jurgen had no hope of reading the message.

"What does it say, Takeshi-*san*? I cannot—"

"My daughter commits *jigaki* rather than live with the stain of your touch! I awoke to find her in her rooms, her legs bound and her lifeblood staining her kimono, with this note tied around the knife she used to take her own life."

His daughter? A young woman had come to Jurgen's room, yes, but he had no idea from whence or why she came.

"Takeshi-*san*, I assure you, I knew nothing of your daught—"

"You sought to rob my family of both gold and honor. This brings shame on your spirit, so now you must redeem yourself in single combat. Or," Takeshi said, motioning with the hilt of his sword, "you may walk into Aokigahara and try your chances with the forest demons."

Demons? What madness was this? All thoughts of propriety left Jurgen and he snatched at the hilt of the sword in Takeshi's hand. As quick as he moved, however, he was not faster than Takeshi's men whose swords came up to reflect the moonlight gleaming down their lengths. Jurgen dropped the sword immediately and backed away from the razored steel of Takeshi's men.

"Go now, Yoo-urgen-*san*," Takeshi said. "Go into the demon forest and cleanse your spirit of its shame."

Jurgen stepped back again. A shiver coursed through him and he stumbled, turning as he fell to catch himself on his hands and knees. For a second he felt the snap of steel against the back of his neck, so sure was he that Takeshi's men would kill him. But the blow didn't come. As he rose to standing, Jurgen heard the metallic rush of blades slid home in their scabbards.

"Goodbye, Yoo-urgen-*san*," Takeshi said, giving a full bow this time.

Jurgen bowed in return and said, "Goodbye, Takeshi-*san*." He turned slowly and stepped into the thin trees at the forest's edge. Two more steps and he felt the darkness surround him, blocking out the moonlight even though the branches above gave plenty of space for the sky to reach down to the earth.

The deeper Jurgen went, the closer the trees became, until he had to push through them to make any progress. Like skeletal fingers, the brittle ends of withered branches tickled the hair on Jurgen's head, and the full lush green of fir and cypress trees seemed like waiting arms come to collect him, embrace him, and hold him forever in their midst.

From behind him, Jurgen heard the rumble of Takeshi's steam carriage disappearing into the night. With a deep sigh, Jurgen halted and made to reverse course. It would be a long walk to the provincial lord's compound, but better that than freezing in a dark wood all night.

He never made the first step back. As soon as he turned, he came face to face with a mournful being, all cast in gossamer and spider silk and hanging in midair so that the diminutive form came eye to eye with Jurgen. The being let out a hungry and pitiful cry, like the wail of a babe left ignored by its mother. Then Jurgen saw the others, a flock of them sailing through the trees from every direction. They came in waves, all with maws agape and full of blood-stained and hungry gnashing teeth that forced Jurgen's scream from his throat, adding it to those echoing through the wood around him.

A Coincidental Theft

By David L. Drake & Katherine L. Morse

9:00 PM, London

Chief Inspector Erasmus Drake stood with his hands on his hips, surveying the unkempt room with the help of a hand-held lantern and what little light filtered through the door from the hall. The walls were bare of pictures; the floor was without a rug. He sighed at the sacks and cartons scattered about without design. He spied a gas lamp on one of the sidewalls.

Using a zig-zagging path that avoided the parcels, he made his way over to light the lamp. He set down his lantern and fetched a Lucifer from his waistcoat pocket. He struck it against the wall. The matchstick spit and flared a brilliant sulfur blaze for a second before the flame relaxed to burning its slender wooden stock. He raised the glass chimney of the lamp, turned on the gas, and set the flame to it.

Just as he returned the chimney to its seat, he heard the distinct *thump-thump* of the door being nudged farther open by a boot. He turned to see Jonathan Lord Ashleigh carrying an overloaded crate of pottery and clay statues. Dr. Sparky McTrowell entered behind the Viscount, doing likewise.

Erasmus spoke as he made his way back toward his friends, "Oh my goodness! You do not need to carry the evidence up here yourself. I will have one of the Scotland Yard patrolmen or sergeants do that."

Lord Ashleigh set the crate down in a clear spot on the floor, replying, "If we plan to make it to dinner by ten, you are going to need all the help you can get. Anu is a wonderful cook, but unforgiving if we are late." With a practiced tug on its chain, Lord Ashleigh popped his watch out of his vest pocket and into his hand in the perfect position to snap open the lid. "Goodness gracious, we only have an hour."

Sparky set down her crate with a grunt. Erasmus could tell by the look on her face that this was not her idea of how to spend the evening.

"I will head downstairs immediately to get one of the lads to tidy up this room and bring all the evidence over from the Fishburn residence. I am also expecting to meet with …"

Erasmus stopped because a slight man with a grey mustache and a dark grey three-piece suit stepped into the doorway holding his bowler and a large leather-bound book.

"Chief Inspector Drake?" he asked.

"Yes! You must be Mr. Mordecai Abercrombie, the occult curator from the British Museum. Come in! This is my fiancée, Dr. Sparky McTrowell, and my friend, Lord Ashleigh."

Mr. Abercrombie stepped farther into the room. "They told me I could find you up here. Pleased to meet you all. I have never been to Scotland Yard before."

Everyone took turns shaking hands. Erasmus continued, "Sorry for the mess. We had to find a room large enough to hold all the evidence discovered today. We are starting to haul up the first wagonload."

Mr. Abercrombie looked around. "Might the item you mentioned be at the station? The Museum would really like to retrieve it."

Lord Ashleigh bent over and scooped up the polychrome jar perched atop the crate he had hauled up. "I believe this is the item you are seeking, the ancient Peruvian wishing jar." He held it out for Mr. Abercrombie. The curator's reflexive response was to pull back away from it, as if to touch it were anathema to him.

"Oh my, no. To begin with, that is an amateurish imitation of a Mayan jar. See those markings on the top? Those are badly rendered reproductions of Mayan glyphs. This jar's clay is too homogeneous and it can't be ancient, as you say. It has no surface deterioration. That jar was made … oh, I would say … in the last twenty years."

Mr. Abercrombie's curiosity got the best of him. He leaned in a bit to look at the jar, adjusting his glasses to focus better in the dim light.

The Chief Inspector added, "Mayan? They lived in Central America, did they not? Not South America."

"That is correct. That jar was not taken from the British Museum. Or any museum worth its salt." At this, Abercrombie chuckled to himself, stood upright, faced the Chief Inspector, and grew serious again. "I came to reclaim the item stolen from our collection four days ago that we must get back into safekeeping. I had hoped you had found it."

Sparky noticed that Erasmus was still mulling over the obviously fake jar and the implications for the events that morning. She spoke up, "For safekeeping?"

"Well, yes. We fear it could still be activated."

Sparky winced. "Are you saying you think the item you're looking for may still have some kind of—magic enchantment? Like in fairy tales and dragon stories?"

The man's entire frame became the embodiment of solemnity. "My dear, there are many things in this world we still do not—understand. Some of the items I watch over have, we believe—caused things to happen. We safeguard the public from these objects. Mostly it is a matter of locking them away. For others, we have to take greater precautions: never letting moonlight shine on them, or allowing blood to touch their surface. We were preventing any human from touching the missing item. As a precaution, mind you."

Looks of shock and concern froze on the faces of Erasmus, Lord Ashleigh, and Sparky. Their collective heads buzzed with the idea of the British Museum taking these objects so seriously.

Lord Ashleigh broke the silence. "Can you describe this object you are seeking? I personally would like to ensure the museum gets it back."

"I can do even better. I will show it to you." He held up his leather-bound book.

Erasmus motioned to the hallway. "My office is downstairs and has much better light. I want to see this."

ഇൠ

Erasmus swept a few papers off his desk into a drawer, making room for Mr. Abercrombie to plop the book open in the center of the desk. It was filled with photographs, rare for 1851, of objects that Mr. Abercrombie curated. He flipped past a few grey-toned images that the circle of friends found unnerving: a jet black orb with a single oriental character carved into it, a mummified baby with an enlarged head, and a scarab-shaped metallic statue that appeared to produce its own hazy glow. Sparky made a couple of *ugh* sounds, to which the rest of the group politely didn't react. With the last flip of the page, the curator exclaimed, "Ah, here it is!"

The image showed a small box engraved with Egyptian hieroglyphs. Sparky stared intently at it and murmured, "Wait a minute …"

Excitedly, Mr. Abercrombie started his explanation of the item, pointing to various places in the picture. "Based on these markings, this box contains an amulet of great power. We have had issues with other items created its maker, the Egyptian High Priest Smendes II. He served during the reign of King Psusennes I around 1047 through 1001 BC. The markings here—and here—state the box contains the 'genie amulet,' the very amulet upon which many legends are based. This, roughly translated, states, 'to wear the stone is to allow three wishes to be granted to your master.' We have never opened the box, since we did not want anyone to touch the object within."

Sparky sputtered, "I—I've seen this box! It was in the flat where I captured—what was his name? Harry!"

Erasmus exclaimed, "Harry is just around the corner in a holding cell! Let's go!"

Abercrombie slammed the book shut and the group hustled out of the Chief Inspector's office.

❧❦

Harry was sitting on a wooden bench, hunched over dejectedly. He looked up briefly when the group of four arrived. Spotting Sparky, he sat bolt upright and held his hands up toward her defensively. In doing so, he showed off a severely darkened black eye on his left, and a swollen cheek on the right.

"Please, don't let 'er near me. Look wat she done to me face! I'll do anythin'. Just keep 'er away!"

Sparky shrugged a bit over her enthusiasm to apprehend the runaway thief. Erasmus, using his deeper, authoritative voice, obliged the captive. "Well then, the 'anything' we would like is to know how you got the box with the Egyptian writing on it, and what you did with it."

Harry looked hesitant. Sparky put her fists up in a mock fighting stance.

"Alright, alright. When I was asked 'ta break in 'ta 'ta British Museum, I was told not ta take anything! W'at a waste o' time, I thought 'ta me'self. So I nabbed 'ta box t'at was in the locked glass case. Wid' 'ta two locks and a chain around it, t'ought it might have somet'ing valuable."

Mr. Abercrombie was beside himself. "Well yes, of course it was valuable! What did you …" His face reddened as if he were trying to hold back a building emotional pressure. He stepped aggressively toward the barred chamber and shouted, "What did you do with the box?"

Harry leaned sheepishly back away from upset curator. "Well t' box is back in me flat. But it's empty."

Lord Ashleigh yelled, "What did you do with the contents?!"

"It was a lovely neck chain wit' a fancy gem. I'm wearin' it."

The man unbuttoned the top of his shirt and parted it to show the dazzling gold chain supporting a walnut-sized green stone. It sparkled like a crown jewel. The gemstone had miraculously tanned and dried Harry's skin in its immediate proximity, as if he had let a hot coal lie on his chest while sleeping off a drunk. He grinned a toothy grin that showed that his gums had receded back to his jaws since that morning. Erasmus had the impression the man was drying up from inside.

Mr. Abercrombie immediately averted his eyes. "Close your shirt! Now!" He looked at Erasmus. "I will get a team together from the museum to retrieve it. This item must be protected. Who is his master? We must find out if he made any requests that could be interpreted as wishes."

Erasmus raised an eyebrow. "Harry has always been under the direction of Lord Fishburn. And believe it or not, he did make three wishes. We can visit him through that door over there. He's also in a holding cell."

℘℘℘

The four stood in front of Lord Fishburn's cell looking at his still body lying on the bench.

Sparky asked, "Should I see if he's dead?"

At that, Lord Fishburn sat up and stretched. "Why, hello, everyone. Why are you visiting?"

"We wanted to see if your three wishes had come true," Erasmus stated.

"Of course they did! I got my just reward! Look at these prison walls! I got exactly what I deserved. The enchanted jar *WORKED!*" He shot his arms up triumphantly to show that his years of searching for occultist proof had finally paid off.

Sparky quietly added, "Well, he *is* correct. The amulet may have honored the wishes the imitation jar couldn't."

Lord Fishburn made an odd face. "What amulet?"

Erasmus, still using his authoritative voice, answered, "The one Harry pinched when you asked him to break in to the British Museum."

The prisoner made a confused face and shook his head slowly. "I didn't ask Harry to break into the British Museum. I confess I had him *procure* many of my treasures from lesser-known museums, but I didn't ask him to get me that jar. It was a gift."

The Chief Inspector asked, "From whom?"

"That's the odd thing. Despite all of my wife's jests regarding my collection, it was she that bestowed the jar on me. I was hoping it was a goodwill gesture to ease the tensions between us. Matter of fact, she was quite ..."

Erasmus cut him off from detailing the particulars. "That's enough fine points for me. Quickly, everyone back to Harry!"

℘℘℘

Erasmus sprinted to Harry's cell. He grabbed the bars. "Harry! Quickly! Who told you to break into the British Museum?!"

"It was 'ta Missus. Lady Fishburn. She said she 'ad a surprise for Frederick, I mean, Lord Fishburn. She told me 'ta make it look like I took somet'ing from the occult vault, but not to take anyt'ing. But I decided ta 'elp meself wit' a little box. I was amazed she asked, 'cause she and I never really got along, if ya get my meanin'. But she paid me well for 'ta errand. So's I got no complaints."

"I must leave straight away to arrest Lady Fishburn as the instigator of this crime. Sparky? Lord Ashleigh? Are you with me?"

The two nodded enthusiastically. Erasmus gestured to Mr. Abercrombie, offering him the opportunity to see justice served.

The curator demurred, "I should stay and guard the amulet."

The three rushed out and hopped into a waiting horse-drawn police wagon, replete with iron bars to restrain prisoners. They squeezed onto the driver's bench with Erasmus in the middle, reins in hand. With a snap of the leather and a whoop, the Chief Inspector broke the horses into a gallop across the cobblestones and into the London night.

Erasmus raised his voice to be heard over the cacophony of wheel and hoof. "Lord Ashleigh, a question if I may. Mr. Abercrombie said it was the 'genie amulet.' Genie stories are Arabic, are they not? How could the Egyptians create a genie amulet?"

"Aha! So you believe I am the expert in all things south and east of Europe? Just joshing you, my friend. Stories of jinns living in bottles are common enough. It is said they are created from smokeless fire. As for the story's origins, Arabia was just a boat ride across the Red Sea from Egypt. It is also very possible that the amulet was crafted to bring the ancient legend to life. So, as you English like to say, who knows which came first, the chicken or the egg?"

℮℞

The Fishburns' butler performed his characteristic derisive sniff immediately upon opening the door. Erasmus wrote it off as his reaction to the paddy wagon sitting at the curb rather than the appearance of him and his colleagues. The butler did his best to block their entry, but within seconds, the Chief Inspector had expertly, but politely, pressed himself and his company past the gatekeeper and into the dining room, where they met Mrs. Fishburn.

"Chief Inspector. Have we not had enough excitement for today?"

Erasmus responded using his deep, serious voice, "Our thief has implicated you in his last break-in. You will need to come with us."

"Oh, poppycock. Harry and I didn't associate. *Very* different classes, as you know. You would be foolish to take his word over mine. If you have no other evidence, you may take your leave. Or contact my solicitor. My man Poole will supply you with the details."

"I see. Perhaps you can clear your name regarding the Peruvian jar. It did not come from the British Museum."

The lady of the house stood up straight and smiled slightly, assuming an air of haughty assurance. "Oh, that thing. I bought it in a curio shop south of the Thames. I even made that rough paper translation guide. I put the pieces of paper in to get him to admit his crimes. What a fool he was. So glad you were there to hear his confession."

Sparky interjected, "How did you know the order he would choose the paper messages?"

"Oh, simplicity itself. I sealed the jar with the same three messages about destroying a false idol. After Frederick removed one of those messages, I secretly exchanged the contents of the jar with two more for revealing a hidden past truth. After he removed one, I emptied the jar and put in the final confession request, and suggested a party. Anything illegal in getting your husband to divulge his past crimes?" She smirked.

Erasmus furrowed his brow. He knew it was Harry's word against hers, and, given her stature in the community, it would be hard to make the charges stick.

Lord Ashleigh broke the silence. "Lady Fishburn, Harry came into possession of an amulet that would have fulfilled his master's three wishes. It is a good thing that you had not ordered him to break into the museum, because that would make you his master, in a manner of speaking."

"So?" came her droll response.

Sparky perked up. "Oh, I see! You created those three wishes."

Lord Ashleigh popped out his pocket watch. "It has been exactly half a day! Confess your crimes, dear Lady!"

Lady Fishburn rolled her eyes. "Oh, poppycock! I do not believe …"

She suddenly grabbed her throat and staggered.

Erasmus carefully quoted, "… publicly confess … past crimes within half a day … if not, they shall breathe their last. Lady Fishburn!"

She grabbed for support that wasn't there and stumbled clumsily. With both hands she ripped her collar open; two satin-covered buttons rocketed off and bounced on the pristine rug. She could not take in or exhale a single breath. The men reached out to catch her, but her knees gave out. She fell to the carpeted floor in a graceless heap.

Dr. McTrowell jumped in and rolled her to her back. The blueness of the lady's face told Sparky there was little she could do.

Lord Ashleigh pleaded, "Lady Fishburn! Confess! Did you send Harry?"

With wide eyes and accentuated motions, she nodded as hard as she could, hoping to defeat her own final wish.

Suddenly, she stopped. With eyes open and motionless, she lay prostrate.

"She's dead," Sparky quietly stated. Erasmus, Sparky, and Lord Ashleigh looked at each other in disbelief.

Erasmus pulled out his pocket watch. "I must tend to this, which will make me late for dinner. Please pass on my apologies to Anu."

"No, no, I will stay to help," Lord Ashleigh added.

"I'm missing dinner because of her!?" Sparky exclaimed.

VICTORIAN POETRY HOUR

By Janice Thompson

Nightfall

Deep, deep within these pages
A cherished, careworn tome
I scarcely feel the ages
Of hours I've been home
Nor notice I the rhythm
The tick of tocking gears
Until the soft collision
When chimes invade my ears
It's ten now by the counting
So close the book, alas,
To stretching yawning frowning
That so much time has passed
Lethargically I struggle
Lift all my tired weight
Then to my bed I shuffle
To dreams I can't abate
Oh wait! The clock needs winding
And have I locked the door?

The will is yet aspiring
But I can do nothing more
Than quietly surrender
Into my bed I fall
And hope that I remembered
The clock, the door, and all.

Antisocial

These uninvited guests
Abrupt and unforeseen
When I was want to rest
Such noisy mirth they bring

With appetites to quell
From pantry light of means
To entertain as well
Though I would rather dream

Of swaying island palms
And languid lapping sea
But brigands raid my calm
With forced comradery

My strength and larder spent
They amble to the door
Each steals a hug and then
I soon become quite sore

Of endless ardent waves
Through doorway growing closed
And I am soon away
In search of sweet repose

Yet as I now recline
My agitated brain
Spins echoes
of the night
To deepen my disdain

Till I becalm my mind
And send the echoes forth
But now I find that I'm
Not sleepy anymore

Morpheus

Sweet Morpheus, envelop me in dreams
Come guide me gently from these feral schemes
That convolute my poorly sorted brain
Till I arise and pace the floor again.
Fatiguing all the more this body spent
This tortured soul as grief will not relent
To lie on linen bathed in moonlight beams
Sweet Morpheus, envelop me in dreams.

FINDER

By Dover Whitecliff

11:00 PM, Valley of the Kings

It seemed hours since Aunty Clarissa had tucked Elle in, hours of pretending to be asleep, hours worrying about the sibilant voice coming from the dark of the cave. Finally, the talking and stories died down, and the others settled in for the night. After another few minutes, Elle cracked an eyelid, listening to the even breathing and murmurs of the rest of the camp, alert for the sounds of anyone still wandering about.

Slowly, quietly, she left her cot, grabbed her boots and small pack, holding them tight against her chest to keep anything from rattling, and tiptoed out of her tent. She waited until she was well away before stopping to knock her boots out, put them on, and lace them up tight. This wouldn't be the time to trip over a bootlace. She slung the pack over her shoulder and made her way back to the cliff, each step more anxious than the last because, instead of the expected sound of purring, she heard a frantic mewling somewhere between fear and pain. Don't worry, Kitty Cat. I'm coming. Elle made the climb, pulled herself onto the ledge with a heave, and crept forward, kneeling to light the small lantern she'd brought with her.

"Shouldn't you be in bed?"

Elle bit back a scream and was actually quite proud of herself when she only knocked the lantern over, rather than breaking it. She turned to see Kilima sitting in the shadows at the side of the cleft.

"Don't look so surprised. You've been sneaking glances up here for the past week. It was only a matter of time." Kilima cocked her head to the side. "Your mother has told me many times of your love of exploring and how you find things others have lost. Why this cave?"

"You won't laugh, will you?"

"I cannot promise, but I will do my best."

"I hear purring." Elle looked at her feet, waiting for the gales of laughter. They didn't come. She looked up slowly to see Kilima with a very thoughtful look on her face.

"Purring like a kitten?"

"Bigger. Deeper. Like a jungle cat." This seemed to decide Kilima. She came forward and knelt, looking into Elle's eyes and putting a hand on her shoulder.

"Then this journey is meant for you alone. I will wait here. Remember well what you have been taught, and be wary of serpents. They like the dark." Elle shivered and nodded, grabbed the lantern and moved to the slit at the bottom of the rock face. She pushed the lantern and her rucksack through ahead of her and wormed through the hole on her stomach, squirming deeper into the darkness. As she made it through to the place where she could stand, she thought she heard Kilima's voice whisper. "Haimaji, protect the young one, and if it is meant to be, let the young Mwokoti find the Cat's Spirit that it may walk the world again."

Then there was nothing but the sound of her own breathing in the dim glow of her lantern as she made her way slowly back down through the cave. But as she moved forward, she began to hear other sounds … slithering, hissing, rhythmic chanting in deep voices, and she blinked as she thought she saw light ahead.

Don't be stupid. She told herself as she started forward then stopped cold. Light means they may know you've come back. Don't just rush in there without knowing what's there. For a slight moment, she thought about turning back and telling Kilima about the voice she'd heard, and the shadow. But then she remembered the look in Kilima's eyes, "Then this journey is meant for you alone. I will wait here. Remember well what you have been taught, and be wary of serpents. They like the dark."

Serpents. Elle had seen the mighty anaconda and the small poisonous vipers of her own jungle home, had even watched the charmers in Cairo with their cobras, but somehow, she knew what serpents Kilima had been describing: the Naga that lived beneath the earth. "I'd better be smart or I'll end up a snack or like the stone statues in Medusa's garden," she thought, and then grinned.

"What would SHE do?" Elle crouched to think about her namesake, H. Rider Haggard's Immortal SHE. She took stock of what she'd brought with her. Her pocket knife. No good for fencing, but might be good for other things. A lantern with some paraffin oil. In the dark, light would give her away to whatever else was down here. A bottle of water. Some string and a plumb bob. A sling and some stones. She shook her head, wondering how on earth she'd thought a few rocks, a pocket knife, and a plumb bob would be enough. No turning back now. I have to find him before it's too late. I suppose I'll have to think on my feet. Elle swallowed, hid her lantern behind a rock, and crept forward.

She had been right about seeing the dim glow of light much sooner than she'd remembered it. The light brightened as she approached and she realized it was coming from flickering torches along the walls. Now that she could see it properly, Elle could tell straight off that the cave wasn't natural, but shaped by hands, and the designs on the walls were a mix of ancient and newly carved.

Elle moved through the shadows, switching sides to avoid standing too near any one torch. The hissing grew more predominant and Elle tried to calm her fears as she kept going, saying over and over to herself SHE wouldn't be scared. SHE wouldn't be scared. Even that threatened not to be enough as she rounded the bend to find that her way still blocked by a serpent. What do I do? Maybe if I crawl it won't see me. Elle eased forward, trying her hardest to keep quiet, but the shape didn't move toward her. So far. So good. Inch by inch. Keeping to the wall. Surely it can smell me by now—surely. Why isn't it chasing me? Is it stupid?

Elle crouched, preparing to run past, then had to slap a hand over her mouth to keep from laughing with relief as she finally realized that the creature, on closer inspection, turned out to be a snake skin longer than the felucca that had brought them to Thebes and almost as big around as the pillars at Karnak. And this snake skin had arms …

Elle forced herself to go forward even though some small voice in the back of her head was telling her to turn right around and head back. If it lost a skin that long, it will be much longer now. How do I stop something like that from eating me? She looked at the cave itself. Up ahead there seemed to be a narrowing of the tunnel and two of the stone torch brackets in the walls fairly close to one another. A glimmering of an idea began to form as she remembered Aunty Clarissa's lecture in Cairo about the cobra. Snakes see better by smell and taste and vibration than by sight. Something thin and motionless might not catch their attention until it's too late.

Elle took out her plumb bob and cut all but two feet of the string from it with her pocket knife. For all that it looked flimsy, it was good solid fishing twine, and as Elle could attest, having been pulled into the frigid stream that ran through Aunty Clarissa's estate by a rather large mirror carp, could hold some bit of weight if it were tied properly. Aunty Clarissa never did things by half and always insisted on good equipment. Elle knotted each end of the twine firmly to the base of one of the stone torch brackets, leaving the twine dangling about four feet above the tunnel floor, ducked under her makeshift trap and continued to sneak along the corridor.

The chanting grew louder as she descended further into the cave, louder and more evil sounding. She could barely hear the purring anymore. Instead the rumble had turned more toward the yowling of an animal in pain. Elle picked up speed at the sound, disregarding caution to get to the troubled animal. When she broke away from the tunnel and into a large vaulted chamber, she stopped dead in her tracks, in awe of what she was seeing.

The chamber was huge, almost as big as the pyramids themselves. Around the edges were several stone nests near warming fires with twitching eggs, perhaps ready to hatch. And in the center stood an altar, presided over by a stone Naga rearing up as tall as the ceiling, her arms outstretched and each holding a bonfire that gave the room its diffuse glow.

But it was the Naga at the altar that gave Elle pause. Each as long as the snake skin she had passed, they circled the altar, slithering in time to the chanting, waving curved blades in intricate patterns in the air, each one closer and closer to the top of the altar. She tried to get a glimpse of the cat in the spaces between the Naga as they slithered past.

She finally saw it clearly when the Naga paused a moment to turn their faces upward toward the statue and—well, she couldn't really call it singing since it was more like nails on a chalkboard.

Only the cat wasn't alive, but a statue of such lifelike carving that she stared at it for some moments expecting it to move before she remembered to be stealthy and backed into the shadows. *Now what do I do? They'll know I'm here for sure as soon as I get any closer. I'm lucky they're too busy chanting to have noticed me yet as it is … what would SHE do?*

Elle cast her eyes around the chamber as she crept inward, hugging the shadows on the wall. She could hear the cat whining in pain as the chanting got louder, and a red light began to glow in the eyes of the giant Naga idol, licking the sides of the altar like a snake itself and homing in on the statue.

"Great Goddesssss, Mother of all sserpentsss … dessstroy the ssspirit of the cat … ssuck out its ssoul to feed your eggssss, that they might grow ssstrong."

Elle tried her hardest not to panic, and concentrated instead on how annoying the ssssing was getting. *SSoul ssucking. Can't they even sspeak properly? Eggsss. Hmmph. That's it. Eggs!!* Elle moved through the shadows toward one of the nests at the back. *Ignore the bloody great snakes. Pretend you're playing rugby. That's it.* Elle looked long and hard at the nearest egg, picturing it in her head as nothing more than a mate on the pitch. She tried to figure out how much it weighed by the size. *Don't worry. You can move it. It's only up to your knees. Roll the egg. They'll have to go catch it. Then run for it and grab Kitty Cat.*

She remembered the certainty in Kilima's eyes. *This is for me to do alone.* And then, between one breath and the next she hurled all her weight at the egg and it popped free from the nest, rolling haphazardly down the slope. Elle sidestepped into the shadows, too late remembering the flaw in that plan … snakes see by tasting the air. The shadows wouldn't help. "Intruderssss!

Kill them all and take their ssskinss!!!" What seemed like an army of Naga roared forward and away from the altar, but only one or two made to chase down the egg.

Elle sprinted toward the statue of the cat as the reptilian bodies crashed around her. She jumped up, tromping on a serpent's tail and running along her dry and scaly back, then leap frogged over her shoulders, nearly hitting the Naga's sword and barely evading her grasping arms. Another jump, this one to the altar as another Naga lunged toward her. She landed badly and dropped to her knees, ripping the rough cloth and feeling the sting of abraded skin. Before she had time to think, she grabbed the statue and jumped to the ground, again falling forward. She rolled sideways to protect the statue with her side, then pushed to her feet and threw herself headlong into the passage with the Naga's hissing and writhing close on her heels.

A tail whipped forward, tripping her and tightening around her small form, but Elle, more terrified of being eaten than with any plan aforethought, found scales next to her mouth and bit down hard. The coils loosened, and Elle kicked free, running forward crouched until she could gain her footing. She felt the fishing twine pass above her head as she ran. Hoped it would be enough to buy her some little amount of time. She knew better than to stop and look when she heard the strangled cry, but the smell of burning meat brought her up short and she turned. The Naga in the lead had pulled the stone torches from the wall and was dragging them tangled along behind, much to his own detriment, as he had caught himself on fire. He writhed in the passage, screaming epithets with far too many sssss's and blocking the others from following.

No time to waste. Get moving. Elle berated herself and started back up the passage, the statue secure under her arm. Metal clanged against the cave wall as she skidded to a halt to grab her lantern. Snakes might be able to taste the air, but she certainly couldn't. A wicked looking dagger ricocheted from the stone and glanced off her arm. She yipped in pain and ran, looking over her shoulder to see that one Naga, this one with a cobra-like hood instead of hair, had crawled over his compatriots and was hot on her heels. Elle ran flat out, gasping for air as she rocketed up the tunnel, all the while dodging daggers and the occasional lunge by her pursuer. Her only hope was the opening: it was too small for the Naga … she hoped. The smell of bat guano nearly caused Elle to gag as she gasped for air. There it was, the faint light up ahead. She threw herself forward with the statue and her lantern held ahead of her and her front half slid into the opening.

She could feel the Naga's breath on her back and realized he was going to catch her. She shoved the statue forward with what little strength she had left after the chase. As long as I save him. That's what's important. Kilima will look after him for me. The hands that grabbed her legs were cold and scaly, and began to pull her backward out of the crevice. Elle reached for anything that might help prevent her from becoming a Naga Nibble and grabbed handfuls of guano. She rolled in his grasp, trying to break free.

"You sssshalll pay for defiling the temple. Where is the Sssspirit of the Cat??? Give it to me and you will die lessss sssslowly."

"You sssshould learn to sssspeak lessss ssstupidly, you egg ssssucker!" Elle yelled, with far more courage than she felt, and hurled the double handful of guano into the Naga's face as it lunged down toward her.

The Naga clawed at his eyes and Elle scrambled forward, squirming as fast as she could through the crevice. Rough hands, human hands, pulled her forward and out. Kilima pulled Elle completely free of the crevice.

"Run, Mwokoti." Kilima lit the stick of dynamite and tossed it through the entrance. Elle pushed to her feet, stuffed the guano-covered statue in her pack and began to climb down. Kilima leapt from the edge, snagging Elle around the waist and pulling her from the face of the cliff. She landed in a crouch on the wadi floor as a low rumble echoed from above and the cave collapsed, sending showers of rocks down the face of the cliff that would have swept Elle with them had Kilima not been so quick. Elle stood, only now noticing the cut on her arm from the ricocheted dagger.

"I got him." Elle pulled out the statue and wiped the statue off on the few remaining clean bits of her pants.

"I can see that. And you have made an enemy of the Tribe of the Naga … but we have always been such, and you join an exclusive club by doing so. Now tell me, what kind of cat it is?" Elle looked at Kilima in confusion.

"When I heard him, he sounded like a jungle cat … like a jaguar from home. And I thought I saw spots when I grabbed him in the temple."

"As it should be." Kilima affirmed with a look of wistful sadness in her eyes. "And yet that is not what you have in your hands, is it?"

"The statue has stripes … and it's … it's a female tiger." Elle looked at the statue in awe. Even though her poor attempts at cleaning hadn't done much, the nobility and bearing of the statue was breathtaking. And Elle began to hear contented purring. When she lifted her head to look at Kilima, she could swear she saw the statue breathing out of the corner of her eye. "I must have been wrong … it wasn't very light in there."

"No, Mwokoti, you were right. The last cat to walk the earth was a jaguar. He was a good friend, and it was my honor to be with him when he walked the world. When he was betrayed by the priests of the Naga, the Spirit of the Cat slumbered. Only by finding the spirit have you brought the cycle back to its proper rotation. When you are older, you will understand why the statue is a tiger. But for now, I think the both of you need a bath. Clarissa will not appreciate your smell, Mwokoti ..."

"Why do you call me that? Mwokoti, I mean ..."

"I see it is time to start some new language lessons. *Mwokoti* is Swahili. It means Finder of Lost Things."

℘   **FINIS**   ℛ

About the Contributors

Ian Berget

Ian Berget is an illustrator, graphic designer, and digital sculptor. If he isn't spending his time sitting in front of a computer screen, designing, it's probably because he's spending his time sitting in front of two computer screens, designing. Whatever the objective in question—book covers, character illustrations, anatomical renderings of the third cranial ventricle—he always strives for perfection. Once in a blue moon (when the power grid is down) Ian enjoys studying martial arts, reading classic books, and planning trips around the globe.

Sharon E. Cathcart

Books by award-winning internationally published author Sharon E. Cathcart provide discerning readers of essays, fiction, and non-fiction with a powerful, truthful literary experience. A former journalist and newspaper editor, Sharon has been writing for as long as she can remember and always has at least one work in progress. Her primary focus is creating fiction featuring atypical characters. Sharon lives in the Silicon Valley, California, with her husband and an assortment of pets. Her website is *www.sharonecathcart.wordpress.com*.

Lillian Csernica

Lilian Csernica's fiction has appeared in *Fantastic Stories*, *These Vampires Don't Sparkle*, and *DAW's Year's Best Horror Stories XXI* and *XXII*. Her Christmas ghost story "The Family Spirit" appeared in *Weird Tales #322* and "Maeve" appeared in *#333*. She has also published a pirate romance novel, *Ship of Dreams*, under her romance pen name Elaine LeClaire. Born in San Diego, Ms. Csernica is a genuine California native. She currently resides in the Santa Cruz Mountains with her husband, two sons, and three cats. Visit her at *www.lillian888.wordpress.com*.

Steve DeWinter

Steve DeWinter is a #1 Bestselling Amazon Action & Adventure Sci-Fi Author who has also co-authored two fantasy novels with Charles Dickens. Yes! That Charles Dickens. His books have hit #1 on the Amazon Children's Action & Adventure Sci-Fi Bestseller list, #1 on the Amazon Steampunk Bestseller list, and his adult thrillers reached as high as lucky #13 on the Amazon Action & Adventure Bestseller list. He also has the distinction of having nine books in the top twenty of the Amazon Children's Action & Adventure Sci-Fi Bestseller list all at the same time. His website is *www.stevedw.com*.

David L. Drake and Katherine L. Morse

David L. Drake and Katherine L. Morse are the award-winning, San Diego-based authors of *The Adventures of Drake and McTrowell: Perils in a Postulated Past,* a serialized steampunk tale detailing the adventures of Chief Inspector Erasmus Drake and Dr. "Sparky" McTrowell. The duo's many adventures are provided in weekly penny dreadful style episode. They have produced four novellas since 2010: *London, Where it All Began*; *The Bavarian Airship Regatta*; *Her Majesty's Eyes and Ears*; and *The Hawaiian Triple*

Cross. Drake and Morse won a Starburner Award for the radio show based on their first story that has run multiple times on Krypton Radio. When not cosplaying their alter egos at conventions all over the West, they are both research computer scientists specializing in distributed modeling and simulation. Mr. Drake is a nationally ranked foil fencer. Dr. Morse is an internationally respected expert on standards, but prefers to be recognized for her cookie baking skills. They throw awesome parties, if they do say so themselves. Visit *www.DrakeAndMcTrowell.com.*

Anthony Francis

By day, Anthony Francis programs intelligent computers and emotional robots; by night, he writes science fiction and draws comic books. His short stories in the anthologies *Twelve Hours Later, Thirty Days Later,* and *Some Time Later* are prequels to his steampunk novel *Jeremiah Willstone and the Clockwork Time Machine.* Anthony is also the author of the award-winning urban fantasy novel *Frost Moon* and its sequels *Blood Rock* and *Liquid Fire,* all starring magical tattoo artist Dakota Frost. Anthony lives in San Jose with his wife and cats, but his heart will always belong in Atlanta. To follow Jeremiah Willstone, visit *www.jeremiahwillstone.com* or *www.facebook.com/jeremiahwillstone.* To follow Dakota Frost, visit *www.dakotafrost.com* or *www.facebook.com/dakotafrost.* To follow Anthony himself, visit his blog at *www.dresan.com.*

T. E. MacArthur

T. E. MacArthur is an author, artist, and historian living in the San Francisco Bay Area with her constant companion, kitten Calypso. She received her bachelor's degree in History and spent many an evening in subsequent Anthropology, Geology, Criminal Investigation and Art classes. However, storytelling remains her passion. She has written for several local and specialized publications and was even an accidental sports reporter for Reuters. The Volcano Lady series follows the adventures of Victorian lady scientist Lettie Gantry through the worlds of Jules Verne. The Gaslight Adventures of Tom Turner novellas continue the thrilling adventures of Robur's first mate turned hero. To put it mildly, T.E. has a love for all things Victorian (history and clothing from 1870–1890 in particular) and is having a lifelong affair with the writings of Jules Verne. Her website is *www.volcanolady.com*.

Vicki Rorke

As a young child, Vicki Rorke contemplated one of the great questions of life: Star Trek or Speed Racer? Fortunately, her older brother controlled the TV and she became exposed to, and enthralled with, Star Trek. After attending many a convention (when 50 attendees was considered a raging success!) and reciting dialog by heart, it was only natural that she began creating her own worlds. Her first sci-fi short story was published at the tender age of 14. If you enjoyed Gods/Monsters, you can find more adventures of Shanarra MacGregor and her friends in *The Stolen Songbird*. Vicki passed in 2015. The authors, editors, and publishers of *Twelve Hours Later* dedicated its sequel, *Thirty Days Later*, to her memory.

AJ Sikes

AJ Sikes writes noir urban fantasy and has published multiple short story publications and the alternate history novel, *Gods of Chicago*. He offers professional editing services to writers of speculative fiction, non-fiction, and academic material. He served in the US Army, holds an MA in Teaching English to Speakers of Other Languages, and taught university level ESL writing and composition courses. He's a woodworker and toy builder in his spare time. AJ keeps a blog called Dovetails (*www.writingjoinery.wordpress.com*) where he talks about the similarities between woodworking and writing. Find out more about his editing services at *www.ajsikes.com*.

BJ Sikes

BJ Sikes is a 5'6" ape descendant who is inordinately fond of a good strong cup of tea, Doc Martens boots, and fancy dress. She lives with two large cats, two small children, and one editor-author. She was the chief cat-wrangler for this anthology and two others (*Thirty Days Later* and *Some Time Later*) and has recently released her debut novel, *The Archimedean Heart*.

Janice Thompson

Janice Thompson has been writing poetry for more than fifty years. She composes tightly woven, unforced verses that allow for as many levels of interpretation as are possible. Much of her poetry hearkens back to the English Lake District poets. JaniceT has been an avid fan of the steampunk genre since the early eighties, and its influence on her is apparent in her "steamier" poems, such as "Twist" and "Train of Thought." Her published works include the Echoes, Neo-Victorian Poetry series, as well as *A Compilation of Echoes*. Samples of her work are posted on her blog at *www.janice-t.weebly.com*.

Elizabeth Watasin

Elizabeth Watasin is the author of the gothic steampunk series The Dark Victorian, The Elle Black Penny Dreads, and is the creator/artist of the indie comics series Charm School. She lives in Los Angeles with her black cat named Draw, busy bringing readers uncanny heroines in shilling shockers and adventuress tales. Follow the news of her latest projects at A-Girl Studio, *www.a-girlstudio.com*.

Kirsten Weiss

Kirsten Weiss worked overseas for nearly twenty years in the fringes of the former USSR, Africa, and Southeast Asia. Her experiences abroad sparked an interest in the effects of mysticism and mythology, and how both are woven into our daily lives. Now based in San Mateo, California, she writes genre-blending steampunk suspense, urban fantasy, and mystery, mixing her experiences and imagination to create a vivid world of magic and mayhem. Kirsten has never met a dessert she didn't like, and her guilty pleasures are watching Ghost Whisperer re-runs and drinking red wine. Sign up for her newsletter to get free updates on her latest work at *www.kirstenweiss.com*.

Dover Whitecliff

Dover Whitecliff was born in the shadow of Fujiyama, raised in the shadow of Olomana, and lives where she can see the shadow of Mt. Shasta if she squints and it's a really clear day. She is an analyst, an editor, and a jack-of-all-trades, but mostly a writer who has been telling stories since forever, and who won her first ten-speed as a fifth grader with a first-place entry into *Honolulu Advertiser*'s "Why Hawaii Isn't Big Enough for Litter" contest. Her short stories in the anthologies *Twelve Hours Later*, *Thirty Days Later*, and *Some Time Later* are companion pieces to her first solo novel *The Superspy with the Clockwork Eye*. She lives in Sacramento, California with her very patient husband and several hundred bears.

ABOUT THINKING INK PRESS

Thinking Ink Press was founded in 2014 by five Bay Area authors with a love for the printed word. Following a preview release of the *24 Hour Comic Day Survival Guide*, our first official release was *The Parents' Guide to Perthes*, a guide for parents of children with Legg-Calvé-Perthes disease.

Since then we have published fiction in a wide range of sizes: the flash fiction postcards *White Mice* and *Finnegan's Firewall*; pocket-sized, origami-inspired Instant Books including *Jagged Fragments*, *Small Surprises*, *Wild Hair*, and *Bees*; chapbooks such as *Sibling Rivalry* and *Beyond the Fence*; illustrated children's books such as *Hip, Hop, Hooray for Brooklyn Bunny!*; full-length fiction anthologies such as *Twelve Hours Later*, *Thirty Days Later*, and the forthcoming *Some Time Later*; and full-length novels, including *Debris Dreams* and the forthcoming *Shattered Sky* and *Luna's Lament*.

Our goal is to find awesome things and to get them into your hands. Our ambition is to find new ways to do that. And our commitment is to produce high quality books that show through and through our love of the printed word. You can find us online at *www.thinkinginkpress.com* or contact us at *contact@thinkinginkpress.com*.

www.ingramcontent.com/pod-product-compliance
Lightning Source LLC
Chambersburg PA
CBHW032122180726
48284CB00002B/664